29/09/20

Janice Preston grew up in Wembley, North London, with a love of reading, writing stories and animals. In the past she has worked as a farmer, a police call-handler and a university administrator. She now lives in the West Midlands with her husband and two cats, and has a part-time job as a weight management counsellor—vainly trying to control her own weight despite her love of chocolate!

THE EARL WITH THE SECRET PAST

Janice Preston

MILLS & BOON

First Published in Great Britain 2020
by Mills & Boon, an imprint of HarperCollins*Publishers*
1 London Bridge Street, London, SE1 9GF

© 2020 Janice Preston

ISBN: 978-0-263-27705-0

MIX
Paper from
responsible sources
FSC C007454

This book is produced from independently certified FSC™ paper
to ensure responsible forest management.
For more information visit www.harpercollins.co.uk/green.

Printed and bound in Spain
by CPI, Barcelona

To Kim Deabill and Irina Wolpers, and all the
other followers of my Facebook Author Page, who
rose to the challenge of naming two of the characters
in heroine Kitty's novel.

The names I picked were Kim's suggestion of Sidney,
for the villainous uncle, and Irina's suggestion of
Minerva, for Sidney's flighty and mercenary betrothed!

Prologue

Hertfordshire

'You *said* you loved me!'

Adam Monroe gazed into huge grey eyes drowning in tears. His throat thickened as he thrust his emotions down.

'I do, Kitty. I… I care for you. Very much. But it's impossible…ye must see it.'

She clutched his hands, her nails digging urgently into his skin. He wrenched his gaze from hers and concentrated on her hands: the slender fingers, the soft white skin, the neatly shaped nails.

It's impossible! She doesna understand the world as I do.

'Kitty… I canna… I can *never* give ye the kind of life ye're accustomed to.'

Too late to regret his weakness in succumbing to that instant attraction that had flared between them the very first time they met. Too late to realise the risk he had run in their clandestine meetings. Those meetings…they had been innocent: walking hand in hand in the woods where they would not be seen, talking and laughing, a few shared kisses, murmured endearments. He'd been naive, not deliberately cruel. He hadn't understood how the heart could so quickly become engaged, how a lonely girl like Kitty might read more into their meetings than he ever intended. Not that he wouldn't elope with her given half a chance. But he had not one tenth of a chance! Not one hundredth! He, an architect's apprentice, she, an earl's daughter.

'Your father…never would he consent to such a lowly match for his daughter and ye know it.'

Adam had never even set eyes on the man, who was away from home, in London, leaving his only daughter alone with just the servants and an elderly great-aunt for company. It was no life for a young lady who craved excitement and company in her life.

'We could run away. We could elope. In Scotland, there is a place…'

Adam laid his fingers against Kitty's lips.

'We canna. Ye would not do that to your father.'

Her head jerked back, away from his touch.

'I would!' Her eyes burned into his. 'I *must* get away before he comes back. You don't understand. *Please*, Adam. Take me with you.'

'Ye would come to resent me. I'm still apprenticed tae Sir Angus for another year, so I canna marry even if I wanted to. I've no income until I build my reputation as an architect. And that could take years.'

And before he could begin to establish his own name as an architect, Sir Angus McAvoy had promised to fund a trip for him to Italy, to study the architecture in Florence and Rome and Sienna. If he searched deep in his heart, he knew he couldn't pass up on such an opportunity; it could be the making of him and of his career. Neither would he betray Sir Angus McAvoy's trust in him, not after the man had been such a good employer and friend to Adam's widowed mother, who had worked as Sir Angus's housekeeper since the death of Adam's soldier father when Adam was barely out of leading strings.

'I would not mind, Adam. I…we could live as man and wife until you finish your apprenticeship. And I can be thrifty. I know I can.'

Adam's heart clenched at the sound of her voice, small and defeated; at the sight of hope dying in her eyes. He closed his own eyes and summoned his strength. Would that he'd had the foresight to avoid this—he should never have indulged himself in meeting with her, but that realisation came too late. He loved her and the thought of never seeing her again tore him apart. But she was only seventeen. Four years younger than he. And it was up to him to be the man. To be strong.

Better she hate him and believe him a scoundrel than she grieve over what might have been.

'Marriage is no part of my plans; not for many years. I'm fond of ye, Kitty, but this was never more than a pleasant way to pass the time when I had an hour to spare. I thought ye understood that.'

She swallowed, her long, slim throat moving. Adam clenched his hands into fists to stop himself reaching for her, comforting her...

'You do not know what I must endure at my father's hands.'

He frowned. Was this some kind of ruse to persuade him to change his mind? She had never before hinted at trouble at home. Loneliness, yes... how could she not be lonely at times, with just herself, her father and her father's aunt rattling around in that huge house? He understood the loneliness of an only child with just one parent. And the natural wariness of a daughter under the control of a strict father.

'Tell me.'

The words left his mouth even as he realised that, whatever her reasons, they could change nothing. He and Kitty still came from, and lived in, two separate worlds and, all at once, he was afraid of what she might reveal—afraid that what he learned might render it impossible for him to leave her. Afraid…selfishly…that, if he felt compelled to act, both of their lives would eventually spiral down into regret, blame and destitution.

He raised his hand, palm facing her, silencing her reply. 'No. On second thoughts, say nothing. It can make no difference. I will still be an architect's apprentice and ye will still be an earl's daughter.'

She was clean, well dressed, well fed. She showed no signs of neglect and he had never seen a bruise marring her white skin. She spoke of endurance…but he had seen the state of the people who lived crammed into the tenements in Edinburgh's old town. There could be no comparison.

He hardened his heart again, knowing he must break hers.

'Return to your father's house and, in time, ye'll see I was right. What ye feel for me isna love. It's infatuation. And, even were we equals, I am but one-and-twenty and in no mind to marry for a verra long time.'

He succumbed to the urge to touch her once again. He cupped her face and looked deep into those tragic grey eyes, the eyelashes spiky from her tears. 'When you meet the man who will be your husband—a man who is your equal in society—ye will look back and ye will see I was right, and ye will be grateful to me.' His hands dropped to rest briefly on her shoulders before sliding down to clasp her upper arms. He squeezed gently before releasing her and then stepping away. 'I have to go. We leave at first light. God bless ye, Kitty.'

He spun on his heel before she could reply; before her pleas could wring a promise from him that he could not honour. A clean break. It was for the best...he must do the right thing for Kitty even though it tore his heart into shreds.

He strode off through the woods, the fallen leaves crunching beneath his boots, his throat aching as he tried, unsuccessfully, to hold back his tears.

He did not look back.

Chapter One

Edinburgh—fifteen years later

'I lied to you. I've been lying to you for a long time.'

Adam Monroe's mother stood gazing out of the window of the Edinburgh town house where she had lived and worked for as long as he could remember—the home in which he'd grown up. Ma's back and shoulders were rigid, but Adam didn't miss the tremble of her hand as she tucked a straying lock of hair away under her cap.

'So you *are* ill?'

Adam's gut churned…he couldn't bear to lose Ma. It had always been just the two of them. Well, them and Sir Angus McAvoy, who employed Ma as his housekeeper and had long stood as Adam's benefactor.

Adam crossed the room in two strides, gently

took hold of her shoulders and turned her to face him.

'Tell me.' His voice rasped. 'Anything is better than leaving the worst to my imagination. What is wrong with ye? We can fight it together.'

She jerked away from him. 'I'm not ill!'

Adam studied her face: her pallor; the quiver of her mouth; the tear-washed eyes. She *looked* sick, to his inexpert eyes. 'What have ye lied about? What happened while I was away?'

He'd been to Lincolnshire, to oversee the completion of his first-ever commission south of the border. He'd travelled home, excited and full of pride at the success of the new stables and carriage house he had designed for a William and Mary country mansion, and with the praise and the grateful thanks of the owner—a Member of Parliament—ringing in his ears. This could be the breakthrough he'd been working for. The chance to attract a better—that was, wealthier—clientele. The chance to get his name known among men of influence. He'd arrived home to find his mother, pale and frail, her eyes haunted, her hands wringing at waist level.

Now, she sucked in a breath and straightened her back, her chin up.

'Sit down, Adam. I have something to tell you.'

He obeyed, sitting at the small circular table in the housekeeper's room, and Ma perched on the edge of the opposite chair. There were only two chairs…there had only ever been two chairs… there had never been any visitors. Ma had always kept herself to herself, even after Sir Angus took Adam on as his apprentice and they were away on jobs for weeks and months at a time.

He waited.

'Your father… I've been lying to you all along. He didn't die. I left him. Ran away and took you with me.'

The air left his lungs in a rush, leaving him to struggle to draw another breath. Ma stayed silent, her expression a mask. No shame. No remorse. No apology.

He ignored the flare of anger that fired his gut. His quickness to anger was now ingrained in him, fuelled by his bitterness at a society that—despite his honesty and his hard-working ethic—deemed him unworthy of an earl's daughter and had cost him his first love, Kitty.

First love? Only love, for he'd never forgotten her and he still had regrets.

He'd learned to control his anger over the years; learned that it was more productive to allow his emotions to subside and his head to clear rather than to launch angry tirades in which words spoken could not be unspoken, even if subsequently regretted.

'He's alive?'

His soldier father…a rifleman…decorated for his bravery. A true hero. Alive?

Adam shoved back his chair and surged to his feet. 'I want to meet him.'

All his life he had regretted never having the chance to know his father…the heroic soldier. And now…and now…

'You cannot. He died six months ago. I'm only telling you now because they're searching for you. Again. But this time…' Ma slumped, her shoulders drooping, her shaking hands lifting to cover her face. 'You deserve to know the truth. He was never a soldier. He was never the man…the father… I told you about. I made it all up.'

Adam frowned, scrambling to make sense of her words. His father was not…? 'Then who was he?'

'An earl.' She looked up at him, her face drawn. 'And you were his only son. I have written to the trustees of his estate and one of them is coming here to meet you and to confirm your identity before escorting you to London to register you as his successor.

'Congratulations, Son.' Her upper lip curled, as though she tasted something nasty. 'You are now the Earl of Kelridge.'

How can I ever forgive her?

His mother had sobbed bitterly after her confession, saying only that she had done it for Adam's own good. But he had only been two years of age when she'd spirited him away from his Hertfordshire home and his father. How could that possibly have been for his own good? And although he could understand why she had not told him the truth as a child, he was now six-and-thirty. There could be no excuse: her silence over all those years had robbed Adam of any chance of ever knowing his father.

Now his imagination was bursting with all kinds of lurid speculation about the father he had never met as Ma stubbornly refused to answer any of his questions about the man, or about why she had snatched Adam away.

'It is only right ye should learn for yourself what sort of a man your father was,' she eventually said, when Adam tried yet again to wring an answer from her.

His temper—sorely tried and brimming close to the surface—erupted. 'And so might I have done had ye told me about him *before* he died!'

He wrestled his anger back under control. Ma buried her head in her hands yet again.

'I did what I thought best at the time, Son. Now, though, I am thinking maybe it *was* a mistake to keep this all a secret and I will not now compound my error by painting his character for ye using the palette of *my* distant memories and experience. You will find out more about him from those who knew him better than I. It's been thirty-four years, and he might have changed since I last set eyes on him. I cannae know the truth of that.'

She lifted her head then, to pierce him with the same blue eyes he saw every time he looked in the mirror. He caught a glimpse of her usual steely determination emerging from the depths of her distress and guessed he was unlikely to get any more from her.

'I willna whine and make excuses for what I did,' she said. 'I acted as I thought best and we were happier without him.'

She might have been happier. But what about him?

More bitter resentment, aggravated by a deep sense of betrayal, settled in Adam's gut over the following few days as he awaited the arrival of his father's trustee. His rage and hurt stopped him from any further attempt to coax the truth from Ma, for to do that he must soothe her, cajole her and tell her he understood.

But he didn't damn well understand.

As the initial shock of the news about his father—and the huge change in his own circumstances—subsided, Adam's thoughts returned often to the past. To Hertfordshire. Remembering the time he had spent there fifteen years before.

Remembering Kitty.

His gut churned with angry regrets, made infinitely worse by the slowly emerging realisation of what might have been.

He and Sir Angus had spent several weeks at Fenton Hall, overseeing the restoration of a wing destroyed in a fire that had also stolen the life of Lady Fenton, the mother of four young children. It had been a tragic story…and when he was not working Adam had taken himself away from the grief as much as possible by going for long walks in the grounds and surrounding woodland, straying beyond the Fenton boundary on to the neighbouring estate, Whitlock Manor. And that was where he'd met Kitty, only daughter of Lord Whitlock.

And Adam had lost his heart to a girl who was so far beyond his reach she might as well have been an angel descended from the heavens.

But now…the truth was that he and Kitty *should* have grown up as equals and as neighbours. He'd consulted a map and Whitlock Manor was less than seven miles as the crow flies from Adam's new home, Kelridge Place.

What might have been possible, had he occupied his rightful place in this world? He'd broken Kitty's heart and guilt had plagued him ever since, even though he'd done it to protect her. Had his mother not snatched him from his father, he and Kitty could have met on equal terms. Their love could have blossomed, instead of withering under the blast of practicality and principle.

If I had known...if only I had known.

And, at first, he'd wished Sir Angus was home, for Adam longed to be able to talk this through with his mentor. But he was working on a project far to the north and wasn't expected home for weeks. Then the second blow fell, when Adam happened to mention Sir Angus to his mother one day.

'I need to tell ye the truth about Angus, too.'

'What truth?'

'He is my cousin, on my mother's side. We were always close as children and, when I came here to build a new life for you and me, he took us in.' She then felled him with another blow. 'Did ye never wonder why a man would take on a woman with a young child as housekeeper? Or make that young child his apprentice?'

He had believed Sir Angus had seen Adam's talent and recognised his hard work and found him worthy of taking on as his apprentice. Adam had been proud of those achievements which, it now seemed, owed nothing to Adam's abilities. It had been sheer nepotism. His sense of betrayal was complete. Sir Angus—his father figure and, as Adam had grown up, his friend—had been complicit in her lies all this time.

How could he ever forgive either of them?

If only I had known the truth.

Where was Kitty now? Would they meet? Would he recognise her? Would she remember him? She'd been seventeen then and fifteen years had passed. They would both have changed and she was bound to be married by now, but he couldn't curb his joy at the thought of seeing her again, even though any meeting would be bittersweet with the knowledge of what might have been.

He couldn't help but wonder how long she had mourned their impossible love—the Earl's daughter and the architect's apprentice.

Two weeks later

'We're here, my lord.'

Adam jolted awake. The carriage had indeed drawn to a halt and he gazed out at the Mayfair town house, with its five steps leading up to the front door and its stucco finish. He craned his neck to fully view it—four storeys, plus a half-basement—taking in the twelve-paned sash windows and the classical stone-pedimented surround to the black-painted front door, which was topped by a batwing-patterned fanlight.

He twisted on the bench seat to view his travelling companion—a compact, humourless solicitor by the name of Dursley, from the firm of Dibcock and Dursley. Once Ma had provided him with the evidence that she was indeed the missing Countess of Kelridge and that Adam was the rightful heir, Dursley had been briskly efficient in apprising Adam of the full extent of his change in circumstances, following which he had maintained a meticulously professional courtesy towards Adam throughout the journey from Edinburgh. There had been no relaxation of his formal manner: no hint of warmth, no friendliness, no reassurance.

'I shall collect you at eleven o'clock tomorrow morning and take you to petition the Attorney General, Sir Robert Gifford. As long as he is satisfied with the validity of your claim to the title of the Earl of Kelridge—and I am confident the documentary evidence your mother provided will prove sufficient—he will recommend the exercise of the royal discretion without reference to the House of Lords or the Committee for Privileges. The Clerk of the Parliaments will then record your name in the Register of Lords Spiritual and Temporal, following which you will receive a summons to take your seat in the House of Lords.

'In the meantime, your butler—Green—will acquaint you with your new household. I instructed the servants to come to London in order

to prepare your town house for your occupation.'
Dursley inclined his head. 'Good day, my lord.'

Adam blanked his expression, keeping his
scowl from his face. Dursley owed him nothing,
other than the legal service he was paid to provide
but, surely, common decency dictated he should
at least escort his client into the house and introduce this Green fellow? But he swallowed back
his angry reaction to the solicitor's treatment, suspecting he would need all the goodwill he could
get in this alien world. It would not do to make
an enemy of his solicitor.

'And good day to you, too, Mr Dursley. Thank
you for providing the transport to London.'

Dursley allowed himself a wintry smile. 'Oh,
the cost will be reimbursed from His late Lordship's estate, my lord. You owe me no gratitude.'

Adam contented himself with gritting his teeth
and a silent vow to appoint a new firm of solicitors as soon as possible. One nugget of information that Dursley had let slip during the
journey was that Adam's heir—his uncle, Grenville Trewin, who would, in time, have inherited
the earldom had Adam not been found—was also
a client of Dursley's firm and he was clearly a
firm favourite with Dursley himself. Unlike, it
would seem, Adam's late father, upon whom the
solicitor resolutely refused to be drawn. No wonder the fellow looked as though he was sucking a

lemon most of the time. He would clearly be happier had Adam *not* been found.

Still. Adam was here in London now and it would be a relief to be released from the confines of the carriage and Dursley's not-so-scintillating company. The man had even flatly refused to stop at Kelridge Place on the way south, deeming time to be of the essence in establishing Adam in his new rank and status.

The sound of the carriage door opening grabbed Adam's attention. A footman in dark green livery stood to attention, his gaze fixed straight ahead. Adam stifled a sigh.

He'd visited, and even stayed in, a few aristocratic households for his work and he really did not care for the rigid structure, the divide between the family and the servants who cared for them. Nor, if he was honest, had he much cared for the arrogance of many of those same aristocrats—the way they simply accepted subservience from others, including Adam, as their due. He supposed that, with Ma being a housekeeper—and he still could not quite believe that, all this time, she had been a countess—he instinctively identified with the servants rather than their masters.

A glance at the front door revealed a man dressed in black tailcoat and grey trousers waiting on the threshold, hands clasped behind his back, and further figures lined up along the hallway.

Adam hauled in a deep breath before descending the carriage steps to the pavement. His new life awaited, with not one familiar thing about it to help him come to terms with all this change. Even his name was not his own, he had discovered. He was no longer Adam Monroe, Scottish architect, but Ambrose Adam Trewin, the English Earl of Kelridge. And he not only had an Uncle Grenville about whom he knew nothing, but he also had a cousin—Grenville's son, Bartholomew, who was thirty years of age.

The weighty dread that had settled in the pit of his stomach over the past two weeks now seemed destined to remain lodged there because, as far as he could see, he had little to look forward to. The only people he knew in this world were those who had hired him as an architect and he was not yet well enough established in his profession to help bridge the gap between him and the rest of the aristocratic world. Neither could he believe those same clients would be overjoyed to find him joining their ranks. He had attended a small boys' preparatory school in Edinburgh, with the sons of bankers, lawyers and business owners, and had not attended university, so he had never mixed with these people, but he must now make his home in this city of strangers and at his new country estate, Kelridge Place, in Hertfordshire.

Adam did not even have the comfort of his

mother. Their relationship had remained strained until he left and although, at the last minute, he had invited her to accompany him, she had refused.

'I am content here, Adam. It's been my home for many years and I have no wish to face the censure of those who remember me from before. You will have a hard enough time gaining acceptance without me reviving that old scandal. You are better off without me.'

'What about *your* family, Ma?'

'There is no one, other than Angus.'

The only truths she'd told him of her own past was that she had been born in Scotland, she was an only child and her parents were dead. He had not known that her father—his grandfather—had been a wealthy banker or that she had gone to London for a Season, chaperoned by her mother and a hired companion. It had been there that an heiress, without male protectors, had proved all too easy prey for the impoverished Lord Kelridge.

'Have you no old friends?'

Her lips had pressed together at that and she would be drawn no more upon the subject. And he—God help him—had not argued, resentment at her betrayal still smouldering deep within him. Now, though, he found that the further he got from Edinburgh and the more distance he put between himself and his mother, the more that resentment gave way to hurt.

Hurt that she had never trusted him enough to tell him the truth. Through his boyhood they'd always been so close. He'd always felt as though they'd shared everything, but now it felt as though his whole life had been a lie.

Now, as he trod towards the front door of his new home, Adam wished he had been more forgiving. Maybe then she would have relented and come with him.

'Welcome to your home, Lord Kelridge. I am Green. Your butler.' Green bowed, stiff and correct, then held out his hand for Adam's hat. 'Please allow me to introduce your staff.'

'Thank you.'

Adam scanned the entrance hall. It was dark and cheerless, papered in dark green stripes above the dado, but the cornices were crisply moulded and showed promise. Dursley had said his fortune was large…he would arrange for the house to be redecorated. Maybe then it would feel more like home?

Give yourself time. Don't rush into hasty decisions.

It was true. He'd only just stepped inside the front door. He would wait. He would see what this new life might offer before he changed anything, including his staff, not one of whom met his gaze or smiled during the introductions. He looked back along the line. They resembled soldiers on parade, standing rigidly, eyes forward. He sighed. It was not their fault. They would behave as his father had expected them to behave.

But…he was not his father and he did not have to continue any of his traditions if he chose not to. And he did choose not to. He was the Earl. *He* could dictate the mood of the house. The only other example he had was the happy household in which he had grown up, that of Sir Angus, who had always treated Ma more like a friend than an employee. *That* was the example he preferred.

Except, a sly inner voice reminded him, *do not forget they were family. Not employer and servant, after all. So how would you know what is correct and what is not?*

Even more confused, he vowed again to take his time.

'Aye. Well!' Adam clapped his hands together and then rubbed them briskly. He saw the momentary shock upon Green's face when he heard the Scottish accent and the devil inside him prompted him to exaggerate it. 'I hae been travellin' a week or more and I'm fair grubby and weary. Mrs… Ford, is it, aye?'

The housekeeper dipped a little curtsy. 'It is, my lord.'

'I should like to bathe, if ye'll arrange for water

to be heated, please. And…' his roaming gaze paused on the chef 'Monsieur Delon, I should very much like a cup of tea while the bath is being prepared. Green… I will inspect the rest of the house, from basement to attics, after I have bathed.'

Green's lips compressed. 'The late Lord Kelridge relayed *all* domestic instructions through myself, my lord. And Monsieur does not make tea. Aggie…' he crooked a finger at a kitchen maid '…will see to that.'

'I see.' Adam scratched his ear. 'But, ye ken, I am *not* your late master. And if I wish tae communicate my needs directly tae the person most able tae satisfy them, then I shall do just that.' He smiled at the butler. 'I do hope we'll no' fall oot over this—or any other—wee detail, Green.'

The butler stood to rigid attention. 'No, my lord.'

'Verra good,' Adam murmured. 'Now, will ye show me the ground floor while Aggie fetches me that cup of tea?'

Chapter Two

'Stepmama? Are you in here?'

Kitty, Lady Fenton, laid aside her quill pen with a quiet sigh. 'I am.'

This was the problem with trying to write here in London—at least at home at Fenton Hall she had her own parlour where she could remain undisturbed, whereas she could hardly bar members of her family from entering the salon of their town house. Kitty twisted in her chair to find her seventeen-year-old stepdaughter, Charis, regarding her with a smile and a teasing light in her eyes.

'I am sorry to interrupt you, but I have such exciting news I cannot wait to share it with *someone* and Robert has gone out. *Again*.'

Kitty suspected that Robert—Charis's older brother, and thus Kitty's stepson—had not gone out, but had yet to return home from last night. A not uncommon occurrence. At twenty-six, however, that was his affair—he was his own man and Kitty had neither the inclination nor the right to interfere in his life. Fortunately, her relationship with all four of her stepchildren was an affectionate one and she trusted Robert—Viscount Fenton since the death of his father five years before—not to succumb to the wilder excesses of some of his peers.

It was a relief Charis was far too innocent to realise the half of what her brother—and most young men in the *ton*—got up to.

And long may she hold on to that innocence.

Love for her stepdaughter filled Kitty's heart as she rose to her feet, then linked her arm through Charis's and gently urged her towards the sofa.

'Then you shall share it with me, love. I dare say it is time I took a break from writing…the words prove somewhat reluctant this morning and I fear my prose is somewhat stilted.'

She bit back a smile at the disgust in her own voice. When would she accept that it would never be an easy matter to transfer the images in her head into interesting, or even compelling, phrases and sentences on paper? The late Miss Jane Austen had made the entire process seem so much easier than it proved. Kitty's attempts to follow in her footsteps had resulted in the publication of one novel—albeit anonymously—but it was proving even more daunting to write a second and, try as she might, it seemed impossible to confine her story to family and community as Miss Austen had done with such sly, observant wit. No. Kitty's characters inevitably seemed to stumble into thrilling dramas and her own prose veered towards exaggeration no matter how hard she tried to rein it in.

'You may tell me about it later,' said Charis, who delighted in Kitty's covert double life as a novelist and often helped her to work through any sticky patches that arose in the plots of her romantic adventures. 'But, first… I received this from Annabel.' Miss Annabel Blanchard and Charis had been firm friends from their first meeting at the start of this Season, when they had both made their debuts. Now, Charis thrust a note covered in painstakingly neat writing—presumably Annabel's—under Kitty's nose. 'Talaton has spoken at last!'

'At last?' Kitty laughed. 'You young girls are always in such haste! To my certain knowledge, Annabel only met Lord Talaton for the first time this Season. So that is…now, let me see…' She tapped her chin, puckering her brow and raising her eyes to the ceiling as she pondered.

'You are teasing me, Stepmama.' Charis pouted, then nudged her shoulder into Kitty, who dropped her pose and laughed again.

'Well, how could I resist? Your delight in such exaggeration makes you a most satisfying target for my poor attempts at wit. But it is true, nevertheless. Annabel and Talaton only met two months ago and that is a very short time in which to form a lasting attachment.'

Kitty clamped down on her mind's attempt to drag those old memories from the depths where they had lain safely buried for fifteen years. She had long made it a personal rule not to look back. Not to tolerate regrets of any sort. She lived in the present and she looked forward to the future. It was enough. But she did not forget that hard-learned lesson in how easily the heart could be fooled into thinking itself in love.

'Well, *Annabel* was certain of her feelings from the first moment they met and now her father has given his consent, and it is *all arranged*. I cannot wait to hear all about his proposal.' Charis clasped her hands together in front of her chest, her hazel eyes shining. 'It is *so* romantic. I wonder when it will be my turn.'

Kitty fought the compulsion to warn Charis to be careful, loath to quash her natural enthusiasm. She could not help but worry for her stepdaughter, lest she lose her heart to the wrong man—Kitty's own painful experience had left her determined to guard her own heart well, but she tried not to allow her fears to curb her stepdaughter's youthful dreams.

She contented herself with saying, 'Do not be in too much hurry, Charis. This is only your debut Season and you are still very young to be thinking of marriage.'

Charis pouted. 'Annabel is not the first of my friends to be betrothed.'

'Have you a particular young man in mind?'

'No. No one.'

Kitty almost laughed, Charis sounded so despondent, but she managed to swallow her laugh and, instead, she hugged her stepdaughter and dropped a kiss on her fair head.

'Don't despair, sweeting. The right young man will appear to sweep you off your feet one day. In the meantime, shall we call upon Annabel and her mother later and share their excitement?'

Charis threw her arms around Kitty and hugged her. 'Thank you, for I know you do not much care for Mrs Blanchard. You are the *best* stepmother anyone could ever wish for.'

'I am in wholehearted agreement, Charis,' drawled a voice from the doorway, 'but is this excess of enthusiasm due to anything in particular, or is it merely a general statement?'

Kitty looked up, laughing, at her stepson—tall and broad with his father's golden-brown hair and dark brown eyes—who filled the doorway. He was clean-shaven and dressed in his riding clothes and looked nothing like a man who had spent the night carousing, so she had clearly done him a disservice in suspecting he had not returned home last night.

Not for the first time, she counted her blessings. Edgar, her late husband, had been over twenty years Kitty's senior, but their marriage had been quietly content despite Edgar's tendency to treat her as a surrogate daughter in need of instruction. His motives, she knew, had been good and he was a kindly spouse, but his gentle comparisons between Kitty and Veronica, his first wife—in which Kitty inevitably came off worst—had left her with the feeling of never being quite good enough.

Ironically, being a mother—or, strictly, a stepmother, as she had never been blessed with a child of her own—had been the one role at which she had surpassed Veronica, who had not been the maternal type. And even there, Edgar had not failed to puncture Kitty's self-esteem with his monthly 'joke' that it was fortunate he had already produced his heir and spare when Kitty, yet again, proved not to be with child. Kitty had found that joke unfunny to begin with but, as the years passed, it became increasingly hurtful, especially as she became aware that her barrenness, in Edgar's eyes, was all about him. He never once seemed to consider that Kitty might be upset by her failure to become a mother in her own right—and she had hidden her distress from him, and from the children, for she could not love any of Edgar's four children more had they been of her body.

Robert was the eldest, followed by Edward, currently serving in the army, and Jennifer, who had been married for two years now. Charis was the youngest and Kitty deeply regretted Edgar had not lived to see her grow into such a fine young woman. Since Edgar's death, Robert had become more like a brother to Kitty than a stepson—a steadfast support and ally. She was happy and secure, both in her stepfamily and in her place in society. She had her marriage portion and the Dower House if she chose to live there, but, for the time being, she still happily remained at the family home, Fenton Hall, running it on Robert's behalf until he was ready to settle down.

'Good morning, Robert,' she now said. 'Your sister's enthusiasm is her customary over-exaggeration at my offer to visit Miss Blanchard to share in her celebration. But I must allow Charis to tell you the details, as it is her news to tell, not mine.'

'Where were you, Rob? I looked for you first because I was bursting to tell—'

'*Bursting?* That is hardly a ladylike expression, Charis.'

Charis pouted as Robert continued, 'And I was not here because I went out to pay a visit to an old…acquaintance, I guess would be the correct description. But tell me your news first, Charis, and then I shall tell you mine. Although I doubt it will mean much to either of you, as you never knew the gentleman in question.'

Charis quickly relayed her news to Robert, who—to the disappointment of his sister—failed to match her excitement.

'I dare say they will suit well enough,' he said dismissively, 'but you need not envy your friend, Charis, for Talaton is an awful windbag. You should hear him prosing on in the Lords. But, never mind that…now for my news. You will both be thrilled… I know how hostesses vie with one another to be the first to present a prestigious newcomer to their guests. There is nothing quite like stealing a march on one's rivals, is there? Well. Be prepared to crow over the rest of 'em, for *we* are to be the first to welcome the new Earl of Kelridge to our dining table. Tonight! I've listed a few names we might include on the guest list.'

He reached into his pocket and thrust a sheet of paper covered in his heavy black script at Kitty. She glanced down at the list of ten names—three couples plus a few unattached ladies and gentlemen, all Hertfordshire residents. She frowned up at Robert.

'They finally located Kelridge's heir, did they? They believe this one to be genuine?'

Over the past few years, as the late Lord Kelridge's health failed, the search for his missing wife and son had intensified, but to no avail. Several charlatans, however, had tried their luck, claiming to be the missing Ambrose Trewin. Their claims had been easy to disprove, but of Lady Kelridge and her son there had been no trace.

'There is no doubt. Lady Kelridge wrote to the executors of Kelridge's estate herself…she is still alive and living in Scotland. I'd have paid good money to see Grenville Trewin's face when he found out—I'll wager he was spitting feathers! To get so close to the prize, only to have it snatched away again…one could almost feel sorry for him, although it would have been at least seven years before the Committee for Privileges would even consider declaring Kelridge's son and heir dead.'

'*I* cannot help but sympathise with Mr Trewin's son,' said Kitty. 'It would have meant a very different life indeed for Bartholomew Trewin, who has always struck me as a pleasant gentleman.'

Robert smiled. 'He *is* a good man and a good friend. Let us hope the new Lord Kelridge will have a temperament more like that of his cousin than his late father.'

'Indeed.' Kitty had heard tales of the late Lord

Kelridge's violent temper. 'Well, I admit it will be quite the coup to be the first to entertain Lord Kelridge, although—'

'Although you do not consider yourself in competition with the rest of the hostesses?' Robert grinned. 'I know you always protest against any hint of competitiveness, but can you not admit you will enjoy a certain smug satisfaction at being first in this instance?'

Kitty laughed. 'Well, just between us, I *shall* admit to it, if only because I shall not then have to listen to the other ladies boasting of their success. But, how did it come about? Why is Lord Kelridge to dine with us? Did you meet him last night?'

'No, but I met up with Tolly—that is, Bartholomew Trewin—and *he* told me his cousin had trained as an architect and you will never guess! He might be a stranger to most of the *ton*, but not to me. He actually *stayed* at Fenton Hall.'

An architect? Unease stirred, deep inside Kitty.

'Ooh! Then do I know him, too?' Charis's face lit up.

'Not you, Sis. You were too little. And it was before Father married Stepmama, so I doubt they would have met.' Robert's brown gaze settled on Kitty's face. 'Do you recall when the library wing was rebuilt after the fire?'

Those stirrings lurched into boiling, roiling agitation. She nodded, her mouth dry, those locked-away memories clamouring to be set free.

'Well, the new Lord Kelridge—it turns out he was the architect's apprentice. They stayed at the Hall during the final stages of the restoration and although Adam, as he was then called, was much older than me—I was eleven at the time—he was always patient and made time for me, although I am sure he must have cursed my impudence at times, following him around like a lost puppy as I did.'

A vivid memory struck Kitty, stealing her breath—Adam Monroe, tall and dark, laughing as he described giving young Robert the slip in order to meet up with Kitty. But there had been no malice in his laughter and he'd also spent some of his free time fishing with Robert, knowing the lad was grieving the loss of his mother. She'd thought him a good man. She'd fallen in love with him, wholeheartedly believing that he loved her in return. But he had let her down, with his lies, and she had grieved for his loss—her foolish, tender heart in pieces—when he'd left. She'd dreamt about him at night and fantasised about him during the long, lonely days while she waited for her father's return. *Dreaded* her father's return.

Her father...the one man who should have had her safety and happiness at heart, but another man who had let her down.

Her throat thickened.

'I presume your path never crossed with his, Stepmama,' Robert continued, 'even though we were neighbours.'

Kitty's heart thudded in her chest as though it would beat its way free and disgust at her naivety scoured her stomach. Adam had made so much of the fact they were unequal in status and yet the entire time he had been the son of an earl.

'We were never introduced,' she said. And that was no lie. 'And…this Adam…did he never tell you the truth of who he was?'

'No. And that is the strange thing…it appears that *he* did not know his true identity. He knew nothing about Kelridge until a few weeks ago.'

Kitty felt marginally better. But only marginally. Was that true? He had lied before, about loving her. He might easily be lying again.

'And Lord Kelridge is to dine with us tonight, you say?'

'Yes. I hope you have no objection? I was aware you had no plans to dine out tonight and, as I said, it is the perfect opportunity to steal a march on the other hostesses.' Robert slung his arm around Kitty's shoulders to give her a quick hug. 'Not that you care for such petty rivalries, of course. But many of the others *do* care…a very great deal.'

He winked, and Kitty couldn't help but smile

at the wicked twinkle in his eyes even though her insides were in turmoil. She scrabbled for an excuse. Any excuse.

But—if this is the truth, and not some dreadful nightmare—I shall have to meet him some time. He will be our neighbour in Hertfordshire. I cannot avoid him for ever. And would it not be better to meet for the first time when I am prepared for it? Adam. Oh, dear God. Adam.

She swallowed down the swell of emotion. Ignored the heat that washed beneath her skin. Pressed a hand to her belly to help quell her agitation as the memories she'd held at bay for so long shot to the surface, one after the other.

The taste of his lips.

His scent.

The feeling of rightness, of safety and security in the haven of his arms. The feeling that was a lie.

Kitty... Kitty...what are you doing to me?

Those words that were lies.

Kitty quelled a shudder, quashing those memories, forcing her attention back to the matter under discussion.

'Have you spoken to Lord Kelridge? Has he accepted your invitation?'

'That,' said Robert, 'is where I have been this morning. To call upon His Lordship and remind him of our connection. He was happy to accept.'

'And is there a Lady Kelridge?' Her breath stilled in her lungs as she awaited Robert's reply.

'No. He is a single gentleman. And, now I think about it...' Robert tweaked the list from Kitty's slack grip and scanned the names, '...this may be a touch overwhelming for him—all these strangers. Should we restrict the guest list to a chosen few? Two or three couples, perhaps?'

A shudder ran through Kitty at the thought of being so exposed. Better by far to be one of many rather than risk bringing his attention to her too often.

Will he remember me? Will he even recognise me?

She would be introduced as Lady Fenton. Their...*friendship*...had taken place over a matter of weeks, fifteen years ago. Why should he remember her? She shouldn't flatter herself it had meant as much to him as it had to her. He'd made it quite clear—*brutally* clear—that he'd merely been dallying with her affections. Oh, and how easy she had made it for him...so desperate to escape her father and his plans for her that she had practically begged Adam to wed her. She had even, God help her, lowered herself enough to offer to live with him unwed. It was a miracle she had retained her innocence for, looking back, she had been so besotted she had little doubt she would have succumbed to any attempt at seduction. Willingly.

Another wave of heat—this time the burn of shame—swept over her skin, resulting in another shudder.

'Stepmama?' Charis frowned as she eyed Kitty. 'Are you quite well?'

Again, Kitty tore her thoughts out of the past, the years of controlling her emotions—hiding them from both her father and from Edgar—coming to her rescue. She gathered her customary poise and stretched her lips in a smile.

'I am quite well, my love. No need for concern. I was simply pondering the issue of the guest list. Robert… I think we should invite as many as we can sit. With us three, and Lord Kelridge, that makes ten other couples—twenty-four in total. Charis, you may assist me in compiling the guest list and writing the invitations and, Robert…will you ask Vincent to request Mrs Ainsley to attend me at her earliest convenience to discuss the menu?'

'Will we still have time to call upon Annabel?'

Charis's hesitance suggested she knew the answer, but Kitty refused to put Adam before her beloved stepdaughter. 'Yes, my love. We will *make* time.'

Her nerves continued in turmoil as the rest of the day unfolded, but she did as she always did—rose above her personal concerns and concentrated on the practicalities of what lay before her. Life with her father had instilled in her the belief that, for a female in their world, duty outweighed all other considerations.

The passage of time, however, had never been less predictable: on the one hand, it dawdled past with the speed of a snail and yet, in complete contradiction, the dinner hour swept towards her with the speed of a runaway horse. She approved the menus Mrs Ainsley presented to her; she arranged flowers; she and Charis called upon Mrs Blanchard, staying for no longer than the usual thirty minutes; and, between all that, Kitty visited her bedchamber on at least three different occasions to examine her gowns, each time making her choice, only to return later, having changed her mind.

She prayed Adam, or Kelridge, as she must now think of him, wouldn't recognise her. Yet, as soon as that prayer formed in her head, she realised she couldn't bear it if he had forgotten her—her heart would rip to shreds if he had no memory of those romantic trysts that had meant the world to her. And while she was woman enough to hope he would still find her attractive, she determined to treat him as no more than an ordinary guest, with the reserve and courtesy expected of any society hostess.

And as the clock ticked by, so her thoughts and her insides jumbled and tumbled.

'Which gown do you wish to wear tonight, milady? I shall need to press it for you.' Effie, her maid, looked at her enquiringly when Kitty wandered, yet again, into her bedchamber.

'Oh. I...' She could not continue to prevaricate, but...which gown should she select? She thrust away her disgust at her fickleness. It should not matter what she wore or what she looked like. But it did. 'Why do *you* not choose, Effie?' Kitty smiled winningly. 'I want to look my best—something simple and elegant without frills or fuss. Which gown do you suggest?'

A delighted smile lit the maid's face. 'Ooh, milady. I've always loved this one, but you so rarely wear it.' She reached into the press and withdrew a gown of butter-yellow silk, simply adorned with a few silk rosebuds and with a trim of blonde lace at the neck and the hem. 'It shows off your hair something lovely, it does.'

It was a gown Kitty had not even considered. And yet...yes. It was perfect. It skimmed over her slender figure, the skirt falling in graceful folds that swayed as she moved. The scooped neckline was low enough to be flattering, but not brazenly so.

'Thank you. Yes, I shall wear the yellow silk. With my wedding pearls, I think.'

There, Mr Adam Monroe—or Lord Kelridge,

or whatever your name might now be. You *might not have wanted me, but someone did.*

Edgar's gift for his young bride had been an exquisite pearl necklace, matching drop earrings and a pair of pearl bracelets.

Thank goodness for Edgar. Without him...

Once again, she dragged her thoughts out of the past. Edgar might have been insensitive at times, but he was at least gentle, clean and respectable and they had each rescued the other and fulfilled a need. His, for a mother for his young children and a life companion for himself. Hers, to escape her debt-ridden drunk of a father and his petrifying plan to clear his gambling debts by selling his young daughter's hand in marriage to Algernon White, the lecherous owner of several gaming clubs. White, her father had informed her, had ambitions to expand his business empire and was therefore eager to gain respectability through marriage into the aristocracy. And, as for her— well, what use was a daughter unless to make an advantageous marriage? Her father had never forgiven her for being born a girl and she had never forgiven him his cruel plan.

Thank goodness for Edgar indeed. Kitty had been grateful for his solution to her dilemma and she had tried to be a good wife to him, even though she was sadly aware that she had never quite measured up to the perfection of Veronica.

Chapter Three

Two days after his arrival in London and Adam's feet had barely touched the ground.

So much to take in about this new life…none of which he had asked for or, if he was honest, much wanted. He'd spent much of his time with his solicitors, all of whom, so it appeared to Adam, subscribed to Dursley's opinion that the earldom and the Kelridge estates would be far better off with Adam's uncle, Grenville Trewin, at the helm. Not that they said it outright, of course. It was the subtext of what they said, under the guise of educating Adam about his new responsibilities…the sly insinuation that the estate was bound to deteriorate under new stewardship. More than ever he was determined to appoint new solicitors as soon as all the legalities around his return had been completed.

He'd received his summons from the House of

Lords and had taken his seat yesterday, his skin prickling with the weight of so many stares even though, according to one speaker, attendance in the chamber was surprisingly thin. Adam sat there, watching and listening, feeling nothing like a lord. He did not belong in this world of the aristocracy where, although everyone was curious about him—where he had been, where his mother was, why he had not come forward until now—still he could sense the reserve of the people he met. He had always prided himself on getting along with any man, no matter his birth but…this was different. It was no longer simply a matter of polite interaction with these people. Now, he must, somehow, fit into this world. *Their* world.

He'd enjoyed the debate, in which he had not taken part as he knew next to nothing about the application of duties to imported timber. When he'd returned home, however, the thought had come into his head that he perfectly embodied that old saying, a fish out of water. His servants had resisted all his efforts to create a less formal relationship with them. It seemed they had their own peculiar pride and had no wish to serve a master who, in their opinion, crossed the line between upstairs and downstairs. They wanted a master they could take pride in serving…not one who tried to blur the boundaries between his world and theirs.

Adam belonged neither with the aristocracy nor with the servants and, during the night, he had decided to cut his losses with London and its strict hierarchy, and travel to Kelridge Place that morning.

Until Robert knocked on his door.

Robert, Earl of Fenton. How strange… unsettling, even…to realise the scruffy, grieving eleven-year-old lad who had dogged Adam's footsteps during his stay at Fenton Hall was now a man. And another lord. How many were there in London? It seemed every person he met had some kind of a title within their family. And the remainder of the population seemed to exist simply to make the lives of this privileged elite easier. He'd known, of course, it was the case and that it was the way of the world, but never before had it been thrust in his face in quite such a blatant manner.

So now, Adam had an invitation to dine with Robert and his family that evening which meant he must delay his departure for his Hertfordshire estate. And this afternoon, rather than venture forth to sample the delights of the promenade hour in Hyde Park, where he would be subjected to even more stares and speculation, he opted to stay at home with a bottle of claret and…brood, Ma would call it. He huffed a laugh. She'd be right, too. He *was* brooding…all these changes—

so many in so short a space of time—dominating his thoughts until he had little space left to think about anything else.

He jerked to attention as the door opened and Green entered the room to present him with a card.

'Mr Bartholomew Trewin has called, my lord. Are you at home?'

Adam frowned at yet another example of the stiff formality he so disliked.

What if I was to say, no, I'm not at home? This house is not so vast that my cousin could fail to hear Green speak to me.

But he was curious to meet his cousin, and so he said, 'Yes. I will see him, and please bring another glass and a fresh decanter, Green.'

His cousin had evidently been the one to inform Robert that the new Earl of Kelridge was the same person as Sir Angus McAvoy's apprentice, who had stayed and worked at Fenton Hall fifteen years ago. As ever, the thought of that time sparked memories of Kitty. He'd discreetly enquired about her father, only to discover he'd died and the title and estate had been inherited by a distant cousin. Adam had been reluctant to include Kitty in his enquiry because they'd never officially met.

He stood up as a gentleman walked in through the door. Green glided across the room and set a fresh decanter and a second glass on the table next to Adam's chair before silently leaving and closing the door behind him.

'Mr Trewin?' Adam bowed. 'I am Adam, your cousin. Please, take a seat.'

His cousin bowed, then strolled across the room to take a chair near Adam, giving Adam the opportunity to study him. Thirty years of age, according to Robert, Bartholomew had until recently been a captain in the cavalry and was a veteran of the war against Napoleon and of Waterloo, that epic battle where the tyrant was vanquished at long last. He had a handsome, boyish cast to his face, if one ignored the livid scar that slashed diagonally from forehead to left cheekbone. His missing left eye was covered with a brown-leather patch and his light brown hair was carefully styled to conceal the upper part of the scar, but did nothing to hide the scar that puckered his cheek.

'I'm pleased to meet you, Coz,' Bartholomew said, his tone—as with so many in this world, Adam had discovered—a light, amused drawl. 'Do call me Tolly. All my friends do. That is, if you care to be friends… Rob tells me you seem a decent sort and I trust his ability to read a man's character.'

'Tolly it is, then.'

Adam didn't know Robert the man well enough

yet to know if his judgement was truly sound, but he'd told Adam that Tolly was a good man and Adam was willing to believe it until proved otherwise.

'Claret?'

'Thought you'd never ask.'

Adam grinned and poured another glass of the rich red wine, handing it to his cousin.

'Robert tells me ye served in the cavalry.'

Tolly grimaced, lifting his hand to his eyepatch. 'I did. I got this at Waterloo. Best to get that out of the way from the start, otherwise it becomes the one thing nobody dares to mention and that's enough to stifle many conversations.'

'It must have been painful.'

Tolly shrugged. 'It has its compensations. The ladies seem to love the piratical look…happy to soothe a fellow's pain. They're not called the caring sex for nothing, y'know.'

He raised his glass as though in a toast, then swigged the wine. Adam puzzled over that hint of sarcasm…almost as though Tolly were mocking himself. Then he caught up with his cousin's purpose.

'And in the spirit of getting awkward subjects out into the open…' Adam favoured the straight approach, too '…how do ye feel about my reappearance after all this time? It would be natural if ye bore some resentment towards me.'

Tolly put his glass down and leant back in his chair. 'I knew I'd like you. Rob said you were direct. And to answer your question, I am pleased you have returned. My old man—your Uncle Grenville—would die rather than admit it, but the burden of responsibility is beginning to weigh on him.'

'He's been running the estates since my father fell ill, so I understand.'

'And before that! He resigned from the cavalry thirteen years ago, went home to Kelridge and took over. Your father, my Uncle Gerald, was never interested in the estate, or in dealing with business matters, and was happy to leave it all to my father.'

'Why?'

At Tolly's questioning look, Adam elaborated. 'I mean, why was my father not interested in the estate? And why would *your* father be content to give up his independence and take on such responsibility?'

'Near as I can fathom it, my uncle was too busy living the high life after your mother left and cared not if the estate went to rack and ruin as long as the rents came in and funded his pleasures. My father, on the other hand, adores Kelridge Place.' Tolly shrugged. 'It's his family home…taking over meant he could live there after he left the cavalry and that he could run it in the way he saw fit. It suited them both.'

'So...' Adam frowned, thinking. 'Your father...he is unlikely to welcome my return?'

Tolly's eye narrowed. 'It *could* prove a little awkward after all these years of him being in charge. He is a mite set in his ways and you may need to tread warily at first, until he gets used to you. But *I* still think your return is a blessing in disguise for him.'

'Thank ye for the warning. What about...does your mother also live there?'

'No. She died when I was seventeen. It's just Father and me now.'

Tolly left soon afterwards, leaving Adam with plenty to think about until it was time to change for his dinner engagement at Robert's house.

Some time later, Adam trod up the steps to the elegant town house belonging to Robert, Lord Fenton. The door swung open before he reached the top.

'Lord Kelridge.' And still he felt like an imposter saying that name.

The butler bowed. 'Good evening, my lord.' He clapped his hands and a maidservant hurried forward. 'Allow me to take your hat and then please follow me.'

As the butler handed the hat to the maid, Adam

took in the surroundings—the graceful open-string staircase, with its triple barley-twist balusters topped by a polished dark wood handrail that finished in an elegant spiral at the foot of the stairs. He then followed the butler upstairs to a pair of double doors, which he flung open.

Adam stepped past him and over the threshold into a spacious salon papered above the dado rail in a fashionable grey-green floral design wallpaper and crammed, it seemed, with people. He halted, striving to keep his expression blank. Robert had assured him that they would dine *en famille*, with one or two additional guests. This... *this*...was too much. Every muscle in his body tensed as a hush descended upon the room. Without exception, every single person was staring at him. Appraising him. *Judging* him. His mouth dried and his breathing quickened, causing his pulse to pound as he stared back at the pale, featureless mass of faces. Then a movement broke the moment and Robert emerged from within that mass, striding towards him with a smile on his face, allowing Adam the time to recover his composure, determined to conceal how uncomfortable he felt in his new situation.

'Kelridge! Welcome, my friend. Come...' Robert ushered Adam further into the room '...allow me first to introduce you to my stepmother, Lady Fenton, and my sister, Miss Charis Mayfield.'

Adam's mouth stretched into a polite smile as his gaze skimmed over the two ladies. He bowed. 'Delighted to make your acquaintance, ladies.'

Is that correct? Should I have said Lady Fenton and Miss Mayfield?

Neither lady appeared scornful or, worse, laughed at him, so he hoped he had not committed a faux pas in front of all these strangers. He breathed easier as the two ladies bobbed curtsies, Miss Mayfield—a pretty girl with greenish-hazel eyes and fair hair—eyeing him with unabashed interest while Lady Fenton lowered her eyelids and had yet to look directly at him. As she rose from her curtsy, however, the crescent of her thick, dark lashes lifted to reveal a pair of clear grey eyes and, as their gazes collided, recognition hit Adam with the force of a lightning bolt.

Kitty!

He had hoped they might meet, but he'd not expected it so soon. He'd even wondered if she might prove difficult to find without revealing their previous acquaintance. Deep inside him, a bud of pleasure unfurled, radiating happy contentment. But even as his lips began to curve in a smile, so he recognised the signs that Kitty did not share his joy at meeting again. There was the frosty directness of her stare. The tight line of her lips. The fine groove etched between her eyebrows—a groove that deepened by the second. The stubborn tilt of her chin—a familiar habit from fifteen years before.

Adam blanked his expression yet again, recalling the bad terms on which they had parted, realising that while *he* knew he had denied his love for her in order to protect her from a naive mistake, Kitty had not been privy to his reasoning. There was no chance for explanation, however. Not yet.

'Welcome to our home, Lord Kelridge. I am pleased to meet you.'

Not by a flicker did Kitty reveal they were already very well acquainted and the spread of joy that had already stuttered to a halt now shrivelled and died.

Adam studied his hostess. Robert's stepmother…but *Robert* was Lord Fenton, which made Kitty a widow.

No. Not *a* widow. *The* widow…of the Lord Fenton who had appointed Sir Angus to design and oversee the restoration of his fire-damaged house; the Lord Fenton who had lost his wife, the mother of his children, in that same fire. Robert's father who—so Robert had informed Adam that very morning—had married unexpectedly within two weeks of Adam leaving Fenton Hall.

Two weeks! She swore undying love and claimed her heart was breaking, yet, within days, she accepted another man's hand?

Adam's head spun. Had she lied? She *must* have lied! If she'd truly loved him as she'd claimed, she could never have given herself to another man so soon. He had never quite recovered from his youthful love for Kitty—no other woman he had met had come anywhere close to banishing his memories of her—and yet she had forgotten all about him within two short weeks and married another man. And not just any other man, but Lord Fenton.

God, I'm such a fool! A stupid, blind, trusting fool!

Fenton must have been...what? At least forty years old at the time Adam had known him. Forty years to Kitty's seventeen? Adam's gut clenched. What the devil had possessed her to throw herself away on a man so much older than her, a man with four children already, to boot? No wonder she did not look happy to meet him again. He was no doubt an unwelcome reminder of her youthful infatuation and would be mortified should her stepchildren discover the truth of her behaviour.

Adam struggled to rise above his pain, vowing never to let her know for how long he had ached for her after his return to Edinburgh...not when she had moved on to another man without a second thought.

Lies! They all lied to me—Ma. Sir Angus. And now Kitty.

He reined in his anger and struggled to contain his sense of betrayal as he continued to study her.

She was still relatively young—only thirty-two—and she had matured into a fine woman indeed. Her pale yellow gown draped enticingly over a slender but lush figure—curvier and more womanly than he remembered. Unsurprising in view of her youth when they had last met. He wrenched his attention from her body to her face—the same face that had haunted his dreams for many months after his return to Edinburgh. It was older, but no less appealing: the plump smoothness of a young girl's cheeks had given way to high, sculptured cheekbones; the rosy robustness to a more subtle creamy glow; the brief smile she afforded him was measured rather than eager to please—no sign now of the dimples he had adored—and the eyes that had been a window to her every thought and feeling were now guarded. The full pink lips were the same, as was the glossy mahogany-brown hair, but they were physical features—they did not reflect the person...the character...

She was a stranger now, that was the truth.

Who knows what has happened to her in the past fifteen years, or what sort of a woman she is now? And this... He cast a glance around the salon and its occupants. *This is a new world to me...the* haut ton...*the aristocracy... Mother warned me how disapproving this world can be.*

He would be wise to move through society with a cautious tread until he could better understand it and, if Kitty chose not to reveal their past acquaintance, then he would respect that wish.

'I am honoured by your invitation, my lady.'

Another smile flickered over her lips and was gone. 'Robert will introduce you to our other guests, sir', and she turned away to greet the arrival of yet more guests.

Robert guided Adam towards the nearest of his fellow diners and the following half an hour became a jumble of names and a blur of faces, although he found his gaze drawn frequently to Kitty despite his best efforts to ignore her.

Robert assured Adam there were no more than four-and-twenty diners—all of them, evidently, Hertfordshire residents and, therefore, neighbours of Adam's seat, Kelridge Place—but it seemed like twice that number. Some of the guests were cautiously friendly. Others appeared more suspicious. But every one of them was curious and they vied with one another to slip intrusive questions about Adam's past into the conversation, as though trying to catch him out.

Just as he began to despair of ever reaching the end of the introductions, Robert gripped his elbow to turn him, whispering into his ear, 'This is the last of them, I promise. I should warn you, though…she is the highest-ranking lady in our area of Hertfordshire and she expects to be treated according to her consequence. But she's not a bad old trout.' He raised his voice. 'And this is the Marchioness of Datchworth. My lady…please allow me to present the Earl of Kelridge.'

The Marchioness had swept into the salon only moments before and Adam bowed for what felt like the hundredth time. The lady in question was around sixty years of age, with an upright posture and a sprightly, energetic step that surely rendered the slender cane she carried in her right hand superfluous. She was dressed in a peacock-blue gown and sported a turban of the same hue, trimmed with a fluttering white feather. In her left hand she held a white lace fan.

'I knew your mother.' The Marchioness pinned him with a piercing look from her sharp blue eyes. 'Has she ever mentioned me? Araminta Todmorden? That was my maiden name.'

'I'm afraid not.'

'You are very Scottish-sounding.' She continued to eye him suspiciously.

'Aye. That is because I *am* Scottish.'

'Do not be ridiculous! You are as English as I. You were born in Hertfordshire. I remember it very well.'

'Aye…well…' What the devil did the woman want him to say? 'I—'

'Lady Datchworth…'

A floral scent with a hint of citrus wreathed through Adam's senses. He half-turned and there was Kitty at his elbow. The scent was unfamiliar… it did not conjure up the girl of his past. He must get used to it. *That* Kitty was gone…vanished into the mists of the past…and this lady, this stranger, occupied her space in the world. But he couldn't deny she had matured into a very attractive woman— one who stirred his blood as effortlessly as the younger Kitty, despite the pain caused by that revelation of her speedy marriage to Fenton.

'It is time to eat,' Kitty said. 'Will you take Fenton's arm to lead the way to the dining room, ma'am?'

'Not on this occasion.' The Marchioness, although shorter than Kitty by a good three inches, still managed to look down her nose at her. 'Kelridge will escort me. I expect him to be seated next to me. I have *questions*.'

Far from looking put out by Lady Datchworth's edicts, Kitty bit back a smile as her eyes danced with amusement.

'Of course, ma'am.'

The Marchioness snapped her fan closed and tapped Kitty upon the arm. 'Do not imagine me blind to your insolence, young lady. You always were too opinionated for your own good. Young gels these days…full of new-fangled notions and opinions. It wasn't the same in *my* day. Come, Kelridge. Let us proceed. I know my way, even if you do not.'

Adam slid a sideways look at Kitty, intercepting her glance at him. Her expression was as blank as he strived to make his own, leaving him at a loss as to how to she truly felt about them meeting again and about his change of circumstances.

He vowed to speak to her privately before the evening was out.

Chapter Four

⁂

Trust Lady Datchworth to tread her own path, Kitty thought. Had anyone else suggested that Lord Kelridge give her his arm, she would have speedily pulled rank for, as the lady of highest precedence, she would expect to be escorted by—and seated next to—Robert, her host. Kelridge and the Marchioness strolled from the salon and Lord Radwell, as the highest-ranking gentleman, proffered his arm to Kitty, who accepted with a gracious smile. The remaining diners would, she knew, follow in no specific order, unlike at a formal dinner where they would enter, and be seated, strictly according to order of precedence.

For the first time she wondered how Adam would adjust to the unwritten rules and etiquette of this world so alien to him. Nothing would come naturally to him.

Her eyes sought him, taking in his height and

the breadth of his shoulders. He was so much larger than she remembered—his sheer size as intimidating as his direct blue stare—but he was just as handsome. She guessed he was not a man to be thwarted as she watched him lean over to listen to what Lady Datchworth was saying, nor one to be easily controlled...and Lady Datchworth was a woman who thrived on manipulating others into doing her bidding. But Her Ladyship's acerbic tongue concealed a kind heart for anyone in trouble and Kitty hoped Adam would be patient with her when she annoyed him, as she surely would.

Kitty cast her mind back to the young man she had known. Had he been patient? Impatient? She was hard put to recall.

He had lied to her. *That* she remembered. He had broken her heart.

The manner of their parting overshadowed all that had gone before and all that had raised her young hopes. His fine words had proved false. Words with no meaning or substance or truth in them. Words to cajole and persuade a young starry-eyed girl to relinquish her heart...and thank goodness it had not been her body, too. She did owe him thanks for that, for he had never even attempted to go further than a few kisses and caresses—although she doubted the man he had become would be so hesitant.

She had not missed the admiration in his blue eyes when they first came face to face, or his subtle scan of her person, and she was conscious of the number of times he had sought her out with his gaze in the interlude before dinner was served. Her fear he would not remember her had proved groundless. He remembered her all right and he clearly still found her attractive. But she would not allow herself to be flattered into lowering her guard against him. Never again. So many men could not be trusted…she had learned that hard lesson early, from both her father and from Adam.

'Lady Fenton?'

She turned to Lord Radwell, seeing the kindly concern in his eyes.

'You tutted.' A smile creased his face. 'Is there aught amiss?'

She smiled back. 'No, indeed, sir.'

He quirked a brow. 'I am pleased to hear it.'

She need not elaborate and he would pry no further, of course. He was a gentleman. He had been a close friend of Edgar's and he and his wife had proved a great support to the family when Edgar died.

Radwell helped seat Kitty at the table and sat by her side. Adam was at the far end, between Robert and Lady Datchworth and, throughout the meal, Kitty responded by rote to her neighbours' conversation, drawing on her years of practice as a hostess. She even initiated a change of topic by referring to the forthcoming coronation of George IV in July but, the entire time, her attention returned again and again to Adam.

But that did not mean her interest was in any way personal. It was natural curiosity. It was understandable.

Everyone here is curious about this newcomer...why should I be exempt?

His hair was still dark as night and he still wore it a touch on the long side. Was it still as soft? His face...it was the same, but older, of course. And, perhaps, harsher—no longer the open, sunny smiles of his youth but all hard planes and chiselled, brooding looks, with dark brows drawn low over those percipient blue eyes. And his mouth... his lips...

The memory of his kiss shivered through her and she shook it off, only to find Lord Radwell watching her with a slight frown. She smiled at him.

'Tell me, my lord...how fares your mother these days? It is several years since I have seen her in town, I believe?'

'She grows frail,' he said. 'But that is only to be expected for a lady almost eighty. She is not strong enough to travel and so must remain at the Manor and hope for the occasional visit by friends and neighbours.'

Oh, dear. And now I am obligated...

'I am sorry to hear that. When we return to Fenton, I shall make sure to call upon her.' Radwell Manor was less than ten miles from Fenton Hall. Many of their guests, deliberately, had been drawn from their local society in Hertfordshire, for the same families were also neighbours of Kelridge Place. 'And how are the rest of the family?'

While the Earl told her about his adult children and their families, Kitty's thoughts returned to Adam.

Should I try to talk to him? In private?

But she shied away from the idea. What was there to say? Nothing she hadn't said to him at the time and nothing that could possibly alter the fact that he had walked away from her, having lied.

I must be grateful for Lady Datchworth's interest...she will no doubt keep him occupied for the rest of the evening.

But Kitty had not reckoned on Lady Datchworth developing the headache and leaving before the gentlemen finished their port.

'I am so sorry you are unwell,' Kitty said, as she escorted her from the salon, having already instructed Vincent, their butler, to order Her Ladyship's carriage to be brought to the door.

'As am I, for I had hopes of finding out more

about the newcomer in our midst. He plays his cards close to his chest, does that one—bluntly refused me his mother's direction, would you believe, even though I demanded it outright! I am persuaded she would not object, for we were friends in our younger days, you know, and I wish to write to her, but he simply would not budge.'

Kitty smiled at Lady Datchworth's outrage—being thwarted was a novel experience for her—as they made slow progress down the stairs.

'Mayhap his mother does not wish to revisit her past?'

'Stuff and nonsense!'

Male voices reached them from the landing above as the gentlemen began to leave the dining room. Lady Datchworth halted.

'I shall pay my respects to my host, my dear, if you would be good enough to summon him?'

'Of course.'

A hand stayed Kitty as she turned to climb the stairs again. 'And, while you are there, you may tell Lord Kelridge that I wish to speak to him before I leave. He is an interesting man and he would, I believe, be a splendid match for that stepdaughter of yours. Do you not agree?'

'*Charis?* No, I do not. He is far too old for her.'

'Poppycock, my dear. Look at how content you were with Fenton...there were more years between the pair of you than there are between

Kelridge and Charis. And think of the advantage in having her settled so near to Fenton. Not like poor Jennifer, so far away in Yorkshire. I am convinced you will be happy to have Charis so near.'

With no idea what to say without revealing her prior acquaintance with Adam, Kitty merely nodded and continued up to the landing. She passed Lady Datchworth's command on to Robert, who grinned good-naturedly and headed for the stairs. Kitty scanned the other male guests as they quit the dining room. Adam was the last to emerge and his gaze immediately settled on Kitty, capturing hers. She swallowed past the sudden constriction of her throat.

'Lady Datchworth is indisposed and is about to leave. She expressed a wish to speak with you before she goes.'

A sardonic smile stretched his lips but failed to reach his eyes. 'A wish, you say? I should rather believe it a command. I suppose there is no getting out of it? An excuse ye might pass on to Her Ladyship on my behalf?'

'You suppose correctly, sir.'

'Sir? There was a time ye called me Adam without hesitation, Kitty.'

Anger flashed through her, shocking her with its intensity. Hearing her name on his lips…as though he believed he had the right—No! He forewent any such right the day he walked away from her and left her to the mercy of her father and his greedy, heartless scheme.

'It is Catherine, Lord Kelridge.' She kept her tone measured. Not for the world would she reveal how rattled she was by his reappearance in her life. 'And that was in another lifetime. Time has moved on and I with it.'

How many years had it been since anyone had called her Kitty? Edgar had always preferred Catherine, deeming Kitty childish, and she had raised no objection because the name brought back too many painful memories of Adam. She drew in a breath and straightened her shoulders, raising her chin.

'I should deem it a favour if you forget we ever met.'

His expression gave nothing away, the planes of his face hard and still, his eyes shadowed by the fall of hair over his forehead.

'As ye wish.'

He spun on his heel and headed for the stairs. Kitty followed, her heart thumping erratically, her mouth dry.

They descended to the hallway where a maid was helping Lady Datchworth to don her tippet ready for the journey while Robert waited patiently by the open front door. Her Ladyship waved her hand at Robert in regal dismissal as Kitty reached the ground floor.

'I have already thanked you for your invitation, Fenton, so you may go now. Catherine will see me out. You must attend to your guests.'

Robert flicked a sideways glance at Kitty, and his lips quirked. He bowed to Lady Datchworth. 'Goodnight, my lady.'

Adam also bowed. 'I'll bid ye goodnight as well, my lady.'

'You may hand me into my carriage, Kelridge.' Her Ladyship's gaze shifted to Kitty, then back to Adam again. 'And do not imagine I have forgiven your stubborn refusal to give me your mother's address, for I have not.'

'It seems I am doomed to disappoint the ladies this night.' Kitty steeled herself not to react to his jibe. 'Yet I have offered to forward your letter to my mother—whether she then chooses to share her whereabouts with you is, I would suggest, her prerogative. My lady.'

Lady Datchworth peered down her nose at him, but then she caught Kitty's eye to reveal a twinkle in her own blue orbs. 'This one,' she said, 'will need watching, Lady Fenton. He is a rogue.'

With that, she marched out into the street, ignoring the groom standing ready to assist her into the carriage, and waited for Adam to hand her in. It was only when she was settled on to the seat that she deigned to say goodnight to Kitty, who was therefore obliged to stand outside as well. She shivered as the carriage pulled away and turned for the warmth of the house.

'It is chilly for the time of year,' she remarked as they went indoors.

'Not in my experience.' Adam stood aside to allow Kitty to precede him. 'You southerners are no' hardened to a cold climate.'

Vincent closed the door behind them and then trod sedately towards the back of the house as Kitty began to ascend the stairs, back straight, chin high, incredibly conscious of Adam following behind her. At the top, he grasped her arm. His touch on her bare skin set her nerves tingling, and her breath caught in her throat.

'Kitty. Give me a minute. I have something I need tae say to you.'

He stood close to her, his sheer size almost intimidating, but there was no fear in her heart. Rather, his touch and his nearness resurrected memories. Memories that, in their turn, dragged long-suppressed feelings to the surface and stirred forgotten yearnings that Kitty could not bear. She could not allow him to sweet talk her into…into… into *anything*. She snatched her arm from his grip and drew her shoulders back.

'Unhand me, sir! You will bring scandal to me and to my family and I will not allow it.'

He took her hand this time and no amount of

tugging could break his hold as he stared down at her.

'There is no one tae see us and we will hear should anyone approach.'

She stilled, loath to give him the satisfaction of struggling against him, but if he imagined she would fall for his false charm again he was sorely mistaken. 'Say what you must and then allow me to return to my guests.'

'I…'

His chest rose as he heaved in a breath and his thick brows drew tight into a frown. She averted her gaze, feeling her nostrils flare with anger. How dare he come here, to her home, and put her in this odious position?

'Say what you have to say.' She aimed her words at his chest, determined not to be put at a disadvantage by looking up at him.

'I know ye're angry with me, Kitty. But *I* behaved as I did for the best. I explained it tae you that day and—even were ye then too young and innocent of the ways of the world tae fully understand—ye *must* look back now and know I was right. But *you*…' He paused.

They were so close she could smell his cologne…musky and spicy…and feel the heat radiating from his body and the warmth of his breath as it stirred her hair. Slowly, his words penetrated the fury that clouded her brain. Even though she longed to throw his words back at him, she could not deny he had been right about the impracticality of what she had asked of him fifteen years ago. What she had *begged* of him.

But it does not change the fact that he lied to me. Over and over.

She reassembled her righteous anger and glared up at him.

'But I?' she prompted.

'Ye wed just *two weeks* after I left!'

'I—' Her eyes narrowed. 'How do you know that?'

'Rob told me. Ye lied tae me...ye swore ye loved me, but ye didna!' As his anger strengthened so, too, did his accent, bringing the young man she had known even more forcefully to mind. 'It wasna *me* ye wanted—ye'd take *any* man tae be your husband, ye were that eager to snare some poor soul...sae desperate ye'd even take a man auld enough to be your own da.'

Only as those accusations tore from his mouth, as though ripped out of him, did Kitty understand that his desire to speak to her without being overheard had nothing to do with currying favour, or with trying to cajole her...to rekindle their love, or passion, or friendship, or whatever it had been... but everything to do with venting *his* anger. And that realisation revived, in all its heart-wrenching agony, the pain he had caused her.

She was the injured party here. It was she who had suffered…what right did he have to be angry?

'And I bless the day I married Edgar.' She snatched her hand away again, this time freeing it. She clutched the handrail on the balustrade to help steady her trembling frame, for she was shaking with fury at the injustice of him blaming her when it was he who had led her on, raising her hopes with his false declarations of love. She dragged her gaze up and down him, allowing her scorn full rein. 'You were *nothing*! He, at least, was a real man. And I still mourn the day of his death.'

She fled along the landing, heading for the safety of the salon and other people. Once inside, she crossed the room to sit with Lady Radwell and Lady Charnwood to join in their conversation about the last few weeks of the Season, including Lady Charnwood's ball the following night. Once again Kitty conversed by rote, at least half of her thoughts occupied with a silent diatribe against that despicable rogue, Kelridge. How dare he twist everything, insulting her and accusing *her* of inconstancy? Although, in all fairness, he *was* right that a match between the two of them would have been a disaster, given their unequal places in society. If, of course, he hadn't known all along that he was the son of an earl. How was she supposed to know the truth when he had lied before?

She fixed her gaze on her two companions and resolutely refrained from looking to see if he had followed her into the room.

She did not care.

She would not care if she never saw him, or spoke to him, ever again. And she didn't even want to *think* about him. She hoped he would soon tire of his new life and return to Scotland and leave his estates in the hands of his uncle and his steward, who—it was said—had run the place during much of the late Lord Kelridge's time. Eventually, however, a shadow fell across their trio and, when her companions fell silent, Kitty had no choice but to acknowledge Adam's brooding presence.

His bright blue eyes bore into Kitty. 'I must bid you goodnight, Lady Fenton. My thanks for your hospitality.'

'You are most welcome, Lord Kelridge. I trust meeting so many new faces has not proved too onerous?'

'Not at all.'

'Lord Kelridge,' Lady Charnwood addressed Adam. 'If you are free tomorrow evening, might you honour me with your attendance at my ball?'

Kitty stiffened in dismay. How had she not foreseen that he was likely to be invited to the same entertainments as her family? She needed time, and space, to think about his return without being thrust headlong into his company. It would be nigh on impossible to avoid him for the remaining weeks of the Season. Her nerves skittered as her stomach turned over.

Adam bowed to Lady Charnwood. 'It would be my pleasure, ma'am.'

'Splendid. I shall send the invitation in the morning…no need for a formal reply.'

Adam smiled at her before returning his gaze to Kitty. 'I wonder if I might beg the indulgence of a private word, Lady Fenton?'

Kitty kept any sign of emotion from her expression. If only she could refuse without giving rise to speculation and rumours she would do so, but the wretch knew very well good manners would force her to agree. She rose unhurriedly to her feet, smoothing down her skirts with hands that trembled with that suppressed fury.

'Pray excuse me, ladies,' she said and trod steadily and deliberately over to the nearby window.

'What more can you possibly have to say to me? Have we both not said enough?'

'I regret my outburst and I apologise. Blame my upbringing if you will.'

His wry tone indicated that he knew all too well the rumours flying around the *ton* about his life as a boy and a youth. Few facts were known about those years and the man himself was less than forthcoming, so speculation filled the void. All that was known of him were his professional qualifications and glowing testimonials for his work as an architect from a handful of well-connected clients, but they revealed nothing about the character of the man.

Kitty forced herself to face him, fixing her gaze on his mouth…a mistake, as it happened, because her treacherous mind insisted on conjuring up the slide of his lips over hers…the stroke of his tongue…and her heart, annoyingly, fluttered in her chest. She did not want these memories, or the feelings they aroused, but…*oh*, those kisses! She stifled her sigh. Edgar had never kissed her in such a manner. She did not even know if it was natural, for she had never kissed a man other than those two. She dragged her gaze from his mouth to his eyes.

'I will,' she said. At the lift of his brows she elaborated. 'I shall blame your upbringing. A true gentleman would never say such things to a lady.'

'Ah. No. Of course he would not.'

'Have you quite finished? I must return to my guests.' She started to step past him.

'One more thing.'

Kitty paused. 'I am listening.'

'When we meet, might we agree to do so with at least the appearance of civility?'

Civility! Who would have thought all that youthful passion could be distilled down into mere politeness? Kitty buried her hurt, telling herself it was a false emotion, borne out of memories and broken dreams, and it had no place in the present.

'I pride myself on my civility, sir, no matter the circumstances, and you have my word that I shall treat you no differently to any other gentleman of my acquaintance when our paths cross during what is left of the Season. Now, it has been interesting to renew our acquaintance, but I see our guests are beginning to depart and I must say goodbye.'

She inclined her head and moved past him to join Robert as he bade farewell to the Radwells. There was a flurry of departures and, when Kitty had the time to notice, Adam had gone.

Chapter Five

The following evening—quite late, as it was already dusk—Adam presented himself at the Charnwoods' house for Lady Charnwood's ball, his mind full of Kitty, as it had been all day, even after he'd lain awake half the night, going over every single word, every single look they had exchanged the night before. He told himself it meant nothing. There was nothing left between them… certainly no tender emotions. Only hurt and rejection and deceit. But despite that, and despite his hurt at the speed and the ease with which she had recovered from their ill-fated romance, he had looked forward all day to seeing her again, knowing she would, without doubt, be here tonight.

He entered the ballroom and stopped short. If the Fenton dinner had been intimidating, *this* was utterly overwhelming. So many people. So much chatter and laughter. The ballroom soared two storeys with three massive chandeliers suspended from its high ceiling, and wall sconces all around were lit. The effect was magical as jewels glittered, reflecting the candlelight, and gowns in a myriad of hues swished and swirled around the dance floor. The dancing had already begun, accompanied by a quartet of musicians sitting on a raised dais at one end of the room, and the combined heat from bodies and from candles was already tangible despite the row of French windows along the wall opposite having already been flung wide.

Adam tamped down his unease as he searched the crowd for his hostess and finally spied her standing with Tolly and another lady. His anxiety subsided. At least he had two acquaintances in this heaving mass. He threaded his way through the guests and bowed to the group.

'Good evening, my lady. Tolly.'

'Oh, you have come. I *am* pleased.' Lady Charnwood turned to the other lady in their group—a stunningly beautiful female of around twenty, he guessed, with hair of a deep golden colour and eyes the exact same hue. If ever a woman could be described as the epitome of femininity, it was surely this one. 'Lady Phoebe Crawshaw, allow me to introduce Lord Kelridge.'

Adam bowed as Lady Phoebe curtsied. Her unusual eyes examined him with a frankness he found refreshing. 'I am pleased to make your acquaintance, my lord.' Her voice was deep and somewhat husky. 'I have been wondering when we would meet.'

'How so, my lady?'

She shrugged gracefully. 'You must know you are much discussed and speculated upon in these circles. And I…' she slanted a look through her lashes at Tolly '…am of a naturally curious disposition.'

Tolly sucked in one cheek and his eye narrowed. Tonight…presumably in honour of the occasion…he had swapped his leather eyepatch to one made of silk. 'You will not persuade me, my lady, so you may as well save your breath.'

Lady Phoebe pouted. 'Then there is no point in conversing with you further, Mr Trewin. Lord Kelridge…a waltz is about to begin and I am in sore need of a partner. Would you care to ask me to dance?'

Adam bowed. 'It will be my pleasure, my lady.'

He held out his hand. Lady Phoebe laid her gloved hand in his, but then hesitated.

'I presume you do know how to waltz?'

Adam laughed. 'Scotland is quite enlightened, my lady. Aye, we know the waltz.'

He led her on to the floor and found a space, conscious of the many looks in their direction, not all of them benign.

Adam placed his hand on Lady Phoebe's waist and took her right hand in his left.

'Why do I get the feeling there is something here I dinna understand?' he asked. 'We appear to be the centre of attention.'

She shrugged and smiled up at him prettily. 'The men are envious of you and I imagine the ladies are envious of me.'

She was no shy miss with her opinions, that was for sure. 'And what is it that Mr Trewin will not be persuaded of by you?'

She laughed, revealing small and even white teeth. 'I *knew* you and I would get along. I do like a man who gets straight to the point. I requested to see Mr Trewin's scars and he is being most disobliging in that respect. That is all.'

Adam laughed and, as he did so, he glanced across the room, his gaze clashing with Kitty's as she stood in another man's embrace awaiting the opening bars of the music. The suddenness of it took his breath away and his heart lurched in his chest. He tore his eyes from hers, cursing inwardly, telling himself again that it meant nothing.

He forced himself to concentrate on dancing because—for all his brave declaration about the waltz—in truth he was not at all well practised in the steps. Time and again, though, he found his attention on Kitty as she glided gracefully around the floor in her partner's arms, her pale blue gown floating around her ankles.

'Are you acquainted with Lady Fenton, or is it Lord Silverdale commanding your interest, sir?'

His partner's slightly mocking question jerked Adam's attention back to her.

'I dined with the Fentons last evening,' he said, 'and I was wondering where I had seen Her Ladyship's partner before. Now you have said his name, I do recall it was in the House of Lords the other day.'

He forced himself to concentrate on Lady Phoebe until the end of their dance, when he led her from the floor, back to where Tolly stood with Robert, Lady Charnwood having moved on. The other men immediately vied with one another to pay Lady Phoebe the most extravagant compliments and Adam took advantage of their preoccupation to take his leave of them. He then patrolled the perimeter of the ballroom, scanning the guests. It wasn't long before he spotted Kitty at the very moment she slipped out through one of the French windows. Adam headed for the open window nearest to him and paused.

He welcomed the cool of the night air after the heat of the ballroom and breathed deeply as he took stock of the narrow, stone-flagged terrace outside. Lamps were set at intervals along the house wall, throwing alternating areas of light and shade across the paving. There were a handful of others on the terrace but, of Kitty, there was no sign. A growl of disapproval rumbled in Adam's chest and he stepped out on to the flagstones even as his common sense roared at him not to be a fool, that to follow her outside would be to suggest an interest in her that even he was not certain existed. A wise man would bide his time and sort out his own inner turmoil first.

He ignored his own advice.

He would just make sure she was safe. He strode to the balustrade that edged the terrace and slowly rotated. Finally, he spied her, standing at the far end of the flagged area, in a patch of shadow, her back to him and her head tipped back as she gazed up at the night sky. The new moon was a mere crescent suspended above the neighbouring rooftops while innumerable stars spangled the vast darkness overhead.

'Ye shouldna be oot here alone.'

He spoke softly, but she started none the less and spun to face him. He could not read her expression here in the shadows, but he *could* recognise the tension in her body.

'Why ever not?'

'Someone might take advantage of ye.'

She laughed, folding her arms. 'Nonsense. I know all the guests here tonight and this garden is entirely enclosed. You may leave me, safe in the knowledge I shall come to no harm.'

Adam stepped closer. She stepped back. He halted, his hands itching to stroke the bare skin of her arm above her glove, and he closed his fingers into his palms, clenching his hands to keep them from straying. How could she have this effect on him? How could he yearn to touch her and yet, at the same time, long to fling her perfidy in her face again? *Her* heartbreak had lasted a mere two weeks, and the urge to retaliate…to hurt her in return…beat deep inside him. But…alongside that urge was the desire to simply talk to her. Connect with her. *Understand* her. And he retained enough awareness to know that would not happen if they argued every time they met. He swallowed down that myriad of confusing emotions.

'I saw you dancing,' said Kitty. 'What did you make of The Incomparable?'

It soothed his wounded pride a little to learn that she had noticed him.

'What is The Incomparable?'

'Not what. Who. Lady Phoebe Crawshaw. That is what she is called by the gentlemen—it is the fashion to be in love with her, you know.'

Adam's eyes had adjusted to the dim light on the terrace and he searched Kitty's expression for a sign…*any* sign…that she experienced any-thing like the tumult of emotions that churned within him, but her expression was serene. His gaze lowered to her décolletage. Did her bosom rise and fall more rapidly than it should? Or was that mere wishful thinking?

'Is it indeed?' he said.

'It is. So I hope you will prostrate yourself at her feet at some point before the end of the Season, or you will be declared a very poor sort of a fellow.'

Her tone lightly mocked. Surely she could not speak of such matters so casually if she still felt anything for him? Not that he *wanted* her to feel anything for him…other than as a sop to his pride. He forced a laugh.

'I concede the lady is beautiful, but I have never been one to follow the herd and Lady Phoebe isna quite to my taste.' He moved closer to Kitty, angling his body to shield her from the view of others on the terrace, and lowered his voice, keen to provoke a reaction beyond that of social chit-chat. 'She is too young and too bold. I prefer my women more refined.'

'Your women…' Kitty spoke slowly, staring up at him, wide-eyed, as her chest rose.

'Aye.'

His voice deepened, turning husky. He succumbed to temptation, against all his better judgement. He reached out with his forefinger and traced her arm from shoulder to inner elbow, her skin warm and smooth, and he noticed her involuntary shiver at his touch. Kitty's teeth captured her full lower lip. He could still taste her, in his memory, and his blood surged. He leaned in to her, his cheek tantalisingly close to hers. Her breathing quickened, coming in little gasps and, encouraged, Adam turned his head to brush his lips over her satin-soft skin.

Tension flowed off Kitty in waves, the air between them charged with expectation, like the air before a thunderstorm. Adam fingered an errant curl, just behind her ear, then he took her lobe between his teeth and nipped gently. Just once.

She gasped and he sensed the shiver that racked her. She turned her face to his and their lips met, tantalisingly, fleetingly, and she gasped again as she jerked away from him.

'No!'

She seemed to fold into herself, wrapping her arms defensively around her waist. 'No. We cannot. We agreed to treat one another with civility. We cannot revive our old…friendship. I have no wish to travel that path again.'

Relief and regret clashed within him in a swirl of confusion, his heart still yearning for her even as his head rejected such romantic nonsense. Why on earth was he playing with fire? Why would he risk his heart again? How could he ever trust her? He dug deep to revive his anger and his hurt over the lies she had told him, both with her words and with her kisses.

'No more do I.'

He cursed himself silently for exposing himself—he couldn't bear for her to imagine he still harboured feelings for her when he could not even unravel his own tangled feelings.

Provoking her anger seemed the safest course, for both of them.

'Let us blame the darkness and us being out here alone together. It was easy…natural, even… for us to slip into old habits.'

Kitty stiffened. 'Old *habits*?'

Why, oh, why had she come out here alone? She had seen him watching her from across the ballroom and *still* she had ventured outside. Then, instead of joining another group, she had wandered alone to the edge of the terrace.

Did I, deep down, hope *he would follow me?*

Whatever her intention, she couldn't deny she had set a dangerous game in motion. She had been a hair's breadth from allowing him to kiss her, and he…her heart lurched…*he* had accepted her lack of refusal as an opportunity. She would end up hurt again.

Adam shrugged. 'You cannot blame me for forgetting our history when we were getting along so well,' he said. 'And you cannot deny we are both considerably less angry that we were last night.'

Stomach churning, Kitty took refuge in attack.

'I *thought* we had an agreement, my lord. Had I suspected you would take my civility as an invitation to intimacy, I would have been considerably less amiable. Allow me to explain. The reason for my conversing with you as I would *any* fellow guest is that, once the shock of meeting you again faded, I realised that anger is a waste of my energy. Such strong emotion about a person or an event can only make sense if my feelings are still engaged and they are not.'

Her emotions roiled and boiled within her, alongside a hefty dollop of shame, but she contained them all, desperate not to reveal how he affected her. Still. After all this time. After all his lies. *This* was why society had rules for young girls—rules to protect their virtue and their reputation. And because Kitty had been unwise enough—and naive enough—to welcome Adam's kisses all those years ago, he would naturally assume her present morals were equally lax.

'We have agreed that we are now as strangers and it surely follows that any feelings that once existed between us must be as though they had happened to two different people. Now, I shall return to the ballroom and I would appreciate it if you do not follow me. In fact, I think it might be for the best if we avoid one another as much as possible. Then, when we do meet again, as I am sure we will, we shall pretend this never happened.'

She pivoted on her heel and walked away, concentrating on keeping her head high and her pace slow, acting the society lady as she had never acted before.

Chapter Six

Two weeks later

Adam gazed gloomily around Almack's, wondering what the hell he was doing there. He had no interest in marrying anyone, yet it seemed that every person he met…well, those who were female, anyway…was convinced he was in the market for a bride. He stifled his snort of derision and sipped again at his glass of orgeat, an insipid light wine that passed for liquid refreshment in this godforsaken place. The choice, he had been loftily informed, was that or ratafia. What wouldn't he give for a wee dram right at this moment?

Lady Datchworth had taken it upon herself to instruct Adam as to the places a well-born gentleman simply *must* be seen and this place had been high on her list. She'd presented him with a voucher as though it were manna from heaven, impressing upon him how grateful he should be that the Patronesses had granted him permission to attend, and all his polite refusals to her request that he escort her tonight had met with the utter conviction that he did not mean it. And he *had* remained exceedingly polite, even in the face of extreme provocation.

And now he was here he could not for the life of him see what all the fuss was about and why so many people vied with one another for a voucher. The dress code was ludicrous—silk knee breeches, indeed—the refreshments wretched and the entire evening promised to be a bore.

'Well, Kelridge? Who takes your fancy?'

He glanced down at Lady Datchworth, seated on a chair, her gloved hands wrapped around the head of her cane which was planted firmly between her legs, spread apart in a very unladylike manner, albeit still covered by her skirts. The head of her cane, which accompanied her everywhere, was fashioned in the shape of a dog's head…a terrier…and that is exactly what she reminded him of. A terrier who, once it buries its teeth into something, refuses to give it up. And, it would appear, *he* was her latest obsession. And he…oh, hell and damnation…to be brutally honest, most of the time he found her company amusing, unlike many of the prattling idiots of the *ton* and despite her highhanded belief that she knew what was best for him—and for everyone else, for that matter.

He sighed. He had to face the fact that he *liked* the meddling auld woman. He would not willingly upset her, but he still had to refrain from throttling her every time she began to blather on about finding him a wife. And what made that worse was that her favoured candidate appeared to be Miss Mayfield, Kitty's stepdaughter, a circumstance that rendered him excessively uncomfortable given his history with Kitty and his renewed friendship with Robert. Talking of Robert, Adam had caught sight of him, his expression one of studied stoicism, not five minutes since—which meant his womenfolk must also be here. So much for Adam's attempts to avoid Kitty since Lady Charnwood's ball. He had not spoken to her since, although he had seen her at several events...had watched her, wondering about that near kiss. But she had appeared utterly indifferent to his presence and so he had continued to avoid her, as that is what she appeared to want.

A sharp elbow nudged him. 'Well? You *cannot* attend Almack's and not stand up for the dances. And, if you are serious about making a match, you will do well to follow my advice.' She looked around her. 'If Miss Mayfield isn't to your taste, what about Miss Penhurst over there...?' She flipped her cane up to point, almost spearing a passer-by. 'Oh! Catherine, my dear. My apologies. I did not see you there. I was intent upon helping poor Kelridge here with his marriage plans.'

A pair of startled grey eyes flew to Adam's face and, to his intense irritation, he felt his skin heat as he blushed. *Blushed!* What was he...a young girl still in the schoolroom?

'I have no marriage plans and Lady Datchworth is well aware of that fact, for I have told her so many times,' he growled, embarrassed both by the subject and by the rush of pure desire through his body.

'Nonsense, Kelridge. You have a title and a fortune, you are getting no younger and you need an heir. Of *course* you must wed—it is your obligation as a peer of the realm. You start at a disadvantage, it is true, but I am sure there are chits here who would be prepared to overlook your unfortunate upbringing if *only* you would wipe that black scowl from your face and *apply* yourself to the task in hand.'

She looked him up and down, and he set his teeth. The woman had as much tact as a charging bull and was as impossible to deflect, but he was grateful for the spike of anger that helped to quell his desire.

'You have a fine figure,' Her Ladyship went on. 'Very manly. Of course, you will not display to advantage on the dance floor—unless you are lighter on your feet than you look—but there are chits who positively favour a man with a muscular frame such as yours. Do you not agree, Catherine, my dear?'

Adam caught Kitty's amused twinkle as she mimicked Lady Datchworth in looking him up and down. His teeth ground together.

'Oh, indeed, ma'am. A *fine* figure.'

The suppressed laughter in her voice wound his temper higher. How dare she mock him? How dare they both presume to treat him like…treat him like…?

As suddenly as it arose his anger subsided and he surprised himself by laughing.

'Now, now, ladies. Please do control yourselves. I must ask…is it entirely proper for ladies to discuss a gentleman's figure in quite so blatant a manner? And within his hearing, no less?'

Lady Datchworth, when she wasn't amusing herself by playing matchmaker, had helped Adam no end with learning and understanding the ways of this world.

She grinned up at him. 'I see you have taken in some of my lessons after all, Kelridge.'

'Lessons?' Kitty arched one brow. 'What, pray, has Lady Datchworth been teaching you, my lord?'

'Oh, this and that.' Lady Datchworth waved an airy hand. 'He is a receptive pupil when he has a mind to co-operate. But he has proved himself remarkably stubborn in certain areas.' She fixed Adam with a darkling look. 'You will do well to heed my advice. You are already six-and-thirty... time is not on your side and, as your poor mother cannot be here to guide you, it falls to me as her oldest friend to step into her shoes.'

Kitty tucked her lips between her teeth, but the sparkle of her eyes gave her away.

Adam looked away, scanning the dancers. *I am pleased my situation is providing her with such enjoyment.*

'Perhaps I will—'

'No!' Lady Datchworth held up a peremptory hand. 'I understand your predicament better than you know, Kelridge, and I have the solution— dance with Lady Fenton here. That will ease you in gently and, in time, you may find the confidence to ask one of the younger, more eligible ladies to be your partner.' She sat back, satisfaction writ large on her face.

'I—'

'That is a splendid notion, ma'am.' Kitty tucked her hand through Adam's arm. 'Come, Lord Kelridge. We shall soon build your confidence.'

Adam found himself manoeuvred away from Lady Datchworth and out on to the dance floor where sets were starting to form. He planted his feet, giving Kitty no option but to stop.

'I have nae need of your charity.'

Her grip on his arm tightened. 'Is the prospect of dancing with me *really* so objectionable that you would prefer to endure yet more of Lady Datchworth's unique variety of persuasion?'

Her voice remained low; her words were forceful, with a hint of anger, but her expression was serene—light-hearted, even—belying her tone.

'The last time we spoke ye could not wait to rid yourself of me. And yet, here you are, nigh on begging me to dance. I wish ye would make up your mind.'

'I have no more desire to dance with you than you do with me, my lord, but I took pity on you as I would on any other harried-looking gentleman suffering the undivided attentions of Lady Datchworth. I have no further agenda, I assure you, and what I said still holds true: what happened fifteen years ago happened to two different people and I have come to the conclusion that we cannot avoid one another for ever.'

'Verra well.' He walked on, leading her among the other couples forming sets. 'As you said before, after fifteen years we truly are little more than strangers. Blame my testiness on Lady D. The woman effortlessly stirs my ire. She is so…' He could think of many words to describe Her Ladyship, none of them suitable for a lady's ears '…

exasperating. So, thank ye for rescuing me from her...um...*efforts* on my behalf.'

'No thanks are necessary. But...do not condemn Lady Datchworth too harshly, Adam. She actually has a heart of gold beneath her overbearing ways.'

His heart twitched at her seemingly unconscious use of his forename.

'I am aware of it, or I would not continue to tolerate her,' he said, then frowned at his own words. 'No. That is unfair. I admit she amuses me more frequently than she frustrates me.'

'That is at least one thing we have in common, then.'

'Indeed.' He glanced at Kitty. 'I confess I am surprised to find ye here. It does not appear the sort of place—'

She tensed. 'In the first place, my lord, you have precisely no idea of my current interests, likes or dislikes. In the second place, I am here as chaperon for my stepdaughter and this is precisely the sort of venue a young lady is expected to attend in her debut Season.'

My lord! Adam did not last long.

'Of course it is. I am still guilty of overlooking the passage of years, it seems. I wonder, though...'

Could he bury his hurt at her betrayal? He kept forgetting how young she had been and he could surely make allowances more easily for Kitty's behaviour than for his mother's lies. It was not Kitty's fault that she had mistaken a young girl's infatuation for love, but it *was* his mother's fault he'd wasted fifteen years of his life believing himself unworthy of an earl's daughter.

'...as we agree we are now strangers, might we also agree to get to know the people we are now a little better?'

Surely that would be preferable to this constant sniping at one another? Kitty slid him a sideways look and her expression softened infinitesimally.

'Yes. I think we might agree upon that. And I admit it is true that I have no great liking for this place but, as I said, I am here for Charis. Almack's is the perfect place for young, unmarried ladies to display their elegance and beauty.'

'It is known as the marriage mart, according to Lady D.' Adam couldn't resist the chance to tease her. 'I assume it is an equally suitable venue for young widows to attract a future husband?'

Kitty frowned. 'Not for this widow, I assure you, for I am resolved to never again marry.'

The dance began, Adam taking Kitty's hands as they circled one another. 'Why are you opposed to marrying again? Was your marriage to Fenton so very distasteful?'

He remembered that stubborn tilt of her chin. The action exposed the pale skin of her throat, and, without warning, a starburst of longing exploded within him. The memory...her skin, warm beneath his lips; the fresh scent of his lass, of crushed grass and the earthy smell of the woods where they held their trysts; the taste of those lush lips, as full and rosy now as when they tasted of the berries they picked.

But her lips were no longer stained with blackberry juice. His heart lurched as sorrow flowed through him. She was not his lass. His Kitty. She was Catherine, Lady Fenton. Fifteen years had changed them both and he still struggled to come to terms with it.

It was the strangest dichotomy: a girl he had known so well, a girl who had taken root in his heart and who had been a part of him—staying the same in his memory for fifteen long years— a girl he had loved, yet here she was...a woman who was a stranger to him. And his feelings for this stranger were...complicated. Undoubtedly, he felt physical desire for her. She was a graceful, beautiful woman and he...*he* was a man. How could he not want her?

They had agreed to get to know one another again, but could he truly move forward and view her afresh? Could he break those chains to the past, chains forged by the pain and the insult to his pride caused by that news of her hasty marriage? He could bury his hurt, yes. But it still existed and still coloured his reactions to her. It still confused him.

He clenched his jaw and dragged his thoughts into the present as Kitty replied.

'My marriage was far from distasteful, but I shall not discuss it with you other than to say I miss my husband a great deal. I shall not remarry because I am perfectly happy remaining with my family at Fenton Hall and I have other interests that occupy me fully. I shall not remarry because I have no need. I shall not remarry because I have no desire to do so.'

Desire. That word on her lips stirred his own desire, even though she did not use the word in that context. Was it nostalgia that returned his thoughts to her and to their shared past so frequently? Or was it the growing conviction that there were still words unsaid between them? He wanted answers. He wanted to know how she had gone from a broken heart to marriage just two weeks after his departure. He wanted to understand how she had so speedily recovered from the anguish she had accused him of causing.

How he longed to sit down with her and talk about what had happened. Perhaps then he might untangle this mass of emotion that knotted his stomach.

But the opportunity to do so was unlikely to present itself here in London. Besides, was there any point when Kitty appeared to be utterly un-interested in him? He was a seething mass of contradictory emotions whereas she revealed no hint of any residual feelings for him.

Except...there *had* been that near kiss. That, surely, meant something?

The steps of the dance separated them, and he partnered others without really seeing them. No doubt he would be branded uncouth... Lady D. had told him often enough that a gentleman was expected to entertain the ladies with gay conver-sation and subtle compliments. Well, his tongue had never been silver. He veered more towards the unvarnished truth. His gaze roamed over the dancers until they found Kitty and, this time, his heart lodged in his throat.

All those months...all those *years*...he had suf-fered guilt over his treatment of her and she... *she*...had moved on without a second thought. All those years that his own attempts to find love had come to nothing because his heart had never been in it. Because they weren't her. They weren't Kitty.

They came together again in the dance and their hands met, but barely...her touch having no more substance than that of a feather lying in his palm.

And this is what we have come to. Two strang-

ers, with an ocean of hurt and mistrust lying between us.

Did he want more from her? Or was he right in the first place and it was simple nostalgia swelling this lump in his throat and weighing down his spirits? But even if he did want more, she had made her position crystal clear.

The decision came from nowhere.

'I leave for Kelridge Place tomorrow.'

Her grey eyes regarded him. He could read nothing of her thoughts. His gaze dropped to her lips as they parted and he mentally swatted aside the sweet nip of desire and tamped down the swell of longing. He must use reason and logic to overcome her effect on him and keep reminding himself that she was a stranger, not the Kitty he had fallen in love with.

'The Season has another two weeks at least before families leave for the country.'

Adam shrugged. 'That holds no interest for me.'

'I thought…' She paused and frowned.

The music finished and Adam bowed.

'You thought?'

Kitty curtsied. 'The dance has ended.'

The tinge of relief in her voice stirred the pain that lurked ever ready in his depths, making him long to lash out at her. To make her feel the same hurt he suffered.

He proffered his arm.

'I shall escort you back to your family.'

Again, he barely registered her hand on his arm and was forced to glance down to assure himself it was there. She roused emotion within him like no other female ever had, but he was hard put to know if it was love or hate. Was it the past casting rainbows over the present that was keeping that sliver of hope alive deep inside him? He could not tell and neither could he tell if she, too, still felt this connection that hovered between them, binding them. She was so guarded, so difficult to understand, and he longed to provoke her into some show of the emotion she claimed was absent, but which he sensed—hoped?—was there, well hidden beneath her serene surface.

'You thought?' His voice harder this time—he would not allow her to wriggle out of explaining herself. He was confused enough, without her adding more questions to the list circling inside his head.

Again, that familiar lift of her chin.

'I thought you would wish to make the most of this time, while everyone is in town, to more fully establish your position.'

'To what purpose? These people mean nothing to me. They are not my friends. I have an interest in politics and I am happy to have my say in the Lords but, as to the rest…' He contemplated his surroundings and the people within. 'I miss the purpose of earning my living. This is not a way of life that I recognise or find fulfilling. I find no merit in lives lived in pursuit of idle pleasures.'

Kitty halted, releasing Adam's arm. Her mouth was tight and, when she spoke, so was her voice. 'You may leave me to find my own way to my companions, Lord Kelridge. I should thank you, I surmise, for your condescension in agreeing to so frivolous an activity as dancing. I trust you will find your estates in good repair when you go to Kelridge.'

'If they are not, I shall soon turn them around.'

Although he did not know quite how he would manage that when he had no clue about running an estate. The flick of her eyebrow before she stalked away suggested that Kitty, too, doubted his bold confidence. Let her think what she pleased. It would be a relief to leave London and its inhabitants behind him and, as for Kitty, maybe putting distance between them might help him to sort through the confusion of his feelings for her. At least he need no longer be burdened with guilt over the past, knowing now that she had not suffered after he left. He could now look to his future and plan his life free from the sentimental, romantic regrets that had plagued him for far too long, regrets over what might have been.

He returned to Lady Datchworth, who cast a glance at a nearby couple, deep in conversation with one another, before patting the empty chair by her side. As Adam sat, the couple moved away on to the dance floor and he recognised them as Miss Mayfield and Lord Sampford. Lady D. watched them go.

'What are those two up to?'

'Shush! Nothing. How should I know?' Lady D. tore her attention from the couple and turned it on to Adam. 'What did you say to upset Catherine? For two people who barely know one another you do seem to rub one another the wrong way.'

'I shared my opinion of high society and she took offence.'

Lady D. tapped his arm with her fan. 'You must learn to dissemble, Kelridge. Bluntness will win you no friends.'

'I do not need friends. I need to go to Kelridge and learn about my inheritance. And, to that end, I have decided I shall leave London in the morning.'

'Tomorrow?'

'Aye. It's time. I've told you many times I have no wish to marry in the foreseeable future. There is no need to stay here longer.'

'But…' Her Ladyship stared at Adam, her lips pursed. 'I need you to escort me to the Change tomorrow. At two o'clock.'

'Two o'clock? Why?'

'A shopkeeper there has a new cane for me. A

very special cane.' Lady D. leaned towards him, putting her hand on his arm. 'Besides…you did express an interest in seeing the beasts in the menagerie…'twould be a pity to miss them.'

'I make no doubt they will still be there next time I visit London. Hertfordshire is not Scotland—it is a short enough journey. Only a couple of hours, so I am told.'

'Precisely! So it will not hurt you to delay your departure. Have you ever *seen* an elephant?'

'No.'

'Then you simply must go before you leave. I insist. You can set off for Kelridge Place *after* you have escorted me to the Change. As you rightly say, the journey is only a few hours so you will reach there long before dusk.' Her voice rang with satisfaction and she sat upright once again, clasping her hands over the top of her cane.

Adam raised his eyebrows and grinned. Really, she was totally impossible. He didn't for one minute believe her excuse of buying a new walking cane, but curiosity prevented him from arguing further.

'Very well. I shall escort you. But I shall not stay for long, so no lingering, mind.'

It would be amusing to discover the real reason for Her Ladyship's sudden desire to visit the Exeter Exchange. Leaving town a few hours later than planned wouldn't hurt him.

Chapter Seven

Kitty tamped down her rising irritation as she stalked across the room, seeking Robert and Charis. How dare Adam, with only a few short weeks' experience of this world, be so judgemental of this life? *Her* life?

How she now wished she had not succumbed to that ridiculous impulse to rescue him from Lady Datchworth's matchmaking mischief. In fact, she had regretted her impulse the second she had taken his arm—the play of muscle and sinew under her fingers had roused long-suppressed feelings within her, feelings that had only intensified as they danced: a peculiar fluttery and yet clenching sensation deep inside her that she hadn't experienced since...

With a silent oath she diverted her thoughts from following that particular trail. They were physical feelings of no use to a widow such as she and she had no intention of either encouraging them or, heaven forbid, indulging in them.

But surely you want to know what it might be like. You are fooling yourself—

She ruthlessly quashed that taunting inner voice as she finally found Robert. She had learned her lesson and she *would* guard her heart from any such misery ever again. No matter how her treacherous body might react to the infuriating man.

Her stepson eyed her, then sighed.

'I recognise that martial light in your eye, Stepmama. Who has upset you?'

'I am *not* upset.'

Robert grinned. 'Let me hazard a guess. Was it the new Lord Kelridge? I saw you dancing.'

'Do not speak to me of Lord Kelridge! He had the utter gall to peer down his nose at us and our friends and acquaintances.'

'Did he, by Jove?' Robert scanned the room. 'Well, it appears he is also unimpressed by the entertainment and refreshments at Almack's, for it looks as though he is taking his leave. Clearly a man of impeccable taste. What did he say?'

'He finds, and I quote, "no merit in lives lived in pursuit of idle pleasures".'

'Ah.'

Robert stroked his chin, a mannerism that indicated he was secretly amused.

'You find that funny?'

'Well…might I point out to you, *dearest* Stepmama, that you have more than once uttered the same opinion?'

'That is entirely different.'

'How so?'

'This is *our* world. *Our* life. *I* am allowed to voice such criticism.'

'It is his world now, too. And he will see the absurdities that, incidentally, both you and I know exist. He is entitled to his opinion, is he not?'

Kitty set her jaw, knowing she was being irrational but loath to back down. 'He may very well be entitled to his opinion, but I wish he would keep it to himself.'

Robert eyed her. 'Was that a metaphorical stamp of your foot?'

His lips quirked and Kitty felt her own quiver in response. Then she could no longer hold back her laugh and Robert laughed with her.

'There. I always was able to talk you down from the high boughs,' he said. 'I hope you weren't rude to poor Kelridge…it is a difficult time for him, you know.'

'I am never unmannerly, Rob. You know that.'

'No. But you can freeze a man with one look, as I know to my cost.'

'I am persuaded His Lordship is too thick-skinned to notice anything as subtle as a cool glance. Besides, he leaves for Kelridge Place to-morrow so we are unlikely to see him again for a long time.'

She shut her mind to a sensation that snaked through her…a sensation that felt very much like regret. She had no wish to explore that feeling further, afraid that if she allowed her thoughts to dwell too much on Adam and the feelings he aroused within her, the defences she had built around her heart would start to erode. And that she could not risk. Look at how he had tried to kiss her at Lady Charnwood's ball…an old habit, he had called her. Surely that was enough of a warning to avoid him—he had matured into an attractive man and it would be too easy to fall under his spell all over again. She must keep re-minding herself of those lies, and of how he had let her down when she needed him. Like her fa-ther, he had used her for his own ends, then cast her aside.

'That is a pity. I had a mind to consult him on a matter concerning Fenton Hall.'

'The Hall? What matter?'

'Nothing much.' His hand rose to pull at his earlobe and Kitty watched him, puzzled. It was another habit of Rob's—this time when he felt uncomfortable, or guilty, over something. 'I've been pondering whether to have another wing built, to balance the one built after the fire. And, as Kelridge was involved at that time and as he is a trained architect, I thought to seek his advice.'

'Another *wing*? But… Rob…the Hall is surely sufficient for our needs? What do we need with more space?'

Robert shook his head. 'You may be right. It was merely a whim and this is not the place to discuss it.' He scanned the dancers. 'Charis is dancing with Sampford, I see. We need to keep an eye on that. I'm surprised the fellow even got a voucher for here.'

'The Patronesses must be lowering their standards. They allowed Kelridge in, too.'

Robert laughed. 'Poor Kelridge! He really has upset you, hasn't he?'

'Not at all.' She changed the subject. 'What is your objection to Sampford?'

'He is hanging out for a rich wife to reduce his debts.'

'Many peers are in similar financial straits. He *is* a little old for her, it is true, but Charis appears to be enjoying his company.'

'That,' said Robert grimly, 'is what I am afraid of. Charis enjoying his company, I mean. He is charm personified. On the surface.'

'Ah.'

Kitty did not ask Robert to elaborate. She had crossed paths with many such men and, in general, they shared the same selfish outlook on life.

Charis deserved much better. Robert collected his sister as soon as the dance ended and the remainder of the evening passed uneventfully.

It was only later that night, as she prepared for bed, that Kitty realised Robert never did tell her why he was contemplating enlarging Fenton Hall and, by the morning, she had forgotten all about it.

'Stepmama?'

It was just past noon the following day and Kitty had hoped to make progress on her story, in which Arabella, her spirited and beautiful heroine, had just innocently interrupted the abduction of her six-year-old orphaned nephew, Arthur—the Duke of Northam—by his dastardly uncle, Lord Sidney Barmouth, whose intention was to gain control of young Arthur's fortune. The hero was about to step on to the page and she had just decided on Jason as the perfect name for him.

Her attention, however, had been wandering all morning—distracted by images of Adam. Last night was the first time they had spoken in the fortnight that had passed since Lady Charnwood's ball and Kitty's unwise foray on to the terrace. Until last night, Kitty had deliberately avoided him at society events and he, true to his word, had avoided her. But he had still regularly invaded her thoughts to the point where she suspected her preoccupation with him had strayed dangerously close to obsession.

How could she have guessed that he would turn up at Almack's of all places? What was Lady Datchworth thinking, dragging him there... unless, of course, she was still intent on throwing him and Charis together?

Kitty refused to examine quite why that idea made her feel so...so...*prickly.* He was unsuitable and too old. That was enough to warrant her objection. It was nothing whatsoever to do with that insistent voice in her head that mocked her for still being attracted to him, despite everything.

'Stepmama?'

Kitty started, rattled that she had, yet again, wandered deep into her own thoughts. She laid her quill aside before facing her stepdaughter with a smile, welcoming the interruption to the constant circling of her thoughts.

Besides, she thought with a despondent sigh, *my stories cannot hold a candle to those of Miss Austen. My first story was no doubt a fluke and I doubt I shall ever be good enough to be published again.*

Somehow, though, the more she told herself that, the more she felt driven to keep striving to improve. Her first published novel had barely caused a ripple of interest, but the drive to write and to have her stories published was a dream she could not quite set aside. She was fortunate that Robert regarded her 'little hobby' as harmless. He had been instrumental in achieving publication for her first novel, but only on condition her name was not known, even to the publisher, because female novelists were still regarded as racy and scandalous by many in society and he feared any notoriety might tarnish Charis by association.

'Yes, Charis?'

'Might we visit the Change today instead of paying morning calls?'

Kitty opened her mouth but, before she could speak, Charis rushed on, 'I know you will say we went there last week, but I am exceedingly eager to go and see the animals again.'

'But...the last time we visited the Menagerie you became distressed at how they are confined.'

'It is true I should rather see such creatures roam wild and free, but I know I shall never have that chance. We will return home soon and I *should* like to see them again.'

Kitty shook her head wonderingly. 'You really wish to spend time today staring at wild beasts at the Exeter Exchange rather than call upon your friends as we planned this afternoon?'

It was not that Kitty disliked the animals—she found them fascinating—but...surely a responsible stepmother should be able to channel her charge's interests in a more suitable direction?

Charis pouted. 'I shall see my friends tonight. Besides, Annabel can talk of little else other than her wedding and how utterly wonderful Talaton is. All one can do is nod and agree, and murmur "How fascinating" at suitable intervals.'

'It was only a few weeks ago you were in alt over their betrothal.'

'*That* was when it was news. We have surely said all there is to say on the subject by now and yet *still* Annabel and Mrs Blanchard prattle on and on, repeating themselves *ad infinitum* until I could happily close my eyes and go to sleep, I am so bored.'

Kitty eyed Charis, sensing there might be more to this than she was admitting.

'Charis...do you feel a little envious of Annabel?'

'No, I do not. She is welcome to Talaton. But I find it increasingly hard to keep smiling when I find myself the subject of pitying looks from both Annabel and her mama because *she* has found a husband and I have not. And there is nothing I can do about it—I cannot protest because they never *say* it, so they rob me of the chance to say I do not care. But it is exceedingly frustrating because I know precisely what they are thinking.'

Kitty took Charis's hand. 'Well, in my opinion, it is you who are the fortunate one. In her debut Season a young girl's head and heart should be

filled with fun and frivolity, fashion and furbe-
lows, dancing and dashing young men. There is
plenty of time to find a husband.'

'But you married Papa when you were my age,
Stepmama. And *you* never even had a Season.'

Adam once again hovered at the edges of Kitty's
mind and she banished him with a silent growl of
irritation.

'That is true. But my circumstances were very
different from yours. And I never once regretted our marriage. How could I, when without it I
would not have you and your brothers and sister?'

*And even though I did not have the baby I so
craved.*

The sudden thickening of her throat and the
sting in her eyes surprised her, for she had long
ago accepted her childless state. Why did that
thought upset her now? Then Adam's face materialised in her mind's eye and she scrambled to
make sense of the connection until Lady Datchworth's words from last night, barely noticed at
the time, echoed through her head: *I was intent
upon helping poor Kelridge here with his marriage plans.*

But…that was just Lady Datchworth on one of
her matchmaking quests. Was it not? Why should
that trigger…? *Oh!* Her Ladyship's voice continued in Kitty's memory. *'You have a title and a*

fortune, and you need an heir. Of course you must wed—it is your obligation as a peer of the realm.'

And the thought of Adam marrying…of him siring an heir…caused that tell-tale prickling behind her eyes once again and fear wrapped around Kitty's heart. Adam had reappeared in her life just over a fortnight ago and already, it seemed, he had begun to break through the barriers she had built around herself.

'And without it, we would not have you!' Charis hugged Kitty and kissed her cheek. 'Now *please* say we may go to the Change.'

Kitty forced her thoughts away from Adam. 'Very well. But you knew I would give way right from the start, didn't you?'

Charis kissed Kitty again. 'You usually do. Thank you.'

Two hours later, Kitty gloomily contemplated the elephant on the upper floor of the Exeter Exchange, marvelling at the sheer size of the beast, at his eyes—disproportionately tiny—and his huge ears as they flapped back and forth. His name, so a passing keeper had informed her on their first visit, was Chunee and he fanned his ears in order to cool himself down as his native land was India where the temperatures were very hot. As she turned from her study of Chunee— secretly agreeing with Charis that it seemed wrong to keep such an animal confined on its own in a small enclosure—she collided with a solid wall of male muscle.

'Oh! I *beg* your pardon.'

'Dinna fash yersel', lass. There's nae harm done.'

Kitty's head snapped up. Adam grinned down at her as he tipped his beaver hat and her heart leapt with what she feared was joy. She did *not* wish to feel like that at the mere sight of him. She gritted her teeth, battling both that visceral response and the near-overwhelming urge to reach out and touch him—his hand...his sleeve...it mattered not which part of him, it was simply a primal *need* to make physical contact. She curled her hands into fists at her sides, reminding herself that men could not be trusted and that Adam would only let her down, as he had before. As her father had.

'What are *you* doing here?' The war in her breast made her snappish.

His brows rose. 'I have come to view the animals. As have you, nae doubt.' His nose wrinkled. 'I confess I hadna anticipated the smell...it is a wee bit on the strong side, is it not?'

He held her gaze for a few minutes as Kitty scrambled for something to say, for normal conversation between two acquaintances. *He* managed it effortlessly. Why was it so difficult for her?

Adam turned to look at Chunee. 'And this is the elephant?' He shook his head wonderingly. 'I have seen drawings of such beasts—and of some of the others up here—but I had no idea of its sheer size.'

Kitty swallowed and forced a level tone. 'Indeed. And have you seen the lion and the tiger?'

'No. And I have nae desire to see them… Kitty…'

He paused and she waited for him to continue as he seemed to wrestle with himself.

'Why did you wed Fenton not two weeks after declaring undying love for me?'

She sucked in a breath at his unexpected question. She raised her chin.

'That, my lord, is none of your business.'

'Aye, it is. Ye owe it to me to tell me why.' His blue gaze burned into her, sending sizzles of awareness chasing across her skin.

'I owe you nothing.' She spoke through gritted teeth. 'When I would have told you the truth about my life, all those years ago, you refused to listen.'

The unfairness of that still festered deep inside and, although back then she had steeled herself to tell Adam about her father's cruel plan to sell her hand in marriage to settle his gambling debts, she was not prepared to expose her pain and shame to this near stranger. 'You did not want to know then and I do not believe dragging up old, forgotten feelings will serve any useful purpose.'

He searched her face and she fought to keep her anger in place as the intensity of his scrutiny aroused a swirl of conflicting emotions within her. She must protect herself, at all costs. Her heart was fickle...what if she fell for him again, despite the past? And if she did, there would only be more pain because even if, this time, Adam truly fell in love with her, it could never lead to marriage. Lady Datchworth was right... Adam *would* need an heir and Kitty could not give him one.

But his silence gave her time to regret her harsh words. 'Besides...' she indicated their surroundings '...this is hardly the place to discuss such a subject.'

He raised a brow. 'Indeed not. With ears that size, the elephant would nae doubt hear every word and trumpet our secrets far and wide.' He grinned, but then his brows twitched into a frown. 'When may we discuss it, Kitty? I think we must. Don't you?'

She could think of nothing more dangerous to her peace of mind. 'I can see no benefit in dredging up the past merely on some whim of yours.'

He sighed. 'Aye...well... I canna say I'm keen on being labelled as a man with a tendency to whims, Kitty, but if it pleases you to think of me in such a way—'

'I would not waste my time labelling you as anything. You flatter yourself, sir.'

She hated hearing the words snapping from her mouth, but she could not help it, she was in such turmoil. Adam, however, merely chuckled, making her feel even more ashamed of her volatile moods.

'I was, believe it not, jesting with you. Have you lost your sense of humour as well as your charge, ma'am?'

'My charge?'

'Your stepdaughter.'

Charis! Kitty spun around, searching the room where the animals were housed. There were several people on the upper floor, but Charis was not among them. Kitty turned back to Adam.

'Have you seen her? Oh! Of course! You must have done, to know she is missing.'

In her agitation, she clutched his forearm, registering the sudden tension in his muscles at the same time as…something…some emotion… flared and died in those intensely blue eyes, triggering a response deep inside her: a tugging, yearning sensation.

'As I said before, dinna fash yersel'. She is downstairs with Lady D., who declined to come up here as she does not care for the menagerie.

She says the monkeys give her nightmares. It was she who sent me to find you.'

'I must go to Charis. I do not understand why she went downstairs without telling me... I thought she was looking at the Arabian camel.'

Adam pursed his lips, his gaze wandering around the room before coming back to rest on Kitty's face. 'I passed her on the stairs. She appeared to be in company with a gentleman. Although...it could be I'm mistaken, but I did think you might wish to know that is a possibility.'

'Do you know who it was?'

'Sampford.'

'*Sampford?* But—' Kitty reeled with shock. That Charis should have met with Sampford here today after dancing with him last night could not be a coincidence.

'I did see them together at Almack's last evening,' Adam said. 'It made me question if there may be an attachment of some sort.'

Kitty could read nothing from his expression.

'You suspect they had an assignation?'

Adam shrugged. 'I thought it possible.'

'But she is only seventeen—far too young to form an attachment.'

His eyes narrowed. 'We both know how headstrong such young girls can be when they fancy they are in love.'

Chapter Eight

Kitty sucked in a breath at that jibe. 'Oh!'

She glared up at him, striving to project every single ounce of her outrage into that one look, then whirled around and marched to the stairs, battening down the swell of hurt his remark had provoked. A low blow, as Robert would describe it. How could she ever have imagined herself at risk of falling in love again with him? He was nothing but a boor and she hoped she never set eyes on him again. On that thought, she slammed to a halt and spun to face him.

'I *thought*, Lord Kelridge, you were to return to Hertfordshire this morning. Another lie?'

Proud at the icy tone she achieved and the fact her voice did not quiver, Kitty turned and hurried down the stairs to street level, where she could see Charis and Lady Datchworth at the far end of the Change, examining the wares displayed on one of the stalls set up outside the shops. Of Sampford there was no sign. She slowed her pace, relief flooding her at the sight of Her Ladyship.

'I enjoyed watching you flounce, Kitty.'

Her pulse rocketed as the low voice sounded in her ear and his warm breath raised the little hairs at her nape. Kitty halted.

'I do *not* flounce, my lord. And, if I did, it would be for neither your benefit nor your entertainment.'

Somehow, she knew not how, he manoeuvred her arm through his and they were again walking towards Lady Datchworth and Charis.

'You do not wish to give Her Ladyship the suspicion we have been squabbling, I hope?'

Put like that…no, she did not, so she accepted his escort with as good grace as she could muster.

'And, in answer to your…um—*accusation* might best describe your tone of voice—I am leaving for Hertfordshire later today. It is only a short journey and the evenings are light enough. I had a matter or two to tie up before leaving town and I wished to say my goodbyes to the few people I can regard as friends. Including Robert, of course.'

Oh, no! Robert wanted to speak to Adam…

'Have you seen Robert yet?'

'No. He was unavailable, unfortunately. May I impose on your good nature—you note I do not say goodwill as you appear to have a scant quantity of that towards myself—to pass on my good wishes and my farewell?'

'You may.'

'I thank you.'

Kitty breathed a little easier on learning Robert had not yet spoken to Adam about this new wing for the Hall. She would persuade him to consult a different architect, although she still couldn't fathom why he had suddenly formed this desire to refurbish the Hall. Unless…could he be contemplating matrimony? She frowned, racking her brains, but she could not recall him paying particular attention to any young lady during the Season—other than the Marquess of Patterdale's sister, Lady Phoebe Crawshaw. But Kitty could not believe Robert's attention to the Incomparable—as the gentlemen had dubbed Lady Phoebe, as they clustered around her like wasps around a ripe plum—was anything more than Robert following the latest fashion. Kitty prayed he had more sense than to view such a female as a suitable marriage prospect for, although the gentlemen were universally captivated by her beauty and her spirit, the ladies of the *ton* were divided upon the subject of Lady Phoebe. The younger ladies thought her fast but fascinating, the older matrons thought her fast and vulgar. Kitty's opinion lay somewhere between the two, but she had found the other woman intriguing as she observed her, drawing upon her antics and mannerisms for Minerva, a character in her novel and the flighty, avaricious betrothed of Arthur's villainous Uncle Sidney.

Kitty and Adam joined the others—Lady Datchworth's sharp gaze switching from Adam to Kitty and back again as Charis sent Kitty a look that managed to be both guilty and apologetic at the same time.

'I followed the keeper down here because I needed to ask him something.'

The rush of her stepdaughter's words did nothing to quell either Kitty's suspicions or her concern.

'And did you find out what you wished to know?'

'I… I could not catch him.'

'And you then met Lord Sampford, did you not, my dear,' said Lady Datchworth, 'which is why you did not *immediately* return to your stepmother.'

A blush lit Charis's cheeks. 'I did not wish to be thought unmannerly by not speaking to him.'

'Well, I thank you both for ensuring Charis's safety and for informing me of her whereabouts,' said Kitty, fighting to keep the disapproval and worry from her countenance. 'Charis, come. It is time we returned home.'

She would not discuss this with Charis in front of others, but she would have plenty to say to her on the journey home. She prayed poor Charis's heart was not engaged if that *had* been a clandestine plan to meet Lord Sampford because—following Robert's revelations about the man—Kitty had no doubt Charis deserved far better than a husband like him. He was utterly unsuitable and had proved he could not be trusted and was no gentleman by encouraging Charis to go downstairs with him, away from her chaperon. Thank goodness Lady Datchworth happened to be there at the right time. Charis was so young... only seventeen...far too young to fall in love.

Kitty sucked in a breath at the significance of Charis's age. Seventeen...the same age she had been when she had fallen in love with Adam. Not that she had truly been in love with him, of course. Infatuation. That was what it had been. He had been right, of course. She shot a glance at Adam and it collided with his knowing gaze. His lips twitched and a gleam lit his blue eyes, drat the man. It was as though he knew precisely what she was thinking—and it was no doubt the cause of his earlier comment about young girls.

'Lord Kelridge.' Lady Datchworth's crisp command brought both Kitty's and Adam's attention back to her. 'I desire a private word with Lady Fenton. Would you be so good as to escort Miss

Mayfield to peruse the wares on that stall over there?' She waved her arm in the general direction of a stall displaying silver-plated trinkets such as snuff boxes and vinaigrettes.

Kitty frowned at Her Ladyship's blatant attempt to throw Adam and Charis together, in no mood to allow the Marchioness to interfere in Charis's future. As soon as Adam and Charis were out of earshot, she said, 'I intend to be straight with you, Lady Datchworth.'

'Oh. Please do.' A smile flickered on Her Ladyship's mouth. 'But, before you speak, allow me to explain that I overheard Sampford last night persuading your Charis to meet him here today, and I thought it my duty to circumvent any trouble.'

'You *knew* about their tryst? But why not just tell me last night? Why go through this charade?'

'Charade?' Her Ladyship's eyebrows shot skyward. 'Allow me to remind you that I have vastly more experience of life than you, my dear. Had you banned their meeting, all you would end up doing is cause resentment and a determination to be even more secretive. *This* way, Charis is both embarrassed and ashamed—and the lesson has been learned that she *will* be found out. Besides, it gave me an opportunity to throw her and Kelridge together.'

'Well, I wish you had not involved Kelridge.

I told you before. I do *not* believe that would be a good match.'

'But you have still not furnished me with a good reason for your objection.'

Kitty's teeth ground together. 'I do not need to discuss my objections with you, ma'am. Suffice it to say that Lord Fenton would disapprove as well and that should be an end to it.'

Her Ladyship shrugged. 'Very well. If you do not wish my assistance, I shall say no more. Never let it be said that I interfere in others' lives even though, as I said, my experience does furnish me with a unique insight into my friends' well-being.'

Kitty swallowed down any further hot words as Lady Datchworth beckoned imperiously at Adam, who nodded and returned with Charis on his arm.

'It is time to return home, Charis.'

'Very well, Stepmama.'

Charis looked suitably chastened and Kitty allowed herself to imagine what her attitude might have been had Kitty been aware of her rendezvous with Sampford and flatly refused to come here today. Irritatingly, she realised Lady Datchworth might have a point about the best way to deal with Charis's clandestine meeting. She summoned up a smile for Her Ladyship even as she prayed Charis had not developed a *tendre* for Sampford, especially in light of Robert's revelations. She was aware it was impossible to protect Charis against heartache, but knowing she was powerless did not stop Kitty from wanting to do her utmost to protect her precious stepdaughter against any and every sorrow.

'I am grateful for your sage advice, ma'am.'

Lady Datchworth's lips stretched into an answering smile. 'You are most welcome, my dear.'

Adam bowed. 'Good afternoon, Lady Fenton, Miss Mayfield. It's been a pleasure to meet you both again.'

'Likewise, sir.' Kitty inclined her head as Charis curtsied. 'Good afternoon, Lady Datchworth, my lord.'

As they walked away she heard Lady Datchworth's peremptory tones float after them.

'How the devil did you contrive to provoke her this time, Kelridge?'

Kitty increased her pace to prevent any prospect of overhearing his reply.

'Hi! Adam!'

Adam paused with one booted foot on the carriage step as his cousin, Tolly, sprinted up the street, a valise in one hand. He waved and increased his pace. Adam lowered his foot and waited. That valise presented a strong clue that Tolly had decided to travel to Kelridge Place with him after all, although he had declined the offer last evening, when Adam had met him at Brooks's after he had escorted Lady Datchworth home from Almack's.

'Much obliged, Coz.'

Tolly dropped his case and bent forward, hands on knees, panting. Adam waited patiently.

'Thought I'd missed you!'

'Changed your mind?'

'I have.' Tolly straightened, his face red. He hauled in a breath and blew it out again. 'Phew! Not used to runnin'. Bit of a rush, by the time I got home and packed.' He picked up his valise. 'Given my man the day off, too. Never was much of a one for plannin' and so forth.'

Adam was surprised how pleased he was to have Tolly's company. If nothing else, it would stop him brooding about Kitty and obsessing over his ungentlemanly jibe at the Change. He had meant his comment about headstrong young girls to be humorous, but had realised his error as soon as it left his lips. And Kitty's reaction confirmed she had not found it amusing. He had no wish to squabble with her every time they met. Rather, he longed for the chance to question her properly, driven not only by the urge to understand why she had married Fenton, but also by this new burden of guilt over his refusal to listen to her explanation as to why she had been desperate to leave her father's home.

Somehow, he must find a way to have that conversation with her and he now regretted his impulsive announcement that he was leaving Town, admitting—if only to himself—that the heaviness currently weighing on his soul was entirely due to the fact he would not see Kitty again for the foreseeable future.

There was the consolation, however, that when she returned to Hertfordshire it would surely prove easier to find privacy there than in London. Until then, he must try to be patient. But that would be hard, especially since their meeting that afternoon. Her guard had slipped and he had glimpsed very real emotion in her eyes as they had sparred with one another. And that glimpse had given him hope that, maybe, they could work through the events of the past and reach a better understanding. And then…who knew?

He was still unsure exactly what he hoped for with regard to Kitty, but he did know he would rather be someone she trusted than someone she eyed with caution.

'Barlow—load Mr Trewin's luggage on the rack if you please.' The groom on the box jumped down and did as he was bid. 'In you get, then, Tolly, and you can tell me why the change of plans.'

Once the carriage was in motion, Tolly said, 'I

just realised you might appreciate a friendly face there, to help ease you into your new role.

He stopped speaking, his chest still heaving with the effort of his sprint.

Adam leaned back, stretching his legs out and folding his arms across his chest as he settled down for the journey.

'Well, I admit I shall be glad of both your company and your support. Plus, the journey will finally give you the chance to tell me all about my father.'

Adam had questioned Tolly about his father a few times since their first meeting, but Tolly had always fobbed him off—easily done when there had always been other people around. But now it was just the two of them and Adam burned to why his mother had run away from the man, depriving Adam of his father, and her husband of his son and heir.

'Ah. Yes.' A frown slashed between Tolly's eyebrows. 'It is...awkward.'

'As are so many things about this situation. Look... Tolly...my father was who he was. Telling me the truth about him will change nothing. I didn't know the man, so you will not be shattering dreams...' His mother had already destroyed those, when she admitted the soldier hero he had thought was his father was naught but a figment of her imagination. 'I just want to understand what he was like.'

And to know if he was really such a monster that his wife chose the life of a housekeeper rather than remain as his Countess.

'Well…if you put it like that, I can tell you he was quick-tempered and free with his fists, too. Your mother had already left him by the time my parents wed, but my mother did know yours and she told me she didn't blame Esther for running away, even though it created a huge scandal and most of society were unforgiving. Including my own father, I'm sorry to say.' He shook his head. 'Family loyalty, I suppose. I've even heard people say that a wife belongs to her husband and, if he has to beat her, then it's her own fault and she should mend her ways.'

Anger stirred at the thought of anyone beating his mother and Adam clenched his fists on his knees. No wonder she had always been quick to stop any signs of temper in her son. He stared down at his clenched fists and forced them to relax. He might be quick to anger, but he had *never* come close to hitting anyone.

'Did you know him? What did you make of him?'

'We saw very little of him when I was young as my mother disliked him but, after her death, Father sold his commission and moved back to

Kelridge. I was in the cavalry myself by then, but I would visit him there whenever I had leave and I got to know Uncle Gerald better.' Tolly leaned forward, propping his forearms along his thighs. 'I saw more than I wished to: maidservants with black eyes and bruised faces. Staff didn't stay for long and the Place had fallen into disrepair, but my father gradually began to put things to rights.' He looked round at Adam. 'One of the estate men once told me your father used to make you drink brandy, as a punishment.'

'*Brandy?* But… I was only two years old when we left.'

'Quite.' Tolly sighed again and sat up. 'He wasn't punishing you…it was to punish your mother, if she dared to stand up to him. I tell you, Coz…you were better off brought up as a housekeeper's son than if your mother had stayed with that devil.'

Adam leaned his head back against the squabs and closed his eyes, regret coursing through him at his anger with Ma and that they did not part on better terms.

'Did your mother not tell you anything about your father?'

'Not a thing. She said she did not want to burden me with her view of my father. That I should discover the truth from people who knew him better than she did. She thought he might have changed in the years since she left.'

Tolly huffed a laugh. 'No. he didn't change. Your mother, though...she could have chosen to fill your head with poison about your father, but she has allowed you to make up your own mind. She sounds a fair-minded woman.'

'She is. And she has been a good mother to me.' *And I miss her.*

Adam felt even more guilty at his misjudgement. He had been too hasty to apportion blame... jumping to conclusions even though Ma had never given him cause to think her a vindictive woman who would keep father and son apart without good reason. That was a lesson he would do well to remember.

A few hours after leaving London, Adam recognised the turning that led to Fenton Hall, Kitty's home, although the house could not be seen from the road, shielded as it was by a belt of trees.

Half an hour later, the carriage turned on to a quiet, leafy lane and slowed.

'We are getting close now.' Tolly pointed between the trees at a distant Palladian mansion standing proud on the crest of a rise.

As the carriage bowled along the driveway, Adam took in the healthy cattle and sheep grazing the lush pastures. He had a lot to learn about this way of life and he hoped it would prove easier to establish a rapport with the estate workers than with the household staff, most of whom had travelled back to Kelridge that morning to prepare for his arrival. When the house came into view, Adam's first thought was how stark it looked... no wings to soften or extend the outline, just a solid block of a house with a central temple-like portico rising the height of the building. The severe lines were softened only by twin flights of steps rising to the entrance. It didn't look much like a home, but the windows sparkled and the forecourt was neatly raked.

'My uncle had done a good job in maintaining the house and park,' Adam remarked to Tolly. 'Everything looks in good repair.'

'It is. Your father enjoyed the high life and failed to invest much in the estate before he fell ill but, when my father took over, he made sure any neglect was made good. The rents provide a healthy living. You are a fortunate man, Coz.'

There was no edge to his voice, but Adam still found it hard to credit that Tolly did not feel even a little cheated by his reappearance.

'Are you certain you do not resent my turning up again, Tolly, when all this might have been yours one day?'

'Not I. My mother left me funds so I am quite comfortable, and all without the responsibility of running an estate this size. You are welcome to it, Coz.'

Tolly's comment was too breezily dismissive for Adam to believe him wholeheartedly but he kept his doubts to himself. If there were any bad feelings there, they would show themselves in time.

The carriage halted, and both men jumped down before the groom could let down the steps. Adam turned in a slow circle, taking everything in. He'd never felt more lonely and out of his depth in his life, and he was grateful Tolly had decided to accompany him.

'Come on. Let's find the old man and I'll introduce you.' Tolly bounded up the left-hand flight of steps to the door, which remained closed. He paused before opening it. 'Don't expect the fatted calf, Adam. M'father…as I said earlier…he's become accustomed to having the income from the estate at his disposal and he wouldn't be human if he didn't feel some bitterness towards you. He won't like having to return to his former, restricted way of life.'

His comment echoed the doubts Adam had just been having, but about Tolly. He didn't reply as Green opened the front door and bowed.

'Welcome to Kelridge Place, my lord.'

Inside, a soberly dressed man of around fifty was descending the stairs.

'Mr Bartholomew, sir. It's a pleasure to see you.' The man bowed.

'Thank you, Corbett. This is Lord Kelridge. Adam, Corbett is my father's valet. Is Father about?'

Corbett bowed to Adam. 'Welcome, milord.' He didn't quite meet Adam's eye before he turned to Tolly. 'Mr Trewin has just this minute gone up to change for dinner. Shall I have hot water sent up for you both? I dare say you will wish to refresh yourselves after the journey.'

The valet only spoke directly to Adam when he had no choice. 'The master's bedchamber is ready for you, milord, and Mr Bartholomew's chamber is always kept aired in case of a visit.'

'Thank you, Corbett. And, yes, please send up hot water. I shall meet my uncle later.'

Chapter Nine

'So. You're m'nephew?'

Adam nodded at his uncle's rhetorical question.

Uncle Grenville stood before the empty fireplace in the drawing room of Kelridge Place, his hands behind his back as he rocked up on his toes and back down again. He'd adopted the dominant stance the minute Adam joined him in the room to await the announcement of dinner. Adam allowed himself a wry smile and sat on a nearby chair, crossing his legs. He wouldn't take part in games of one-upmanship, if that was his uncle's aim. It mattered not how long Grenville had regarded himself as master of Kelridge Hall—that was now Adam's role.

'I realise my existence must be somewhat… difficult…for you to accept, Uncle, but we cannot change that. I should like to reassure you, how-

ever, that you may continue to regard Kelridge as
your home for as long as you wish.'

Grenville nodded, his expression thoughtful.
He was still a fine figure of a man despite near-
ing sixty years of age. Tall, with an upright posture, and with steel-grey hair that showed no sign
of receding, his shoulders were broad, his belly
still flat and his features chiselled—no hint of a
double chin above his neatly tied neckcloth. A
legacy, maybe, of his years in the cavalry—as
the younger son, that had been his chosen career.

'That is decent of you in the circumstances.
And, as you have so generously made the offer, I
have no hesitation in accepting it. While we are
on the subject, have you a preference as to which
bedchamber I use from now on? When my brother
became too ill to climb the stairs, he moved into
apartments on the ground floor and I moved into
the master's suite of rooms. I have, of course, va-
cated them, since I learned that you...' His voice
trailed into silence.

'That I am alive? It must have come as a...
shock, after all these years.'

Adam had been going to say '*a blow*' but, at the
last minute, dismissed the term as too provoca-
tive. He and his uncle must learn to rub along together. A flash of some strong emotion crossed
the older man's features—gone in an instant.

'A *pleasant* shock, Nephew. I am delighted Gerald's bloodline has not died out.'

At least he *sounded* sincere.

'As to which bedchamber you should occupy, Uncle, ye may choose whichever ye please, other than the Countess's suite—well, that goes without saying, for I am sure you would have no desire to occupy those rooms—or the principal guest bedchamber, which I shall require for guests.'

Uncle Grenville's brows beetled. 'Guests? What guests? When do they arrive?'

'I have issued no invitations yet, but I shall require the principal guest room for any guests I may choose to invite in the future. You surely willna deny me the right to invite friends to stay in my own house?'

After what Tolly had revealed of Adam's father's character—and now he understood better the reasons his mother had fled his father—Adam hoped he could now persuade Ma to come and make her home at Kelridge Place, where she belonged. He did not, however, expect his uncle to welcome that news.

'Very well.' Uncle Grenville inclined his head. 'I shall instruct my man to move my belongings *again*.' He paused, his chest moving rapidly up and down as his jaw clenched. Then he shook his head. 'I apologise if that sounded a touch bitter, Ambrose.'

'Adam.'

'Adam. My apologies. Anyway, I find as I get older I do not care for change. I have had sole responsibility for this place for over five years since your father first fell ill and I also shouldered much of the responsibility in the years before that. It is where I grew up and, although I have my own house near Kelworth village, I have always regarded the Place as my home. Yet now I am to be relegated to a minor bedchamber to give way to *occasional* guests.'

Adam rose to his feet and strode over to the window, staring out unseeingly to give himself time to consider how best to respond. He had learned over the years that was the best way to control his sometimes fiery temper—words flung out in the heat of the moment could do more damage than intended. A temper—he was now aware, his stomach churning uneasily—he might have inherited from his father. His mother's constant correction of his boyish outbursts made sense now. Had she seen hints of his father's temperament in Adam? The very thought made him shudder after what he'd learned from Tolly and he vowed to work doubly hard to keep his anger on a firm rein.

'I am sorry you find change uncomfortable—' he swung around to face his uncle, '—but you *have* had several weeks now in which to become accustomed to the fact I am still alive to claim my inheritance. And, as you have said, you do have a perfectly good house of your own near to the village.'

Grenville folded his arms, his expression stormy. 'It is hardly a fitting home for the son of an earl. Six bedrooms only and a mere thirty acres of land. Of what use is that? A gentleman is entitled to live in comfort. It is what I was born to.'

'It is more than most people have. It is far more than I ever had. And I, too, lest you forget, am the son of an earl.'

'*You* knew no better. Dragged up in a heathen country by that—'

'Take care!' Adam stalked back to face his uncle, but resisted the urge to grab him by the lapels and shake him, the spectre of his father looming large. '*Do not*, if you know what is good for you, insult my mother. Ever. I might have sympathy for your plight, hence my offer for you to continue to make Kelridge Place your home, but do not mistake my sympathy for weakness.'

He swallowed down his rage as his uncle's colour heightened.

'You—' Uncle Grenville broke off as the door opened.

'Good evening. Is this a private party, or may I join you?'

Tolly's amused tones floated into the charged atmosphere and Adam looked around to see his cousin had halted on the threshold, his eyebrows arched. A faint smile played around his lips, but his expression was watchful. He had donned a brown-leather eyepatch and that, coupled with his scrutiny, gave him a somewhat sinister appearance.

Adam forced a smile.

'Come on in, Tolly. Your father and I were just discussing the new arrangements to be made here at the Hall.'

Uncle Grenville's hand landed on Adam's shoulder. 'I spoke out of turn, my boy. This is a difficult adjustment for me...and for us all, you included. I confess I find it hard to forgive your mother for depriving my brother of his son and heir. Surely you can acknowledge how hard that is to stomach?'

Adam stared at his uncle. 'Nay. I canna acknowledge it, as it happens. My mother should have been safe in her own home and yet your brother...my *father*—' even saying that brought the sour taste of bile to his mouth, '—made her feel so *un*safe that she had no choice but to leave.'

Grenville's eyes glittered as he folded his arms. 'Gerald was *my brother* and, for all his faults, he was Esther's husband—the man she vowed to honour and obey. You were too young to know the truth of it. I—'

'Father.' Tolly stepped forward, his voice low and soothing. 'You cannot defend the indefensible. I witnessed my uncle's violence for myself and I can readily believe my aunt feared for her own life and for the safety of her child.'

'The law says—'

'Enough!' Adam paced the room in another attempt to calm himself. '*I* dinna care what the law might say. My heart tells me that no mother should fear for either her safety or that of her child. But what I do care about is that you continue to blame my mother for something that was clearly the fault of my father.'

Grenville shook his head. 'Neither of you understand what it was like, when Gerald and I were growing up.'

Adam sat down and gestured to Tolly to do the same. 'Tell us, then.'

'It was not Gerald's fault he was the way he was. Our father—your grandfather—he had a temper, too. But Gerald…he always protected me…took the beatings…distracted my father when he was drunk and in the mood to lash out. I…' Grenville looked from Adam to Tolly and back again, his eyes glittering with emotion '…I *owed* him. I know he had a nasty temper, especially when he'd been drinking, but he deserved my loyalty. Especially when your mother left him…the humiliation he suffered…his despair at never knowing what had become of you, Amb—Adam. It drove him to even greater excess. He was a bitter man.'

Adam sighed. Having learned the truth about his father's violence from Tolly, he did not now want to feel even a sliver of sympathy for the man. But Grenville's story did leave him with a touch more understanding of both his father's temperament and, more importantly, his uncle's loyalty to him.

'I am sorry for what you and your brother suffered as children,' he said. 'But that is no excuse for the way your brother treated my mother.'

'I accept that. Maybe I could have stopped him, had I been here, but I was away campaigning for much of the time in the early years of their marriage. And, once your mother had gone, all I could do was support him as best I could.'

Adam felt better to have cleared the air and the three men spent the evening together without further discord. By the time Adam retired to the master bedchamber, he felt more hopeful than he had at any time since his mother had told him the truth of his origins.

'I'll show you around the place after breakfast.' Uncle Grenville spoke through a mouthful of devilled kidneys the following morning. 'There's a decent hunter in the stables that'll be up to your weight. You'll be keen to get your bearings, I make no doubt.'

Adam picked up his coffee cup and drained it. 'I am.'

At that moment Tolly sauntered into the morning parlour, bleary-eyed.

'You look as though your night was as restless as mine, Cousin,' Adam said, with a grin.

Tolly yawned widely. 'I stayed up playing billiards after you both retired. Too accustomed to town hours.'

His yawn triggered Adam to yawn in his turn—he had lain awake for many hours in the night, pondering not only what he had learned about his father, but also dwelling on Kitty. And she was still on his mind this morning. Who had she danced with last night? What would she be doing today? Did she think of him at all? And, finally, how soon would she return to Fenton Hall, and when would he get that chance to ask her again about what had happened after he left her fifteen years ago? Learning how he had jumped to conclusions about his mother had prompted him to wonder if he had also made assumptions about Kitty's behaviour. And the only way to know that was to ask her…and keep asking until she told him.

Adam clenched his jaw as he scraped butter

on his toast, pondering his contradictory attitude to Kitty. In London he had vowed not to go out of his way to meet her or to speak to her and it had been easy enough to stick to his resolve. But he'd seen her at a distance—in the Park, across a ballroom, at the theatre, and there had always been the anticipation...the hope...that they might meet, even though he had not recognised it as such. And, somehow, that had been enough. Their meetings at Almack's and at the Change had been all the sweeter for being unexpected, despite the squabbles that had marred each occasion.

Now, though...now that there was no possibility whatsoever of catching sight of her and no possibility of bumping into her in the street or at an event, it seemed as though a little of the light had leached from his world.

He bit into his toast and chewed. This was ridiculous. He knew the Fentons would not return to Hertfordshire until the Season ended. He must banish Kitty from his thoughts and concentrate instead on learning about his new life. Then, when she came home to Fenton Hall, he would go and visit her.

'I should like to meet with the steward today,' he said to Uncle Grenville. 'Carter, isn't it? I'll send a message to him to come up to the house at two o'clock.'

'Yes. Joseph Carter. He should be here at that

time anyway. He's been working on the ledgers in the afternoons this week to ready them for you. He's a good man and knows the business inside out—he's been keeping the books ever since your father took him on, not long before I sold my commission and came home. Numbers have never been my forte—I much prefer the practical side of running the estates—and Gerald always had a haphazard approach to the finances, so Carter's been a godsend.'

'Very well. Tolly? Will you join us this morning? Your father has offered to show me around the estate.'

'With pleasure. But allow me to finish breaking my fast first, or I shall likely fall off my horse and break my neck.'

As it happened, it was Adam who fell off his horse—a bay gelding by the name of Cracker—who reared up without warning as they rode along the lip of a steep-sided V-shaped river valley. Adam was taken by surprise, tumbling from the saddle and down the rock-strewn slope, and was only saved from a more severe bruising and a soaking in the River Kell by a clump of bushes a third of the way down the slope.

Tolly dismounted in a flash and scrambled down to Adam.

'Are you hurt, Coz?'

Adam sat up and touched his forehead, wincing. His fingers, though, showed no sign of blood. 'Only my pride. Although I dare say I shall sport some colourful bruises for the next few days.' He squinted back up the slope and winced again. This time at the number of rocks protruding from the surface. 'I dare say I should be grateful my skull is not broken.'

He scrambled to his feet and discovered, to his mortification, that his knees were like jelly.

'Here. Sling your arm around my shoulders. I'll help you to the top. What spooked your horse, I wonder? He is normally a steady sort.'

'I have no idea.'

They reached the top of the slope to find Grenville had been joined by two men, one of them holding both riderless horses.

'I am relieved to see you are not badly injured,' Grenville said. 'That could have been very nasty. This is Joseph Carter, by the way, and Eddings, one of the farmhands. They saw you fall and came running. And stopped your horses running off, incidentally. Left to me, they'd doubtless be halfway home by now—I was more worried about you, Nephew.'

Adam eyed him, tamping down a rush of suspicion. His uncle sounded sincere, but Adam was conscious he would be unlikely to shed many tears should a fatal accident befall the new Earl of Kelridge.

After exchanging greetings, Carter—a stolid-looking man of around forty, with a ruddy complexion—said, 'I don't know what could have come over the horse, to rear up in such a way.'

'Likely them horse flies,' Eddings said. 'There's been a plague of 'em lately and that's a fact.'

'That could be it,' said Tolly. 'Nothing a horse hates more than a horse fly buzzing around its ears. Never fails to spook 'em.'

'True,' said Grenville. 'I was bitten by one once. Never forget it—I had a huge swelling on my arm. Must have been five inches across.'

Adam, his legs now steady, took Cracker's reins from Carter. Before mounting, however, he checked the horse over, finding only a trickle of blood on his chest to support the theory of a bite.

'I doubt we shall ever know for certain,' he said. 'Carter—are you coming up to the house later? I should like to go through the ledgers with you.'

'Very well, milord. But may I say I am happy to carry on with the bookkeeping on your behalf? If that suits you, of course?'

The man sounded anxious. Understandable, perhaps, if he thought his job might be in jeopardy.

'You may certainly continue as before, at least

to begin with. Then we shall see how it goes, shall we?'

The man's expression was unreadable. 'Very good, milord.'

Carter and Eddings doffed their hats and walked off as Adam and Tolly remounted.

'I suggest you've seen enough for today, Adam,' said Grenville. 'Let us return to the house.'

The next few days were ones of discovery for Adam, not least of which was the gradually emerging realisation that he could not simply banish Kitty from his life. She was in his thoughts constantly and visited his dreams whenever he managed to snatch a few hours' sleep. More than ever, he felt the urgent need to talk to her. Properly. Not those whispered snatches of conversation they had managed in London, the result of which had been more questions to add to the list of things he did not understand.

How soon would the Fentons return from London? And when he called on them, how on earth could he get Kitty alone for long enough to get those answers he craved? He feared he was close to becoming obsessed not only by Kitty, but also by the need to *understand*.

His attempts to distract himself by learning more about the running of the estate were no more fruitful than his conjectures about Kitty. Uncle

Grenville assured him he'd no need to worry his head over the day-to-day practicalities, insisting he had everything under control and that he would see the season through until harvest. Carter explained crop rotations and yields, and the basics of livestock husbandry, as well as showing Adam how the sales and purchase ledgers were kept but he, like Grenville, was reluctant to relinquish control. Conscious of his inexperience, Adam pored over the ledgers, but—between them and the figures thrown at him by Grenville and Carter, who often appeared to contradict one another—he made excruciatingly slow progress towards his aim of understanding the finer points of estate management.

The household staff stubbornly maintained a reserve in their dealings with Adam—deferring to Grenville and treating Tolly, clearly a great favourite, with more warmth than they ever showed Adam. The estate workers, no doubt sensing Adam's ignorance, always turned to Carter or to Grenville when they needed an answer to a question or were looking for instructions.

Adam remained the outsider. He really could not blame the staff for their loyalty to his uncle and he knew it was up to him to work hard to gain their trust. His own father had clearly been unpopular and it was understandable the staff would fear the son would be like the father. Adam knew it was his responsibility to convince them he was different, but he had to battle the urge to turn his back on everything and return to Scotland every single morning. The only thing stopping him was his pride. He refused to tuck his tail between his legs and run away like a cowardly cur. He counselled himself to have patience, with both himself and with the rest of the people who lived and worked at Kelridge Place.

One decision he did make, however, was to write to Ma. Since Tolly had told him about his father Adam felt a growing need to heal the rift with his mother, so he sat at his writing bureau in his library one day and wrote to her, telling her he now understood why she had run away from his father even though he still didn't quite understand why neither she nor Sir Angus had told him the truth once he reached adulthood. He begged her to visit him soon, reassuring her that he would not allow anyone—even Grenville—to be unwelcoming and he told her that Lady Datchworth—or Araminta Todmorden as Ma would remember her—was eager to be reacquainted with her and would she give her permission for him to pass on her address?

He wasn't confident Ma would accept his invitation but, if she did not, then he would damned well go up to Edinburgh himself and make sure he properly cleared the air between the two of them. He had just sealed the letter when Green entered.

'A letter has been delivered from Fenton Hall, my lord.'

His heart thudded with anticipation. 'Thank you, Green.'

Adam took the letter from the silver tray Green proffered, marvelling at the pomp required merely to hand a letter to a nobleman. But he remembered his vow not to be too hasty to change the way things were done. He was in an unfamiliar world and he must give himself more time to acclimatise to it before ploughing a furrow straight through their customs. But that didn't mean he wouldn't say thank you when the occasion warranted it, refusing to be deterred by the sourness of the butler's expression. Some of the lower servants were beginning to respond to his pleasantries with the odd smile, but only when Green was not around.

Adam broke the seal and read the letter, excitement stirring his blood. It was from Robert, who was now back at Fenton Hall, enquiring how Adam was settling into his new life and containing both an invitation for Adam to visit Fenton Hall, and a plea for a favour. Robert planned to build a second wing, to mirror the one built after the fire fifteen years before, and he begged Adam to advise him on the project...maybe, even, to draw up the plans for which, of course, he would suitably recompensed.

Robert's letter continued.

I realise you might view my request as an imposition, when you no doubt have a great many matters requiring your attention at Kelridge Place, and I appreciate that such a favour as I ask would necessitate you staying here at Fenton Hall for several days, but there is no one I would rather trust to steer me straight on a project such as this.

This was just the fillip Adam needed: a chance to escape the Place and its tensions for a few days; a chance to clear his head and order his thoughts; and, finally—and his heart squeezed at the thought—he would see Kitty again. He would be staying in the same house as her. He would get that chance to discover exactly why she had been so desperate to escape her father's house. More than that…he simply did not know, still not certain his interest in her was anything more than a nostalgic dream of the past, fuelled by a natural male interest in a beautiful woman. Still not confident that she would even entertain any revival of their youthful romance.

He sat back down at his desk and drew a fresh sheet of paper towards him.

Chapter Ten

In her cosy sitting room at Fenton Hall—where they had returned, on the orders of a furious Robert, within two days of Charis's clandestine meeting with Lord Sampford—Kitty read through the words she had spent the past hour painstakingly writing. She grabbed the sheets of paper and ripped them in half and then, for good measure, she ripped them in half again before casting them across her desk, watching as a couple of pieces skimmed over the polished wood to the edge and fluttered to the floor. She propped her elbows on the desk and buried her head in her hands. No matter how hard she tried, she simply *could* not lose herself in her story. Her thoughts kept sliding away from her heroine's dilemma and on to…

No! She shoved her chair back and stood up. This was nonsensical. A man she once knew, years ago, had reappeared in her life…but it was not even that, was it? For Adam was *not* in her life. He'd returned, but now he merely existed on the periphery of her life. Somewhere.

It's not just somewhere, though, is it? It's Kelridge Hall. It is not so very far away.

She put her hands over her ears as if she could block out that treacherous voice. But, of course, she could not. It was inside her head. It was always inside her head, reminding her, remembering. And, as time went on, she recalled more of the good times she and Adam had shared, overshadowing the one bad experience…the time he had walked away from her, callously abandoning her to her heartless father, who cared more about paying off his debts than he did about the daughter he had never forgiven for not being a son.

Her heart ached at the memory. If only Father had been an honourable man and acted as a father should, as a protector for his daughter, then she would never have had to humiliate herself by begging Adam to take her with him. Thank goodness Edgar—who had happened across her crying in the woods one day and had listened to the whole sorry tale—had rescued her. She had often wondered, afterwards, if she should have insisted on telling Adam about her father on that last day. On reflection, however, she was glad she had not. He might well have felt obliged to 'rescue' her and Kitty now understood the unbearable strain that would have put on their relationship. Although it had broken her heart, Adam's abandonment of her had been for the best when his own heart had not been engaged.

His words came back to her, floating up from the depths of her memory. *'I will still be an architect's apprentice and you will still be an earl's daughter.'*

He had been right, however much she refused to believe it at the time. The disparity in their positions in society had been a chasm they would never have been able to bridge. And it had all worked out for the best. Edgar had been a decent husband and Kitty loved his children as she would her own, had she been blessed. She now barely noticed the dull ache at never having conceived a baby of her own. Neither prayers nor tears had ever produced the result she craved—a circumstance Edgar had never let her forget, with his monthly joke at her expense—and Kitty had eventually accepted the miracle she had longed for throughout her ten years of marriage would never happen.

She crossed to the window and gazed out across garden to the woodland in the distance. There, in those woods, she and Adam had met and, on the far side, lay her father's land, now occupied by the new Lord Whitlock—her distant cousin—and his family. She had cut all ties with her father as soon as she was safely wed to Edgar, not wanting anything more to do with the man who had caused her such anguish, and he had passed away around the same time as Edgar had died.

Restless, she turned from the window. She'd take a turn about the gardens…cut a few blooms for her room…and hope the solution for that scene in her story might come to her. She knew from experience that remaining at her desk when the words refused to flow merely resulted in more frustration and more stilted prose. She headed for her bedchamber to fetch her shawl and bonnet, then went downstairs.

In the entrance hall, as she paused to tie the bonnet ribbons under her chin, Robert emerged from his business room.

'Ah, well met, Stepmama. Are you going out?'

Kitty indicated her plain dress and faded shawl with a smile. 'Only as far as the garden, you will be pleased to hear.'

'Ah.' Robert's eyes danced. 'Is the writing not co-operating this morning?'

Kitty gave him a resigned smile and shrugged, raising her eyebrows.

Robert grinned. 'No need for words; I know what that look means. Never mind… I have good news for you.' He gestured to his office. 'Might you spare me a few moments of your time?'

Kitty walked ahead of Robert into the room and sat down, wondering if he'd received a communication from her publisher. Robert rounded his desk to sit opposite her and tapped a letter that lay on the surface of the desk.

'This is from Kelridge.'

Hearing his name sucked the breath from her lungs. *Good news?* She did not trust herself to speak, merely nodded for Robert to continue.

'Do you recall I spoke to you about building a new wing here at the Hall?'

Kitty frowned. 'Yes. But I did not imagine you were serious. We have no need for more room here. Do we?'

A frown knit Robert's forehead and he tugged at his earlobe. 'I thought it time to look to the future. The house is adequate for us, but…in time, I shall marry. And I should like the Hall to be suitable for entertaining. I wish to build a wing with a ballroom on the ground floor and additional bedchambers and a nursery suite above.'

'Well…' Kitty quashed down the pain that threatened. It was inevitable this time would come… Charis would marry and move out and Robert, of course, would want to secure the future of the earldom and the estates. She adopted a teasing tone. 'This is unlike you, Robert—planning ahead in such a serious way.'

She watched a blush rise to colour his cheeks

and unease wormed through her stomach. Could she be wrong about Lady Phoebe? Surely Robert couldn't be serious about such a woman? And yet...who else could it be?

'Do you have a particular lady in mind?'

Robert's colour deepened. 'No. At least...no. Not really. I wish to prepare for the inevitable, that is all.'

Kitty bit back the questions she longed to throw at him. He was a grown man now. He would tell her when he was ready. But, one question she simply *had* to ask: 'What has this to do with Lord Kelridge?'

'I asked him to visit us, in order that I may pick his brains about my plans. You know...what is possible. What would not work.'

Kitty breathed easier. She might spend much of her time thinking about Adam, but that did not mean she wanted to meet him more than necessary. Kelridge Place was close enough to visit and return in a day, as that sneaky voice in her head persisted in reminding her. She would arrange to be out on the day Adam came to the Hall. It would be for the best. They seemed unable to meet without the past rearing its head and all *that* served was to stir anger and resentment in them both.

She closed her mind to the truth—that it also raised unbearable longing within her. *False* longing, as she had reminded herself ever since their last encounter at the Exeter Exchange. The Adam who was now Lord Kelridge was very different from the Adam she had known when she was seventeen and he was twenty-one. But her heart and her body could not be as easily directed as her mind. *They* remembered the Adam of old—the thrill of those clandestine meetings; the sublime pleasure of time spent in his arms; the heady rush of his lips on hers.

'And that is his reply?' she asked.

'It is…and more than merely advising me, he has agreed to draw up the plans. Is that not splendid? He writes that he will enjoy the challenge of such a project. Reading between the lines of his letter, I believe he is finding it difficult to settle at Kelridge. Hardly surprising, I dare say.'

'Why do you say that?'

'Oh, well, I doubt Grenville Trewin is thrilled to have him home when he has run the place for so long. And you know yourself how servants dislike change. I don't suppose the new Earl will have an easy time of it at all.'

'I see.' With any luck Adam would decide to return to his old life in Edinburgh. Then Kitty could return to normal and relegate him to the past once again. Where he belonged. 'Which day do you expect him?'

'Tomorrow. You do not mind? I know it is short notice.'

'Unfortunately, I have plans for tomorrow. I have already arranged to call upon Lady Datchworth.' Kitty latched upon the one excuse that Robert would accept that she could not possibly cancel, knowing Her Ladyship's imperious nature. 'I should be obliged if you will pass on my apologies for my absence to Lord Kelridge, but it cannot be helped, and I am sure I could add nothing of value to your discussions.'

Robert stood up, rounding the desk as he said, 'There will be no need for apologies, Stepmama. You misunderstand me...or, more likely, I have not made myself clear. Kelridge will not arrive until late afternoon—he will stay here a few days to give him sufficient time to reacquaint himself with the Hall before drawing up the plans.'

Kitty's stomach lurched as Robert took her hand and assisted her to rise. 'He will be *staying* here?' She stared up at her stepson. 'But...surely he has matters to attend to at Kelridge?'

Robert gave her a puzzled smile. 'Have you an objection? I made sure you would not mind... I know you value your quiet time while we are at home, in order to write, but your path will only cross with Kelridge's at dinner and in the evening.'

'No. I have no objection. I was merely surprised.'

Robert shrugged. 'I dare say his steward will

ride over if there is anything urgent that needs his attention. He will draw up the plans while he is here.'

Kitty recalled Lady Datchworth's matchmaking between Adam and Charis. 'Is he aware Charis is absent from home?'

Robert had packed Charis off to her sister Jennifer's home as soon as they returned to the Hall from London.

'What has Charis to do with this?'

'Nothing really. Only Lady Datchworth seemed convinced that Charis would be a good match for Kelridge and I wondered—'

'Well, don't! I'm very certain Kelridge's interests don't lie in Charis's direction—she is far too young for him. Besides—' his brown gaze pierced Kitty '—have *you* ever noticed him pay any particular attention to my sister?'

'No. But—'

'There you are, then. He is not coming here to see Charis, but to help me.'

Relieved—surely only because of Adam's unsuitability for Charis and not for any other more selfish reason?—Kitty said, 'If Lord Kelridge arrives tomorrow, I must instruct Mrs Kirk to prepare a bedchamber and consult Mrs Ainsley over the menus.'

Robert dropped a kiss on the top of Kitty's head. 'No need to trouble yourself over that for

I've already informed Mrs Kirk and told her to warn the kitchen to prepare. You know as well as I that Mrs Ainsley will be in her element, devising dishes suitable for our guest.'

'How long will His Lordship stay?'

'Oh, a sennight at least, I should think.'

A whole week? Waves of heat rushed through Kitty. How on earth would she manage an entire week with him here? In her home? Could she maintain the façade of gracious hostess for that length of time or would that old hurt and resentment at his lies bubble to the surface? She could not face the humiliation should Robert discover what had happened in the past, nor the mortification should Adam ever realise exactly how much turmoil he still stirred within her.

'Now,' Robert continued, 'I have taken up enough of your time…be gone to the flower beds and allow those plot tangles to unravel in your head.'

Kitty walked away, her stomach tangled in as many knots as her plot and her throat clogged with emotion.

'What the devil is amiss with you, young lady?'

It was the following day and Kitty had called upon Lady Datchworth at her home, Peyton Park.

Her Ladyship raised her pince-nez and peered

at Kitty, continuing, 'You call upon me without warning and then proceed to sit there, pale as uncooked pastry, and fidget your fingers in your lap. If you have no gossip with which to entertain me, you may as well go home.'

Kitty swallowed past the lump of dread that had taken up residence in her throat since yesterday and forced a smile.

'I apologise for my poor company, ma'am. I—I dare say I am missing Charis—she has gone to Yorkshire to stay with her sister.'

'Then the solution is obvious.'

'It is?'

'Indeed. Invite a friend to stay with you. *That* will fill the gap in your life and provide the company you crave.'

Kitty could think of nothing worse. She would rather spend her days writing quietly than having to dance attendance upon guests. Her thoughts flew straight to Adam and his impending visit, and her stomach fluttered. She swallowed again.

Her Ladyship unexpectedly reached out and took Kitty's hand. 'You feel the same as any mother, my dear, whether or not Charis is your own child. You have raised her and you must face the prospect that she will at some time marry and move away from home, and grow away from you. But that is the natural order of things for we women—our fledglings must fly the nest and we must move on, finding new interests in our lives. At least, it is the natural order for *most* people. I could only wish that reprehensible son of mine would settle down. I have tried…heaven *knows* I have tried to find him a suitable bride, but he rejects every single one of them. But, there…we were not discussing my woes…' Her fingers tightened around Kitty's.

'Catherine, dear, I know you have always been adamant you will never remarry, but…mayhap it is time to reconsider?'

Kitty started. 'Ma'am? You surely cannot mean Lord Datchworth?'

The Marquess was a dark, forbidding man with, as far as Kitty had ever been able to tell, no sense of humour at all. She had thought Adam brooding, but Datchworth was twice as bad and she could think of nobody who would make a worse husband, so much so that she'd modelled the villain in her novel, Lord Sidney Barmouth, on the man.

'Foolish girl! I care for you far too much to inflict my son upon you. I might be his mama, but I am not blind to his faults. No… I simply meant in general—is it not time for you to think about marrying again.'

Kitty shook her head. 'I cannot.'

'Cannot or will not?'

'It would be unfair on any husband who did not already have children, when I know I am barren.'

Just admitting that out loud brought a painful lump to Kitty's throat. How she would have loved a baby of her own…but that regret was another that lived in the past and that she tried hard not to dwell upon.

'Are you so sure you are, my dear?'

'I am. Edgar and I were married ten years and my four stepchildren are ample evidence of *his* prowess.'

'Then marry a man who has already produced his heir.'

Again, Kitty shook her head. 'I have no wish to raise a second stepfamily—I love the stepchildren I already have.'

'Then marry a man with older children, or an older man with no desire for children.'

Kitty shrugged helplessly. How had her missing Charis resulted in Her Ladyship deciding she must be ripe to remarry?

Lady Datchworth released Kitty's hand and reached for a silver handbell on the table by the side of her chair. She shook it and the door opened in response to its tinkling sound. A maid entered and curtsied.

'Bring us a bottle of Madeira. Lady Fenton requires stronger sustenance than another pot of tea. And a plate of sweetmeats would be welcome, I dare say?'

She gazed at Kitty, brows raised, and Kitty nodded, knowing agreement was required of her rather than a polite refusal of the offer. Sweetmeats were Her Ladyship's very favourite indulgence and the plate was really for her.

'So, let us think of ways around your predicament, my dear. Which friend might you invite to stay with you?'

'No. I cannot invite anyone for the moment, ma'am. It is impossible.'

'Impossible?'

Her Ladyship bent a look of astonishment upon Kitty but said no more as the maid returned at that moment, carrying a tray which she set on the table. She poured two glasses of Madeira and then offered the plate of sweetmeats to Lady Datchworth, who leaned forward, a line of concentration etched between her eyebrows and rubbing her hands together as she examined the plate.

'Hmmm. Yes… I think…'

She reached out, selected a sugared almond and popped it into her mouth before leaning back and closing her eyes, chewing slowly, an expression of utter delight upon her face. She waved her arm without opening her eyes and the maid offered the plate to Kitty.

'Now. Where were we?' Lady Datchworth had

finished chewing and, despite a longing sideways look at the plate—set within her reach on the side table—she turned her attention back to Kitty. 'Oh, yes. You claim having a friend to stay would be impossible. How so?'

'W-we actually have a visitor arriving today... a visitor for Robert...a man...they will be occupied all week—'

'Who is visiting you? Why did you not say earlier? A man, you say? Is he a gentleman?'

'Yes, but—'

'Then who? I demand to know his identity.'

'It is Lord Kelridge.'

'Kelridge? He has not informed *me* of his intention.'

'You have seen him, ma'am?'

'We have corresponded a time or two since he left London.'

'Well, his visit is only recently arranged and he arrives this afternoon, so he will not have had the time—'

'*This afternoon?* Why are you not at home to greet your guest?'

'Adam...' the sudden gleam in Lady Datchworth's eyes alerted Kitty to her error '...that is, *Lord Kelridge* is not *my* guest. Robert invited him, and he is to draw up architectural plans for a new wing at Fenton. Robert plans a ballroom and additional bedrooms for when he marries.'

'Fenton is to marry? I have seen him pay no particular attention to any lady. Whom is he to marry?'

Relieved to have diverted Her Ladyship away from the subject of Adam, Kitty said, 'He claims he has no one lady in mind. He claims he is planning ahead.'

'Hmm…well now, it will behove me to think carefully about this.' Lady Datchworth rubbed her hands together, a gleam in her eyes. 'I am sure I can come up with the perfect match for him.'

Kitty made a mental note to warn Robert to avoid Her Ladyship for the foreseeable future if he did not want one eligible bride after another—at least, eligible in Lady Datchworth's opinion—thrust under his nose. There was nothing Her Ladyship enjoyed more than a spot of matchmaking.

'Now. It is time you left for home, my dear, for you will want to be there to greet your guest.'

Lady Datchworth rang the bell and ordered Kitty's carriage, then she jumped to her feet with an energy that belied her years and escorted Kitty to the front door.

As Kitty paused at the open carriage door to say goodbye, Her Ladyship called, 'Look after Kelridge, Catherine. He is not nearly as tough as he likes to pretend.'

Chapter Eleven

Adam gazed around with interest as he drove his curricle along the tree-lined carriageway to Fenton Hall. Not much had changed in the fifteen years since his last visit. The lime trees flanking the carriageway were taller. More mature.

As am I.

Mature enough, surely, to persuade Kitty to confide in him without ruffling her feathers with his poor attempts to tease her as he had done the last time they met. He needed to understand if her marriage to Fenton was because she had been desperate to leave her father's house or was it as he'd initially thought—a young girl craving the adventure of being a wife, too naive to realise the implications of tying herself to a man so far beneath her own station in life? But if she had been in trouble, why had she not told him? She must have known he would never abandon her had she been in danger.

But I did stop her from confiding in me on that last day.

That guilt had been added to the other guilt that had tormented him for so long—the guilt of denying his love for her. But the past could not be changed, only the future, and here was his chance to uncover the truth as well as to untangle his feelings for present-day Kitty. Discovering the truth about what had driven his mother to take him from his father—and realising he had leapt to conclusions about her motives—had made him doubt what he initially thought about Kitty's hasty marriage. The Kitty he remembered had been spirited and bright and loving, not a girl who would cynically manipulate a man or lie about her feelings. He now believed he could have been wrong and he would listen to what she had to say.

Then, they would see. Could there possibly be a future for them, or was there too much hurt and suspicion between them now?

This was the perfect opportunity to discover what they *both* wanted while, at the same time, helping Robert with his plans. If nothing else, it would be good to feel useful once again, practising those skills he had learned and honed over many years.

The carriageway passed through the pair of familiar stone pillars that flanked the entrance to the forecourt and he steered his pair around the area, drawing them to a halt level with the front entrance. The front door opened and Robert bounded down the steps, reminding Adam of the young lad he had known.

'Adam! Welcome!' Robert leapt into the curricle. 'I'll ride with you round to the stables.'

'Thank you. It is good to be back… I shall look forward to getting reacquainted with the old place.'

'You'll find not much has changed. Hi! Gresham! Come and see to His Lordship's cattle, will you?'

The Fenton Hall head man emerged from the dim interior of the barn.

'Yes, milord.'

Gresham eyed Adam with the same mix of curiosity and caution Adam had recognised in his own staff at Kelridge Place. He did not begrudge Gresham his restraint—after all, he had known Adam as a simple architect's apprentice—but at least there was no hint of the resentment he detected in the Kelridge men. This time away from Kelridge and that odd, unsettling atmosphere would, he hoped, give him time to work out the best response to the underlying distrust and the hint of disrespect that threaded through much of his interactions with the men. Although reluctant to turn men off, he might have no choice if he could not win them over.

Anyway, he was here now and had a chance to clear his head and to help Robert design a new wing for the Hall. He couldn't wait to begin.

Adam saw nothing of Kitty until he came downstairs after changing for dinner. He made his way directly to the salon and there she was, standing with her back to the door, gazing out of the window. A gown the colour of periwinkles skimmed her curves in all the right places, her shining hair caught up with tortoiseshell combs, a few tendrils spiralling around her ears.

His heart leapt as he drank in the sight. Joy spread through him and his earlier confusion melted away with the certainty that he *did* still harbour feelings for her. But his uncertainty over what she felt about him…*for* him…remained.

'Ahem.'

She spun to face him, her face pale and her eyes wide.

'Lady Fenton, I am sorry to startle you.' He bowed. 'Good evening… I would have waited to be announced, but there was no one in the hall and Robert did say to consider myself one of the family and not to stand on ceremony.'

Kitty inclined her head and glided across to sit

in one of the chairs near to the fireplace. 'Indeed, you must regard yourself at home while you are our guest.' She had swiftly recovered from her shock and now sat primly, her expression serene, with her hands folded upon her lap. 'Please, take a seat while we wait for Robert. I am sure he will be down soon.'

As he sat down, Adam recalled his poorly received joke about headstrong young girls and his other attempts at jesting that had also fallen flat.

'Before Rob joins us—might I apologise for my clumsy attempts to tease you when we last met? I fear I inadvertently upset ye. As I said, they were poor attempts.'

'It is forgotten, sir.'

Silence reigned.

'Do ye—?'

'How are—?'

They spoke simultaneously, and both paused. They laughed at the same time and the atmosphere lightened a fraction.

'Please, do go ahead,' Adam said, willing to take his cue from Kitty as to how they would treat one another.

'I was about to ask if you find the Hall much altered?'

'The house, from what I have seen, is much the same but, of course, the occupants have changed beyond recognition. Your late husband leaves a gaping hole where he stood and, with Edward in the army, Jennifer wed and residing in Yorkshire, and Miss Mayfield temporarily absent, the house seems strangely quiet.'

Kitty's lack of reaction, other than a faint wash of pink over her cheekbones, spurred him into trying to provoke a stronger response from her.

'But *you* are here now, of course. That is the greatest difference. And had our work lasted a mere couple of weeks longer, I should have known all about your marriage. It must have been hastily arranged, for I never heard even a whisper of His Lordship's plan to remarry during my time here.'

Adam fought back that old sense of betrayal that still simmered, driven by his uncertainty over *her* feelings, and despite his newly acknowledged feelings for her. If he continued to prod Kitty in an attempt to learn what she was truly thinking, she would never tell him the truth of what happened and, until she did, they would keep wandering in circles, stuck in the same fog of suspicion that had enveloped them since their meeting in London.

It was possible he had jumped to conclusions about the reason for Kitty's hasty marriage exactly as he had done with his mother and the reasons for her leaving his father. He was still determined to uncover the truth—if it was anyone but Kitty he would suspect she'd been with child, but he knew the marriage was not for that reason. It must have been because of her father.

'Kitty… Catherine…please, might we talk about what happened? We both have questions—'

'You are mistaken. I have no questions. You were very clear at the time and I accepted your decision long ago.'

'But—'

Adam bit back his protest as the door opened and Robert strolled in, looking from one to the other of them with a quizzical expression.

'I beg your pardon. Am I interrupting something?'

Kitty's chin lifted. 'Not at all, Robert. We were talking about the speed of my marriage to your papa. I was about to explain the reason for that to Lord Kelridge.' She switched her gaze to Adam. 'We met quite by chance and fell in love. There was no need to wait.'

The pain, sudden and sharp, stole his breath, but he caught a flash of guilt in those grey eyes of hers.

She was lying. She *must* be lying.

But he could not challenge her with Robert there. He must have patience. He would get his chance to coax the truth from her.

'Dinner is served, my lord.'

The butler, Vincent, stood at the open door, his announcement saving Adam from any further response.

* * *

The conversation between Adam and Robert flowed easily over dinner, with Kitty joining in only when applied to for her opinion. As soon as they finished eating, she rose to her feet and the men followed suit.

'I shall withdraw and leave you gentlemen to your port and your plans.'

'We shan't be long, Stepmama. You will still be in the drawing room when we've finished? Will you play for us?'

Adam was unsurprised when she shook her head.

'I regret I have the headache, Rob. If you do not object, I should prefer to retire early.'

'Then an early night is the best remedy.'

'Goodnight to you both. I apologise for abandoning you on your first evening here, my lord.'

'I hope your headache is speedily relieved, my lady.'

'It is little wonder she has the headache,' Robert said to Adam as Kitty left the room. 'That woman would try the patient of a saint.'

'I...? Lady Fenton? But...?'

'Good Lord, no! I didn't mean my stepmother! She is a diamond!'

He paused as the butler came in with a bottle of port and poured two glasses. 'Thank you, Vincent.'

As soon as Adam and Robert were alone again, Robert continued, 'My comment was aimed at Lady Datchworth. Do you remember I told you my stepmother had visited her today?'

Adam grinned. 'Of course. And now I understand your cryptic comment. Lady D. in full sail could give anyone the headache. I experienced my share of that when in London, as ye know. But, still, I could not help but like her despite her inclination for matchmaking.'

Adam found himself the target of a searching look.

'Speaking of which, my stepmother is convinced Her Ladyship has earmarked you and my sister Charis as a likely match.' Robert's expression remained neutral.

'By no encouragement from me, Rob. Charis is a lovely girl, but much too young for my taste.'

Robert visibly relaxed. 'I am relieved to hear that. Lady Datchworth is convinced of her own shrewdness in matching couples and yet, to my knowledge, she has never yet met with success.'

'I shall be on my guard, but ye need have no fear, Rob—Charis is perfectly safe from me. Now, tell me your plans for this new wing.'

Adam spent most of the following day inspecting the Hall from top to bottom and taking measurements, paying particular attention to the wing

Sir Angus had designed following that devastating fire. Robert assisted him with the measuring and they had a lively discussion about his requirements for the new wing, but once they were done Robert headed out on estate business, leaving Adam in the library, where he had been provided with a desk and a table to work on as he drew up the plans.

Of Kitty there had been no sign all day and, although he resolutely blocked her from his mind as he worked in the quiet of the afternoon, she hovered around the edges as a nagging presence, ready to pounce whenever his concentration wavered. Her announcement that she and the late Lord Fenton had fallen in love so swiftly still did not ring true and Adam was more determined than ever to discover the real reason behind their hasty marriage.

He found it liberating to lose himself in what he still thought of as his 'real life'—his occupation. And it was a relief to be away from Kelridge Place, even though he was aware his time would be better spent in establishing his position as master. It was good to feel he could breathe easily for the first time since coming down from London and so, as he settled down to the business of planning the new wing, not only did he block Kitty from his thoughts, but he also pushed aside his unease over Kelridge Place.

* * *

By mid-afternoon, however, his head felt stuffed full of wool. The weather had turned hot and humid, begging for the release of a thunderstorm to clear the air. Adam had already opened wide all the French doors that led outside on to the flagged terrace that wrapped around this wing of the house—the wing Sir Angus had designed—but there was little relief to be had and he had resorted to removing his jacket, discarding his neckcloth and working in his shirt sleeves and unbuttoned waistcoat.

Finally, craving the relief of a breath of fresh air, he pushed his damp hair off his forehead, laid down his pen and packed his instruments away before striding for the nearest open French door.

'Oh!'

He'd stepped outside without looking, only to collide with someone walking along the terrace. He reacted fast, his hands wrapping around Kitty's bare upper arms, even before he realised whom he had sent staggering backwards. He hauled her upright, her scent of warm woman mingling with that of the mass of blooms she carried as it coiled through his senses.

'Take care! You are crushing my flowers.'

Adam released her. The tingling caused by the satiny softness of her warm skin against his palms only registered with him when it ceased.

He rubbed his palms against his breeches, conscious he had left his jacket hanging over the back of his chair and that his shirt sleeves were rolled up to his elbows. Their eyes locked—hers widening and darkening as a flush bloomed on her cheeks and her lips parted, giving every impression of a woman aroused. Adam's blood surged to his groin. Dare he hope she was mellowing towards him? Could they both let the past go? The tight knot that had lodged in his gut on arrival loosened a little.

'Rather a few crushed blooms than allow you to fall.'

She smiled and it appeared a more genuine smile than the strained efforts of last evening.

'That is true. I spoke out of turn. A few mangled flowers are as nothing compared to a bruised—' She bit her lip. 'That is, compared to a bruising tumble.'

Adam laughed. 'Indeed. I shall take especial care another time I exit the library. May I carry those for you?'

Her smile faltered. 'There is no need... I... that is...thank you.' She relinquished the flowers and indicated the open door. 'We may as well go through the library—I had intended to walk around to the back door to save disturbing you.'

She sent him an inscrutable look from beneath the sweep of her lashes. His gaze lowered to her lips as they parted and sparks of desire sizzled through him.

'You are our guest and I understand you have refused any payment from Robert for your services. While you are under this roof you may expect your comfort to be our highest priority.'

The perfect society hostess had returned and those sparks fizzled out. In his short time in this world, Adam had learned Kitty was renowned in the *ton* for her graciousness, her propriety and her charm. That knot tightened once more as they walked side by side through the library and the familiar uncertainty washed through him. He simply didn't know how to deal with this guarded woman who so rarely revealed any hint of her true thoughts or, more importantly, her true feelings.

'There is a storeroom near the kitchens where I dry herbs and mix remedies and salves, and that I also use for arranging flowers,' Kitty continued as she led the way. 'Are you making progress with the plans? I dare say they will not take long to complete.'

Is that a polite way of enquiring how long I shall stay?

'I haven't begun drawing them yet... I am sketching out a few ideas first and will get Robert's opinion before settling on a final layout. This will be a major investment for him and he needs to be aware of the options available before committing himself.' Her thoughtful expression prompted him to add, 'Do you have any preferences as to what is included?'

'Me? Oh, good heavens, no. This is Robert's home and, when he weds, I shall remove to the Dower House.'

'You will find that lonely after being a part of a family for so long.'

'I shan't be lonely. It is on the edge of the village, so there are neighbours all around. And I shall make it my business to pay regular, lengthy visits to all my stepchildren whether they invite me to stay or not.'

Her grey eyes twinkled as she looked straight ahead, her mind presumably on her family. Clearly there was a great deal of respect and love between them. She paused at a door and opened it.

'If you would kindly put the flowers in that bucket, sir—'

'Adam,' he said.

She was half-turned away from him and, to all intents and purposes, she did not react. But he caught the slight twitch in her jaw that suggested she had clenched it. He sucked in a deep breath, sensing now might be the time to broach the subject of the past and to hear Kitty's side of the story.

'We cannot ignore the fact we once knew one

another,' he said. 'We were close. We called one another by name. I still think of you in my head as Kitty—'

'Catherine!' She pivoted to face him. 'In this family I have always been Catherine. Even my f-father always called me Catherine. I was only ever Kitty to you.'

'Well then. Catherine.' He frowned. Her voice had definitely hitched when she spoke of her father. 'I was sorry to learn of your father's death.'

'Spare me your condolences. I did not mourn his death—we were estranged long before he died.'

'Ah.'

Her expression suggested reluctance to continue the discussion and Adam recalled her long-ago reticence if he asked about her father or her home life. He did know her mother had died when she was a young child and now he also remembered the late Lord Fenton's dislike of his neighbour.

Kitty clasped her hands in front of her and faced Adam, with the look of a woman facing an ordeal. 'He disapproved of my marriage to Edgar.'

'Yet he must have given his consent for ye to wed Edgar.'

'He withheld his permission at first. But Edgar paid him handsomely and he was persuaded to grant his consent.'

'He paid him? That is an odd turn of phrase. What do ye mean?'

She turned abruptly and paced to the window where she stood gazing out, her arms wrapped around her waist. Adam took a step towards her, frowning as he realised she was trembling. He dropped the flowers into the bucket she'd indicated and followed her.

'What is it? You never would talk of your father and the subject obviously upsets you even now.'

Adam had always put her reluctance to talk about her father down to family loyalty, as well as to a daughter's natural wariness of a strict parent and the fear he might uncover their secret trysts.

He stood close enough behind her to feel the warmth radiating from her skin. Her scent weaved through his senses, and his blood quickened. Her hair was caught up with combs and pins, leaving short wisps curling at her hairline, from nape to ears. How he longed to press his lips to that sweet spot on the side of her neck where he could see her pulse thrumming in time with his.

She still hadn't answered him and his anger stirred at her silence.

'Well? What is it ye never told me about your father? Was he the reason ye were so determined to leave Whitlock Manor? And when I refused to help ye ruin yourself ye found yourself a convenient substitute! And do not tell me it was for love, for I didna believe ye last night and I shall not believe ye now.'

She spun around, her eyes flashing with fury. 'That is unfair. You do not know…' She shook her head before sucking in a deep breath. 'No. I am sorry. You are right and this is my fault for not telling you the truth when you first asked why I married Edgar so soon after you left.'

Adam listened, horrified, as Kitty told him of her father's plan to sell her hand in marriage in order to clear his gambling debts. He took her hand as she carried on with her tale.

'My father was still in London when you left and I continued to walk in the woods, dreading his return. I could see no way out of my dilemma. Then Edgar came upon me one day and saw my distress. Somehow, I ended up telling him about my father. As soon as my father returned, Edgar called upon him and offered to pay off his debts in return for my hand in marriage. We married by special licence…neither of us wanted a fuss. And we were happy,' she added, in a defiant voice.

His heart ached for her.

'If only I had known,' he said, reaching for her other hand. 'When we met again…when I found out how quickly you had married Lord Fenton… it made me so angry I couldna think straight. All

I could see was your betrayal. I thought ye had lied about your feelings for me at first, but I did then wonder if I had been over-hasty.' He drew her closer, into his arms. 'I wish ye had told me the truth about your father, sweetheart.'

For a few glorious heartbeats Kitty melted into his embrace but, all too soon, she stiffened, jerking out of his reach with something very like fear in her eyes.

'Do not call me that. I have told you the truth because you deserve to know and I want your pity now even less than I wanted it then. I might have been young, but I did have some pride. And… I thought you felt the same for me as I did for you.'

Her chin tilted defiantly as she faced Adam.

'Thank you for your assistance, Lord Kelridge. Now, if you will excuse me, I have domestic matters to attend to.'

She stalked past him.

'*Kitty…*'

But she was gone.

Adam swept a hand through his hair, cursing himself for his clumsy assumption—or was it wishful thinking?—that her confession would smoothly lead to a rekindling of tender feelings between them. He cursed himself also for being all kinds of an idiot as he thought about the story she had just revealed—her fear of her father's despicable plan and her desperation to get away.

And what had he done to that scared, lonely girl? He, who had professed his love for her so many times, had broken her heart. And her trust.

He stared at the open doorway through which Kitty had vanished. They would have to talk again, but maybe not just yet.

He needed that fresh air more than ever. He headed out for a walk in the gardens.

Chapter Twelve

Kitty rushed from the house, hurrying through the gardens and into the meadow beyond before she slowed her pace. Her chest rose and fell rapidly as she caught her breath, memories flooding her thoughts—her father and his selfishness, and his disappointment that his only child was a girl; Edgar and his gentle fault-finding, leaving her convinced of her uselessness both as a wife and as a woman when she failed to get with child; Adam, the man she had loved with her entire being and the man who had lied about his love for her. The man who had broken her heart.

She had felt herself weaken when he'd pulled her into his arms. For a scant few moments she had thrust all doubts aside and relished the novelty of being held. But, all too soon, those memories had burst into her head, reminding her of her worthlessness and reviving her fear of getting hurt again. The fear of being let down. And she had run away.

Dear God, what must he think of me?

He would be their guest at the Hall for a week... She could not avoid him, or Robert would surely notice and Kitty could not bear the humiliation of her stepson finding out what had happened between her and Adam. Plus, for all that Adam's lies still hurt, Kitty now accepted he had acted in both of their best interests by refusing to take her away with him. The strains would soon have killed off any tender feelings had he succumbed to her entreaties.

She walked on, her mind buzzing as she fanned her face with her hand. Goodness, it was hot. The chip straw hat she usually wore in the garden was still on her head, but she'd not had time to even think about fetching a parasol or a fan. The bodice of her gown was closely fitted with a high neckline, but there were buttons down the front of it and she unfastened the top two to allow a little more air to reach her skin. The woodland at the bottom of the meadow beckoned, with the promise of shade from the sun, although...she scanned the sky...clouds were massing on the horizon, promising a break in the weather and a welcome shower. She ought not to go too far.

She crossed the meadow, stepping high through the long grass which would soon be cut to make hay. Wild flowers were in bloom—meadowsweet, campion, purple loosestrife—and she admired their delicacy after the showier blooms she had cut in the garden.

She reached the welcome shade of the belt of trees. A brook trickled through it and she turned to follow its course towards the larger expanse of West Whitlock Wood, which reached almost as far as her old childhood home. She'd met her father only once after she married Edgar and that had been the year before both he and Edgar had died, when he had called at the Hall to beg for money to pay his debts. Ten years they had been neighbours, yet her father might as well have lived on the moon. He never mingled in local society. Was never seen in church. Never attended society events in London. Never went anywhere respectable as far as she knew. But, so Edgar had told her, he'd still visited those old haunts of his—the gaming hells in St James's and other, less salubrious, areas of London—and still mixed with the villains and reprobates who had brought him so low as to offer his only daughter in payment of his debts. He had never changed his ways.

Thunder growled, far in the distance, and Kitty turned her steps in the direction of home, up through those familiar woods, the woods where she had run to meet Adam whenever she could, breathless with excitement and the joy of seeing him again, of feeling his arms around her, his lips on hers. She dragged her mind away from those memories and the treacherous feelings they evoked. Whatever she had felt, he had not shared her feelings and it still hurt that such lies had fallen so easily from his lips. She had truly believed he loved her, but now she was wiser and would guard her heart against more pain, even though her pulse quickened at the sight of him and the scent of him and at the sound of his voice.

The thunder grumbled again—a long, drawn-out rumble—and she quickened her pace, taking a shortcut up a steep wooded slope that would bring her out close to the back lane that led around to the stable yard. As she neared the edge of the wood, however, she slammed to a halt at the sight of Adam seated under an oak, his back propped against the massive trunk, legs bent, arms resting on his knees. His head, hatless, was tilted back, his eyes closed. Her heart squeezed at the memories that again crowded her head—how many times had she found him waiting for her in just such a pose?

A sane woman would retreat. Quietly.

Kitty walked forward, making no attempt to hide her approach. Adam's eyes sprung open and he raised his head.

'Why are you here?' she demanded. 'Did you follow me?'

He huffed a laugh. 'I did no such thing. I was here first. Besides, ye told me ye had domestic matters to attend to.' He waved his arm. 'I shouldna call these surroundings *domestic*, precisely.'

Kitty pushed a fallen lock of hair back under her hat, aware her face must be pink and shiny with the effort of hurrying up the slope in the heat of the afternoon. Adam, on the other hand, was the epitome of cool and collected as he squinted up at her.

I cannot keep running away. I cannot allow my misreading of a young man's intentions all those years ago to continue to blight our every conversation.

'You're right. I am sorry I left so abruptly.' She clasped her hands together at her waist and inhaled. 'Please forgive my rudeness.'

'I shall forgive you on one condition.'

'Condition?'

'Aye.'

Adam rose to his feet in one smooth movement and Kitty stepped back. He followed, towering over her, but she had never felt intimidated by Adam and she still did not fear him. Not physically, at least. His temper was a touch more volatile than she recalled, but, if she were honest, so was hers. It seemed each sparked intense feelings in the other without effort. And, for all the local gossip that the apple never fell far from the tree, Kitty had never seen any sign of *uncontrollable* anger or any hint of violence in him.

He had been silent for too long, just staring into her eyes. She turned aside. 'Well? Will you enlighten me, or do you mean to make me guess?'

'Yes…sorry… I thought…my condition is that you call me Adam and I call you Catherine.'

She opened her mouth to refuse. Such intimacy would, surely, only encourage those long-ago memories; the memories she worked so hard to suppress. But…could she reasonably say no? Robert and Adam had lapsed into their old familiarity, from when Robert had been eleven and Adam just the architect's apprentice. Adam would remain at the Hall several more days and Rob would be curious if Kitty and Adam maintained a polite distance. He knew Kitty was often informal with her friends, both male and female, and that she called them by their given names. But it still moved her one step further along a path she had no wish to travel, still uncertain of her ability to guard her heart.

She took refuge in teasing to mask her unease. 'Not Ambrose?'

'No. Not Ambrose.' Adam's mouth twisted in distaste. 'I have always been Adam. I am in no mind to fit myself entirely into the mould of a stranger.'

His words, and the bitterness that tainted them, reached into Kitty's heart, beyond her own fear of being hurt again.

'Is it true you had no idea whatsoever of your beginnings?'

'None. My mother saw fit to keep the whole of her past—and, therefore, my past—to herself until she was forced to admit the truth by the fact of my father's death.'

She believed him, despite her initial suspicion he might be lying about that.

How hard that must be, to discover your own mother has lied to you your entire life.

Kitty allowed herself to study him more closely. The harsh lines drawn from nose to mouth…the crease between those dark brows, the etched line that never disappeared completely although it did soften from time to time…the latent anger she had sensed from their first meeting, anger that simmered just beneath the surface to erupt at the least provocation…all these began to make sense. She had been wrong to attribute his anger solely to her, but there was no doubt that some of it was, for she certainly seemed able to provoke an eruption with little effort, just by her presence. As he provoked *her* anger with ease. Their shared history had left its scars on both of them.

Unbidden, Lady Datchworth's final words of

the day before whispered through her mind. *'Look after Kelridge, Catherine. He is not nearly as tough as he likes to pretend.'*

Was she right?

'Very well. I agree. Adam it is. And… I am sorry our meeting again has been difficult for us both. I hope we are truly able to put the past behind us now.'

'As do I.'

They were still standing, several feet apart, facing one another. Adam's gaze roved over Kitty's face, as gentle as a caress, and her pulse stuttered as she willed herself to remain still.

'And just so you know,' he added, softly, 'I *did* feel the same as you, fifteen years ago.'

Kitty stared at him, unsure how to react but, before she could speak, thunder cracked overhead. She started at the suddenness of it and cast an anxious glance up through the canopy of leaves to the ominous sky above.

'We must go back to the house or we are likely to get drenched.'

She took Adam's proffered arm, thankful for the reprieve, her stomach tightening at the warmth of bare, hair-dusted skin beneath her hand. They set off, emerging from the wood into a meadow where sheep huddled together, their backs to the rain which by now had started to spatter down in huge drops as the wind gusted.

The lane that led back to the Hall was across the meadow and it was not long before Kitty's gown was uncomfortably damp and clinging to her legs.

'Is there anywhere nearby we can shelter?'

Adam splayed one large hand to the small of her back, urging her to hurry, and Kitty found herself trotting to keep up with him.

'Yes! This way.' She tugged at his arm, turning him aside and heading for the hedgerow that edged the meadow. 'There. Look.' She pointed out the old gamekeeper's cottage behind the hedge. 'It is a bit rickety, but it still has a roof. Hurry!'

The rain worsened, soaking through Kitty's gown in seconds. Lightning split the sky, followed quickly by another crash of thunder, louder than before.

'There it is.'

They hurtled the last few paces to a gap in the hedge and slammed through the already ajar door into the stone building.

'Phew!'

Adam shook his head, scattering drops as the rain drummed on the slate roof, dripping through in several places. He returned to the door and shoved against it to push it shut. The hinges groaned in protest, but eventually the door closed against the downpour. Kitty, still panting from that mad dash through the rain, scanned the dim

interior of the cottage, the sole source of light one
grimy window. A pile of sacks in one corner—a
corner free of leaks—caught her eye, and she approached gingerly to poke the pile with one foot,
fully expecting to see mice scatter. None emerged
and her breathing steadied. She discarded the up-
permost sack and picked up the next one, conscious that her drenched muslin gown must be
nigh-on transparent and would no doubt cling to
her body in a scandalous fashion. She pulled off
her sodden hat and draped the sack around her
shoulders, banishing her distaste at the thought of
the dust and dirt that would transfer to her clothing and of the likely former use for such sacking
found in a gamekeeper's cottage.

She turned to Adam. His shirt, beneath his
waistcoat, clung to the heavy muscles of his chest
and she glimpsed a hint of dark curls at the open
neck. Her pulse quickened again, the sound of her
now ragged breaths thankfully drowned out by
the drum of rain on the roof. She averted her gaze
and thrust a sack in his direction. There was one
rickety wooden chair and she stalked across to it
and sat as another crack reverberated around the
cottage. Lightning flashed simultaneously, illu-
minating the room with its ghostly glare.

'Thunderstorms usually pass quickly. We shall
not be stuck here long.'

Her voice shook, irritatingly. She stared straight

ahead, avoiding looking directly at Adam, but from the corner of her eye she saw his lips widen in a smile as one brow quirked up. The dratted man was fully aware of her discomfort at being closeted with him in this tiny cottage, but at least he made no move to approach her. Instead, he spread his sack on an area of dry floor next to the cottage wall. He sat down, adopting the same pose as he had against the tree trunk earlier, as the lightning flashed again. After a short delay, the thunder crashed, more distant this time.

Kitty wished she could be on her own to think about what he'd said, but they were stuck there and she could not run away this time. If he hadn't lied about loving her, if that was what he meant, then why had he said those hateful words fifteen years ago? Words that had haunted her for years.

'I'm fond of ye, Kitty, but this was never more than a pleasant way to pass the time when I had an hour to spare. I thought ye understood that.'

Words that had added to her feelings of worthlessness all these years.

His eyes were on her, watching her, and she shivered. If it was true…if he *had* loved her, all those years ago…what then?

'Why did you say what you did? That last day?'

He heaved a sigh and gave her a rueful smile. 'I thought it would make it easier for you. Better to think me a liar and a scoundrel than to grieve over what might have been.'

She should feel mollified to hear that after all this time. But fear wound around her heart as her anger drained away for, without anger to cling on to, she felt…naked. Lost. *Vulnerable*. And she thought that, maybe, the awful truth was that she had been holding on to that anger to shield her from the feelings Adam had roused within her since his return. Unwelcome feelings. *Frightening* feelings. To allow herself to care for another man—and *this* man in particular—was to risk more heartache. A risk that scared her more than she cared to admit.

'Thank you for telling me,' she said, striving to sound calm. 'I accept that I was naive…too young to realise the strain we would both have been under. You did the right thing.' Kitty stood, her heart a touch lighter now the air had been cleared between them. 'It sounds as though rain has stopped. Let us return to the Hall while we can.'

Adam leapt to his feet. He came to Kitty and took her hands in his. 'I still wish you had told me, Kitty.' His voice rasped with emotion and her heart leapt with joy. And with hope, even though it was far too late. 'We would have found a way. I—'

'No, Adam.' Kitty tamped down her whirling emotions and disentangled her hands from his.

This roused fear in her heart. What good could come of them raking over coals grown cold, even if a tiny spark still lingered? Even if she was still drawn to him, as a moth to a flame, she could not risk getting burned again. 'Please, let us not rake it over again. We cannot alter the past and, as we have both said before, we must not mistake the people we were then for who we are now. The past fifteen years have changed us both. Please. Let it be.'

His eyes searched hers, and she concentrated on smoothing her expression. She'd sworn to never again allow any man the power to hurt her. Look forward. Not back. She'd been in danger of forgetting that one rule by which she lived her life. The rule that kept her sane.

She enjoyed her steady, unremarkable life. She could live vicariously through the characters in her stories—love, hate, quarrel, laugh—she could explore every emotion, all without risk to her peace of mind or to her heart. And that was how she wanted it to stay.

'Very well. If that is your wish, I shall respect it. For now. But I have never been a man to give up easily, Kitty.' A smile flickered on his lips. 'You remember that.'

Chapter Thirteen

What was Kitty afraid of? Not of him, Adam was certain—he hadn't mistaken that flash of joy when he took her hands, before she successfully masked her feelings. He longed to haul her into his arms and to kiss her, as he used to.

The last vestiges of anger and hurt had drained from him when she explained why she had married Edgar and hope had flowed in to fill the gaps those negative emotions left behind despite Kitty's assertion that the past could not be altered. Because—although both he and Kitty had changed on the surface—deep inside Adam was confident she was the same Kitty and he was the same Adam. His doubts about his own feelings for her had melted away as completely as his anger and his hurt, and he was as sure as he could be that Kitty was still the woman for him. They belonged together.

For whatever reason, though, she didn't fully trust him and had erected a barrier to keep him at bay. Was that to protect her feelings? He was not mistaken about her interest in him—her eyes, so guarded when they had first met again, now could not hide her response to him. The instinctive response of a woman to a man she desired.

So, she was afraid of getting hurt again. By him.

She had accepted that he had only denied his love for her in order to protect her, but that didn't change what he'd done. She'd had fifteen years of believing he hadn't cared and that he'd lied. It would take time to build her trust and the way to do that was to give her time to get to know him again. To start again, from the beginning.

This time, they were equals. This time, he was going nowhere. This time, he would court her as though they had only just met, as a gentleman would court a lady, and he would do everything he could to change her mind about remarrying.

He tugged open the cottage door and peered outside.

'You are quite right. The rain has stopped,' he said, 'and the thunder has moved away.'

He turned to Kitty, smiling as he spoke, then stepped aside and half-bowed as he swept his arm around, indicating she should leave. She picked up her discarded bonnet, squeezed it, then gave him a rueful smile.

'I think I shall just carry this.'

She stepped outside and they walked side by side across the meadow towards the lane that would take them back to the Hall. Adam deliberately did not offer her his arm to lean on, but clasped his hands behind his back to control his visceral urge to touch her. She, he noticed, retained her grip on that old piece of sacking, clutching it tight across her breasts.

'When we danced at Almack's you spoke of other interests, apart from your stepchildren.' Adam, alive to every nuance and change in Kitty's countenance, noticed delicate pink wash across her cheeks. 'Will you tell me of those? How do you occupy your time here at Fenton Hall?'

She slid him a sidelong look. 'You speak as though a house the size of the Hall can run like clockwork, with nothing more than a quick wind of a key from time to time.'

'I know that is not the case, but...' *But I hunger to know all there is to know about you.* 'I am curious as to what interests you have that occupy you fully, as you put it.'

When she did not reply, he continued, 'After all, as you said, we are as strangers now. And strangers who spend time together—as we shall, while I draw up those plans—can surely indulge in a little polite conversation in order to get to know one anoth—'

A loud retort interrupted him and his immediate thought was that the storm had returned but, even as that idea formed, another bang, followed by a searing pain in his arm, swept it away. He gasped, clutching his upper arm, and then Kitty grabbed him, tugging him to the ground.

'Stop shooting,' she screamed. 'There are people here.'

Adam, his heart thundering in his chest as he scrambled to make sense of what had happened, looked up at Kitty. She was on her knees, above him, staring back across the meadow towards the woods. Adam grabbed her, wincing at the pain in his arm as he tried to pull her lower.

'Get down!'

She struggled against his pull and he tugged harder until she overbalanced and landed on top of him, face to face. He wrapped his arms around her, holding her still even as she wriggled, trying to free herself.

'Stop fighting me, Kitty.'

She raised her head and captured his gaze, her grey eyes wide with shock. 'That was a *gunshot*, Adam. Whoever it is needs to know we are here, or we might get hit.' She struggled to bring her hands between them and began to push against his chest, trying to free herself.

Adam tightened his grip, clenching his jaw against the pain. Kitty's eyes widened further.

'You're hurt! Adam!' She struggled again to free herself.

He forced his words between his gritted teeth. 'Be still, Kitty. Please.'

His arm burned and stung like the devil, but he was certain the bullet had just grazed him and had not lodged inside. Kitty lay still, breathing fast, her head on his chest, her hair tickling him under his chin.

At any other time...in different circumstances...

He swatted the thought aside. This was hardly the time to be lusting after her. Cautiously, he lifted his head and scanned the woods, about twenty yards distant. There was no sign of anyone, no movement, no sound. He frowned. Could it have been poachers? But why would poachers be out in a thunderstorm? Granted, there would be a lack of keepers or other estate workers around, but surely the wildlife would also take shelter at such a time.

'I can't see anyone. Or any movement,' he said. 'Hopefully your shout scared whoever it was away.'

'Robert will be furious about this...he *will* find who is responsible,' Kitty said. She had also raised her head and she captured Adam's gaze again. 'Where are you hit?'

'It's a scratch. Nothing more. It stings a bit, but I'll live.'

His brain ordered his arms to release Kitty, but the message was ignored. Now he had her in his embrace, he wanted to keep her there. For ever. His gaze moved to her mouth and, as her lips parted to release a faint gasp, he fought the urge to kiss her. He forced his gaze back to hers. Her eyes had darkened and his hand had started its glide up between her shoulder blades to cradle her head—to hold her ready for his kiss—by the time sanity returned. He halted that movement of his hand.

'It was most likely an accident, but we should not take any chances,' he said. He rolled her off him and instantly breathed easier. 'I will see if it is safe. Stay there. Do not under any circumstances move, or even raise your head.'

'But—'

'And do not argue!'

Kitty scowled. '*You* are the one who is injured! *You* should be the one to lie still while *I* see if it is safe.'

His heart melted. She had always been full of courage and spirit. It was one of the things he had loved about her. 'Kitty…allow me to do this. Please. Allow me to protect you this time.'

Her scowl smoothed over and she stilled. Then she nodded. Adam rolled on to his side, facing the woods where the shot had come from, then propped himself up on one elbow. Kitty grabbed his hand and he glanced back at her.

'Take care,' she whispered.

There was still nothing to be seen and no further shots. Adam sat up. Then stood. Nothing happened. He bent, holding out his hands to Kitty.

'I think he…they…have gone.'

He'd forgotten his injury in the tension of the moment and, as he pulled Kitty to her feet, his arm shrieked in protest and he could not disguise his wince. Kitty gasped.

'Adam! All that blood. You *said* it was a *scratch*.' Her small fist punched his other arm, punctuating her words.

'Steady, or I'll end up with both arms out of action.'

'Sorry.' Kitty stepped closer and, in one swift movement, she tore his bloodied shirt sleeve apart to expose the wound. 'We need to get you home and clean that up,' she said. She slipped one arm around his waist. 'Put your uninjured arm around my shoulders.'

'There's no need, Kitty. I'm quite capable of walking unaided.'

'Adam…' She fixed him with a stern look.

'You have suffered a shock and you have lost blood. Lean on me.'

It didn't take them long to reach the house. Kitty led the way to the same side room where they had taken the flowers and pushed Adam down on to a chair.

'Stay there. Take off your shirt while I fetch hot water.'

She hurried from the room. Adam stood up again to pull his shirt free from his breeches, then stripped it off over his head. It was ruined any-way—beyond repair, even if the bloodstains could be removed—so he dropped it on the flagged floor. Then he sat down again and examined his upper arm. He sucked in a sharp breath as he probed the groove gouged out by the bullet with the fingers of his left hand. His right hand gripped the edge of the chair seat as pain spiked through him.

'Don't touch it!'

Adam looked up as Kitty bustled into the room, carrying a bowl of water and with a linen towel draped over one arm. He straightened, his hand dropping away from his wound to grip the opposite edge of his seat, bracing himself for the pain he knew must come. But Kitty halted before she reached him, her eyes widening as her gaze travelled across his chest and his upper arms. Her tongue darted out to moisten her lips and heat flooded him as his blood quickened. Her eyes dropped lower and that blood surged to his groin. He shut his eyes, willing his body back under control, desperately forcing his thoughts on to the question of who had been shooting out in the woods in a thunderstorm and away from what he would like to do to Kitty…with Kitty…right here. Right now.

'Adam…?'

He opened his eyes at her soft enquiry. She'd set the bowl on the table and now stood close enough to touch…close enough for her scent to envelop him. Need overcame judgement and he reached for her, sliding one hand around her slender waist as he searched her expression.

Too soon, you fool. You'll scare her off.

But *she* was the one who acted, stepping even closer and cupping his cheek.

'I can't bear that you're hurt,' she whispered. 'I need… I just…' She sucked in a quick breath. 'You could have been *killed*.'

She stroked lightly down the side of his face and along his jaw until her fingers rested on his lips, which parted without volition. He closed his eyes once more, the soft sough of her breaths stirring his blood as her light citrus scent wove through his senses. One finger entered his mouth and he closed his teeth gently on it. The soft moan that escaped her had him hard, and hot, and heavy in an instant. He tightened his hold and pulled her on to his lap and their lips met in a fiery, urgent kiss, all hungry lips and duelling tongues as their quiet moans mingled.

She cradled his head, her fingers tangling in his hair as she pressed against him, her curves moulding to him, driving him wild. He shifted her, bending her back over his uninjured arm, allowing access to her breasts. His fingers explored her neckline, unbuttoning her bodice and gradually working her gown off one shoulder until he could release one breast from her stays.

Oh, God! His fingers closed around perfection, her skin satiny as the firm globe filled his hand, her nipple taut against his palm. Adam bent to her breast and drew that nipple into his mouth. Her hands fisted in his hair and she arched as he flicked that hard bud with his tongue, then suckled. Her soft moans drove him wild…he slowly tightened his embrace, raising her as he trailed open-mouthed kisses from her breast to her neck and again to her mouth, savouring the taste of those lush lips, holding her close to him, relishing the softness of her breasts as they pressed against his bare chest.

Then her hands were between them, palms flat against his chest, pushing him away, and he released her, the madness and urgency fading to be replaced by regret that he had so readily succumbed to temptation so soon after vowing to court Kitty slowly. From the beginning.

'Kitty?'

The look she cast him was stricken. Guilty. *Ashamed*. His heart clenched at the thought she was ashamed of her response to him. He began to wrap his arms around her again, until a searing pain reminded him of his injury. He gritted his teeth against making a sound, but Kitty had noticed, for she took hold of his forearms and gently moved them to release her. As soon as he released his hold again, she scrambled from his lap.

Chapter Fourteen

Shame flooded Kitty as she adjusted her neckline and made herself respectable. Adam was injured. She was meant to be caring for him but, instead, she had as good as ravished him.

The fear of what could have happened had that shot hit a more vital spot had overridden any other consideration. No. It had overridden *every* other consideration. Her only thought…no, not even a thought…her only *instinct* had been to assure herself that he was safe. Unhurt. And to be close to him, physically.

That fear still lurked, her heart still pounding as she hurried to the cupboard where she kept strips of clean cloth and grabbed a handful together with the flask of brandy she also kept in there and returned to the table. She soaked one strip in the still warm water and squeezed it out. Only then did she allow herself to look at Adam.

His blue eyes—bright and direct—fused with hers and she swallowed at the heat banked in them—heat that confirmed he still found her attractive. But Adam had been attracted to her before, even spoken words of love—which he now claimed he meant—but that hadn't stopped him breaking her heart.

That unexpected surge of desire within her... that sudden compulsion to touch Adam, to kiss him...had shaken her to her core. What did this mean for them? Was she really foolish enough to risk her heart again for the sake of physical desire? Better, surely, to continue to protect herself and avoid any further hurt. She had learned the hard way that men could not be trusted. Her father. Adam. Even Edgar—kind, benign Edgar—had hurt her, without meaning to...whittling away her confidence with his gentle comparisons with the perfect Veronica. No. She had no wish to again place her life in the power of any man so she would never marry again. And she mustn't forget that Adam would need an heir and she could not give him one. So any deeper relationship than friendship could never be permanent.

'That gash needs cleansing,' she said. 'It will hurt, I dare say, but there is no other way.'

He shrugged his broad shoulders, causing the muscles in his chest to ripple in a most fascinating way. Kitty set her jaw and dragged her attention to the wound in his upper arm. She frowned, bending to peer closer.

'There are fibres stuck in there, from your shirt.'

His hand came up as if to probe the gash again and, without thinking, she grabbed it.

'I *said* do not touch.'

Adam's fingers closed around hers, sending sparks tingling up her arm, and Kitty abruptly straightened, catching her breath, her heart racing as he raised her hand to his mouth and pressed a kiss to it.

'I'll behave.' His voice a husky murmur that sent heat washing through her body in waves. 'Do your worst.'

Kitty swallowed again, her knees jittery, and she prayed her hand wouldn't shake. With her left hand on his shoulder, she bent again so she could see what she was doing.

'Wait!'

Adam stood up, so close the heat emanating from his bare chest did nothing to cool Kitty's blood, and neither did the close-up view of those crisply curling hairs that spread across his chest like outspread wings, then arrowed in towards the waist of his breeches. She dragged in a breath to calm herself, but only succeeded in flooding her senses with his scent: musky, spicy, manly. She stepped back, almost stumbling in her haste, and his hands shot out to grip her shoulders.

'I am sorry. I startled you.'

His voice and words were so matter of fact they steadied her and she looked up at him. Their gazes fused again…but he appeared unaware of her visceral reaction. There was no knowing gleam in his eyes, no raised eyebrow, no quirk of those sensual lips to ruffle her anger and help her maintain her guard. He, unlike her, appeared totally unaffected.

'It will be easier if I sit on the table. You will not have to bend and there will be better light from the window on to my arm.'

'Yes. I…yes, of course. That is a good plan.'

Adam rounded the table and hoisted himself up to sit on it, the muscles in his arms bulging as he raised his body.

Without volition, Kitty licked her lips. 'That is an improvement.'

And it was, as far as cleansing the gash was concerned, but it also put that chest on a level with Kitty's eyes and mouth. His nipples—and their flat, dusky areolae surrounded by whorls of hair—proved yet another distraction.

Resolutely, Kitty tore her attention from the expanse of bare male skin and directed it at that gouge caused by the bullet. And the very thought of the bullet quashed any further lustful thoughts.

Someone had *shot* at Adam. Her heart stuttered and her mouth dried. Who could it have been? And why? Her mind tumbling with conjecture, Kitty steadied Adam's arm with her free hand as she bathed the wound, sluicing water through it to wash it clean of dirt and fibres.

'Do you think it was deliberate?' she asked as she worked. Adam sucked in a sharp breath. 'Sorry. I am trying to be gentle.'

'I know you are. And...'

Kitty paused her ministrations when Adam failed to continue, her gaze flicking to his frowning face. 'Well? Do you?'

Adam's brows rose. 'Yes. I do. It makes no sense otherwise. No poacher would be out in a thunderstorm—he would know the animals have more sense than to be out and about in such weather. And the same goes for gamekeepers. I dinna wish to alarm ye, but I can think of no explanation other than one of us was the target. And, of the two of us, I would say that I am the more likely, would you not?'

Kitty bit her lip, considering, pleased that he had answered her honestly.

'Ye have to think about that?' Adam tipped his head to one side. 'Why on earth would anyone wish to shoot at you?'

'Oh! No! That is not what I was thinking about. It is... I was thinking how refreshing that you have admitted that to me. Most other gentlemen would try to hide the truth…they believe that ladies ought to be protected from the harsh realities of life, that their sensibilities are too delicate to cope with being told the truth. But you…you answered my question with a direct answer. Thank you.'

Adam's eyes narrowed as he studied Kitty and her face heated at his scrutiny. But she held his gaze. She made her mind up there and then. She would keep strong those barriers surrounding her heart, so that he could never hurt her again, but she *would* be his friend and be honest with him, as long as he treated her as an intelligent being and not as a grown-up child to be sheltered and humoured.

Adam smiled then and Kitty's heart leapt even though she silently scolded herself for her foolishness. But he was so handsome. So masculine. He stirred her blood in a way that no one had since… *no*. She must be honest with herself as well. *No one* had ever stirred her blood like this, not even Adam when they had known each other fifteen years before. She had been too young, maybe, to fully understand the full depth of the sensual attraction that could exist between a man and a woman. Her marriage to Edgar had never been one of passion and it was only now—at the age of two-and-thirty—that her body was awakening to the full potential of sexual attraction between a man and a woman. Lust and the promise of physical fulfilment. And far from being shocked at herself, as she had been mere moments before, she was now intrigued.

She turned away, to give herself time to compose her features now that this new understanding of herself—not to mention these new, hitherto unsuspected feelings thrumming through her—had seemingly sprung from nowhere. Was she strong enough…brazen enough?…to explore physical desire without risking her heart? Men managed to keep the two separate—look at Adam just now. Utterly unaffected while she was a jittery mess. Many women, both widowed and unhappily married, indulged in *affaires*. But…could she? Uncertainty swept through her. Now the idea had occurred to her, however…did she not owe it to herself to at least consider it?

She took her time, picking up the flask and unscrewing the top before she faced Adam again. He still watched her, his eyes alert. Intent. A faint crease between his brows.

'This will sting,' she said.

He took the flask from her hand and raised it to his mouth, taking a swig. 'For fortification,' he said. 'And it is good for shock.'

She stepped closer, her skirts brushing his leg, his musky scent creating strange sensations within her as it coiled into her depths, awakening all her senses.

'Keep still,' she whispered and placed one hand on his shoulder as she trickled the spirit on to his wound. He stiffened, but made no sound, and she glanced up at him, capturing his gaze. She caught her lower lip between her teeth and his gaze lowered to her mouth. Then, and only then, a low groan emerged, seemingly wrenched from deep within his chest.

'Kitty...'

His throaty growl reached deep inside her, grabbing and squeezing. She gasped as heat spiralled through her and an aching need gathered in the feminine folds between her thighs.

This is desire. This is lust.

All thought of guarding her heart fled. Excitement thrummed through her as she moved between his legs and pressed close, tilting her face to his, aware of every tiny change in his expression—the flare of his nostrils; the unmistakeable craving in those dark eyes; the slight compression of those sensual lips before they relaxed, parting as he hauled in a ragged breath.

Long fingers curled behind her head, taking a fistful of hair as he angled her face to his.

'May I kiss you, Kitty?' A tortured whisper.

'Yes. Please.'

He lowered his face to hers, until their lips

met. Not a kiss of uncontrolled passion—not the frantic onslaught she craved…a kiss like before, a kiss she could lose herself in—but a gentle caress as his lips glided over hers. And she lost herself anyway, her eyes closing as every nerve in her body homed in on the meeting of their mouths. Then his tongue traced the seam of her lips and she opened to him. Adam gave a groan and his tongue swept inside.

Possessive. Assured. Masterful.

Her arms wound around his neck and she gave herself up to these wonderful new sensations, her entire body tingling…coming alive. His tongue plunged, mimicking the timeless rhythm that she recalled from her marriage, but now…this time… with this kiss…it felt as though an invisible thread ran straight through her, connecting her mouth with her breasts—full and heavy, and *aching*— and with her womb, which wanted…needed… *craved*…in a way she had never felt before.

Boots ringing in the stone-flagged passage outside wrenched her back into the present and she tore her lips from Adam's and stepped away, feeling the heat burning in her cheeks, her knees trembling. Adam looked no less discomposed as their eyes met. He could do nothing, sitting on the table as he was, so—as the door opened—Kitty began to sort through the strips of linen lying on the table. She selected the longest.

'I think this will suffice.' She held it aloft, then spun to face the door, pasting a look of surprise on her face as though she had missed their visitor's approach.

'Adam! What is this I hear? You have been hurt?' Robert strode into the room, his eyes filled with angry concern and fixed on Adam. 'Is it true?'

'It is. As you may see, Lady Fen—Catherine is about to bandage my wound, having cleaned it thoroughly. And painfully.'

'What happened? A shot, Vincent said.' Robert grabbed Adam's elbow and moved his arm to get a better look at the wound. 'It looks painful.'

'Someone,' said Kitty, nudging Robert aside so she could bandage Adam's arm, 'was shooting out in the woods. We had each gone for a walk to get some air and met quite by chance in the woods. Then we were caught in that thunder shower and took shelter in the old keeper's cottage until the rain stopped. We had just started on our way home again when we heard the shot.'

'And, as you can see, he missed.'

Robert frowned at Adam's sardonic comment. 'Are you saying it was deliberate?'

Adam shrugged. Robert's frown deepened. 'We've had some trouble with poachers, but as long as they are local and restrict themselves to taking the odd rabbit, I turn a blind eye. But they usually use snares, not guns.'

'You're forgetting the thunderstorm,' said Kitty. 'The animals can sense such a change in the weather and they normally take cover long before the storm strikes. Any countryman worth his salt would know *that*.'

Robert stared at her, still frowning. 'That is true.' Then he started, as though seeing her for the first time. 'You will catch your death of cold, Stepmama. Look at the state of you.'

Kitty glanced down at her wet, muddy gown. 'We were already wet through before we were forced to dive to the ground.' She shook her head. 'A muddy gown is the least of my worries.'

'Your stepmother is too modest, Rob. It was her quick thinking that saved us—she dived to the ground and took me with her even as I was still trying to work out what had happened.' Adam smiled ruefully.

'I had no idea whether that shot was an accident or by design, but I wasn't prepared to take the chance it was a deliberate act.' Kitty shivered then, as the reality of what had happened hit her again. 'Who knows what might have happened had whoever it was shot at us again?'

Her stomach churned and she wrapped her arms around her torso as though she might contain the tumult of emotions that erupted from nowhere. Adam muttered something beneath his breath and jumped down from his perch on the table.

'Thank you for your help, Catherine. You need to go and change out of your wet clothing. In fact… Rob, I think your stepmother would benefit from a warm bath.'

Robert wrapped his arm around Kitty's shoulders and, grateful for the support, she sagged against him even as she castigated herself for her weakness. She hadn't noticed the chill of her damp gown before and the fear about what had happened—and what *might* have happened—only now seemed to have caught up with her.

Still, even though she longed to do as Adam suggested, she felt she must protest. 'It is you who have been injured, Adam. Not I. And you are equally as wet.'

'And Adam will no doubt go and change into dry clothing now his arm has been bandaged,' said Robert, steering Kitty towards the door. 'Come on. I shall help you upstairs.'

'I can manage, Robert. There is no need for all this fuss.'

'Caring is not fuss. Now do as you're told.' Robert paused as they reached the door. 'I'll have hot water sent up to your bedchamber, Adam,' he said, 'and I will send my man up to assist you.'

Kitty, glancing back, saw Adam's attention on

her, his eyes brimming with concern. She forced a smile and was rewarded by a smile in return.

'Come, now, Stepmama.' Robert tightened his grip as they stepped into the passage. 'You know Charis will never forgive me should you succumb to a chill on my watch. Let me help you upstairs.'

Chapter Fifteen

When Adam, freshly washed and clad in clean clothes, descended the stairs a short while later, Vincent awaited him in the hall.

'Where might I find His Lordship?'

'He is out riding, my lord. With some of the men.'

Adam's brows rose. 'Out in the woods?'

'I believe so. He desired me to tell you on no account were you to follow him and he will come to see you the minute he returns.'

Adam's instinct was, indeed, to follow, but common sense warned him he was unlikely to be much use and his arm had stiffened up enough to make him reluctant to attempt to ride.

'Very well. You may consider your duty discharged, Vincent. I shall continue my work in the library, so that is where I shall be when His Lordship returns.'

The plans he had been working on had completely slipped his mind in among everything that had happened that afternoon and, although his wound might render fine draughtsmanship as tricky as horse riding, he could use the time to sketch out rough ideas and plans. That would help to distract him from that shot and from what Robert might discover.

Nothing, however, could distract him from Kitty.

'How fares Lady Fenton?'

'I believe Her Ladyship is resting in her room, my lord. Might I bring you refreshments to the library?'

'Thank you, Vincent.' What he really wanted was a dram of whisky, but Robert did not keep that *heathen spirit* in the house. 'A glass of brandy would be most welcome.'

He strolled to the library, his heart full of fear and his head full of images of Kitty.

She could have been killed.

He'd been aware of that ever since the shot rang out, but so much had been happening that the full horror of it had been kept at bay. Now, though, alone with his thoughts as he entered the library, that knowledge hit him with force. It would be impossible to concentrate on work, so he swerved away from the desk and, instead, headed for a wingback chair by the centre window. Vincent appeared a moment later, carrying a tray with a decanter and two glasses, and set them on a table within reach of the chair.

'Two glasses?'

'For if His Lordship wishes to join you in a glass upon his return, my lord.'

Vincent poured brandy into one glass, bowed, and then left the library, closing the door softly behind him.

Adam reached for the glass, drained it in one and then refilled it. He closed his eyes, tilting his head to rest on the back of the chair, and willed away the utter terror that now paralysed him at the thought of what could have happened.

She could have been killed!

Images again filled his brain.

Kitty... I've only just found her. I could have lost her again.

Had it been deliberate? Aimed at him? If it was...there was only one culprit he could think of.

'Uncle Grenville.'

The rustle of fabric reached his ears seconds before the scent of flowers with a top note of citrus registered. 'My thoughts precisely.'

His eyes flew open. He sat up straight and glared at Kitty. 'Ye should be resting.'

'As should you.'

'I am.'

A brief smile flickered on her lips. She gestured, indicating the chair in which she was now sitting. 'As am I.'

He scowled. 'Will ye please stop humouring me? Ye should be in bed.'

With me. A new, mouth-watering picture now filled his head... Kitty, in bed, the covers rumpled, her hair loose around her shoulders, her eyes heavy-lidded with desire. He thrust aside that image.

'But I am too restless. I want to talk about what happened. Or, more to the point, talk about who might have been responsible. And it would seem we have reached the same conclusion.'

'I was thinking aloud,' Adam growled. *God, I just want to hold her. Protect her always.* 'Ye weren't meant to hear that.'

Her brows arched. 'Of course I was not, because I am a lady and must therefore be shielded from the brutal reality of this world.'

That was close to what she had said before. She had been so happy he had told her the truth...and he could not disagree with her point. She was— and he could verify it—no child.

'What you mean,' she continued, 'is that you would not say such a thing to me because I am female. I should be prostrate upon my bed because I am female. We spoke about this earlier—I need neither protection nor cossetting. It happened. I was there. Someone shot at us...with you as the most likely target...yet I am expected to quash any conjecture or curiosity because of my sex?'

'Put like that, no. Of course not. But ye *were* in a state of shock when I last set eyes upon ye.'

Her eyes narrowed. 'As. Were. You. And yet...' again, she gestured '...here you are and here am I.'

Adam sighed and shook his head. 'Ye're just as stubborn as I recall.'

Her smile lit her face. 'And, you will find, just as opinionated. So...may we discuss your uncle and his possible involvement as adults or is it your intention to exclude me entirely from what you and Robert will surely talk about upon his return?'

How could he deny her? She was beautiful and charming and graceful: the most desirable woman he had ever known—and he included her younger self in that—but, more than that... so much more...she fascinated him. Now they had cleared the air between them, he felt he could talk with her for hours and never grow tired of listening to her, watching her. He wanted her, physically. But that could wait. For now, what she was asking him was that he treat her as an equal...as though he were talking with another man. And so that is what he would do. And he would always strive to respect her wishes.

'Let us talk, then.' He cocked his head to one

side. 'Would ye care for refreshments? Shall I ring for Vincent?'

'You may pour me a brandy, if you will,' said Kitty. 'There is no need to disturb Vincent when there is a spare glass just begging to be filled.'

'Is there no end to your rebellion? Brandy in the afternoon? Quite shocking!'

She grinned and, for the first time since they had met again, those beloved dimples made an appearance. 'It is good for shock. You said so yourself.'

Adam poured the brandy and handed her the glass. She grew serious then, staring reflectively into the amber liquid as she swirled it gently.

'Seriously, Adam…do you truly suspect your uncle?'

He didn't want to think it, but what other explanation could there be? *If* it had been a deliberate act.

'I think we are agreed it was unlikely to be a stray shot from poachers,' he said, still pondering, 'and *someone* pulled that trigger. Twice.'

'So…you do not believe it was accidental?'

'No. And, as I can think of no one I have angered enough to cause him to wish for my death, I fail to see we can reach any other conclusion,'

'Or her.'

'Her? No!'

'Because a female would never kill?'

He huffed a laugh. 'Not a bit of it. Women, I am sure, nurse grievances and think murderous thoughts just as men do. I meant I can think of no female I have angered enough for her to wish to end my life.'

'No other young ladies you have wooed and then abandoned?'

He started at her question.

'I apologise.' She looked contrite. 'Now it is my turn to squirm at an attempted jest that has fallen flat.'

Adam did wonder how much truth lay behind that question. He'd known she'd be upset when he left, but... He raised his brows. 'Tell me ye never hated me enough to wish me dead, Kitty.'

'No. Of course not. I cannot imagine hating *anyone* as much as that.'

'I am relieved to hear it. And, in answer to your question—no.'

'Which leaves your uncle. Or...' A frown knit her brow.

'Or?'

'Your cousin. Bartholomew Trewin. Your uncle is your heir and, after him, your cousin.'

'Tolly? No...surely not. He is...that is...he seems a good man. And he is a friend of Robert's, is he not?'

He felt his colour rise under her scrutiny. 'Do

you believe that good men cannot be driven to do bad things, given desperate circumstances?'

'Why, of course not. But… Tolly…what circumstances? He gave nae hint of debts or such.'

He desperately did not want to suspect his cousin but, now the notion had been put into his head, he could not deny Tolly would probably have more cause to wish Adam dead than Uncle Grenville. Tolly was still at Kelridge on the day Adam left, so either man could have ridden over to Fenton Hall and stalked the woods. But…to what purpose?

'As a plan, it left much to be desired,' he said. 'What if I had been more conscientious and remained working at my desk? How long would my assailant wait, hoping to take a pot shot at me?'

'Hmmm.' Kitty tapped her lips with one forefinger, frowning. 'Tell me…did you establish a routine of any sort while you were at Kelridge?'

Adam eyed her with admiration. He hadn't even considered that, but it was logical. 'I did ride out most afternoons. It became something of a habit.'

It had become a necessity, if he was honest. Anything to get away from that stifling atmosphere in which he'd felt more and more of an interloper. Maybe he should air his concerns, especially as they pointed more definitely at his uncle as the culprit.

'To be honest, I found it difficult to settle at Kelridge. There was this…oh, I don't know… I suppose you'd call it an undercurrent. And not a pleasant one.'

'I am sorry to hear that, but you must have expected it to be a difficult period of adjustment. Not only for you, but for everyone at Kelridge Place.' Kitty frowned. 'Was your father popular among the staff? I had heard he could be… difficult.'

'He was, without doubt, *un*popular.' And that was an understatement. 'Did you never meet him?'

'No. Edgar knew him, of course, but our paths never crossed. I *have* heard that your uncle has improved the estate a great deal since he took over running it, though.'

'So I have been told. Many times.'

'It makes sense, therefore, that the servants and other workers will view him favourably.'

'Without doubt. That message was made clear in numerous subtle and not-so-subtle ways by many senior members of my staff. Grenville Trewin is still regarded as the true master of Kelridge Hall, no matter what the laws on primogeniture and entails might decree.'

And he was beginning to wish he had never learned the truth. That his mother had kept her secret to her grave. Except…he would not then have met Kitty again. And that was unthinkable.

'Hopefully that will all change once I have an heir of my own.' An image of Kitty with a babe in her arms appeared in his mind's eye, filling him with hope and contentment. The future looked rosier than it had for many, many years. But he was rushing ahead of himself. He must keep to the topic at hand. '*That* would soon quash any random hopes that my uncle will ever fully control the reins again.'

Adam emptied his brandy glass. Without a word, Kitty leaned forward and refilled both his glass and her own. She sat back and sipped as she stared at the window, her fine brows drawn together.

'Maybe,' she said, after a few minutes' reflection, 'they fear you are your father's son? If he was a cruel master, they will fear a return to that regime.'

'But I have given them no reason to suppose I am like my father. In fact, I have been at pains to be friendly in my dealings with them.'

Kitty tucked her lips between her teeth. Adam scowled at her. 'What is so funny?'

'Servants, my dear Adam, do *not* appreciate their masters trying to make friends with them. They want to serve a man they can look up to and respect. A master who can make them feel superior to servants in the neighbouring houses. You must understand that they have their pride, too. And a nobleman is expected to behave as such.'

'I do not wish to live in that manner of household. I want a more relaxed feeling, like when I was growing up. I canna believe they wouldn't appreciate that.'

Kitty smiled at him. The tenderness in her look evoked a swell of longing, but a longing tinged with a sadness he couldn't place until Ma's face materialised in his mind's eye. Sadness and guilt, that was it. He thrust his fingers through his hair, sweeping it back from his face.

'Anyway. We are straying from the point. Yes, I established a routine of sorts, but why would my uncle or anyone else suppose I would continue that routine at Fenton Hall?'

'That is true, and the theory has been disproved because you did *not* ride out. You went for a walk.'

'And we are no nearer to finding out who might wish me dead.'

Kitty shuddered. 'It is a horrid feeling. It may not, of course, be about the money. It might be the lure of the title. I heard Tolly was hanging out for Lady Sarah Bamford—a duke's daughter might lower herself to wed an earl, but I doubt either she or her father would countenance an offer from plain Mr Trewin.'

Adam laughed. 'You have a lurid imagination there, Kitty. You believe Tolly might commit murder for love? You should write novels!'

She stared at him blankly for a moment. 'Now there is a thought. I take it you disapprove of such mindless drivel?'

'I neither approve nor disapprove. I have never read one and I have no wish to waste my time on such an activity. Do I take it ye are an avid reader of novels?'

'I am. I particularly enjoy the work of the late Miss Austen—she has a sharp wit and holds a mirror up to society with all its faults and contradictions. Her books are amusing, but also interesting in their insight into human behaviour.'

'Well, I have no objection to others indulging in such a pastime if they wish to waste their time. It is not for me, however.'

'And you can state that without ever having read a novel?' Kitty shook her head, leaving Adam feeling he had somehow disappointed her. 'Anyway…to return to the matter in hand, I do not say Tolly would kill for the sake of love, but I would urge you to keep an open mind. People *do* kill for love…there was a case recently where a man poisoned his wife in order that he might be free to marry his mistress. I agree to the *feeling* that Mr Grenville Trewin is the more likely culprit, but that is illogical. My instinct is simply because I *like* your cousin and I really do not know your uncle very well. However, being less likeable does not make a man guilty.'

'Ye're right. I'll keep an open mind. I hope Robert might discover something in his search of the woods.'

Kitty started up from her chair. 'Robert is searching the woods? Adam…why did you not stop him?'

Adam surged to his feet and caught Kitty's arm as she headed for the door. 'I didna know until after he had gone. But ye need have no fear. He has taken men with him. He will be in no danger.'

'Oh! Of course. How silly of me. I did not think… I dare say I am still more rattled than I thought.'

'Ye're trembling.' Adam wrapped his arms around Kitty. 'There's nothing to be afraid of. I promise.'

She leaned into him and he tightened his embrace as he breathed in her scent…the scent he now recognised as Kitty. This Kitty, not the girl he had loved, but the woman she was now. He tipped up her chin and lost himself in their kiss as her arms encircled his waist and she hugged him close.

The sound of the door opening sent Adam's heart leaping into his throat as he and Kitty sprang apart. His face burned as he turned to face Robert, who sauntered into the room, his expression innocent of even a hint of suspicion. Adam's pounding heart slowed as his breathing eased—he needed all the friends he could get at the moment and he had no wish for his feelings for Kitty to drive a wedge between himself and Robert.

'Robert! You are back!' Kitty's voice was too high-pitched and even though Robert appeared not to have seen their embrace, Kitty still managed to look and sound panicky as she launched into speech. 'I... Lord Kelridge and I were discussing what happened. I was so afraid you might be shot at too. I...we...'

Her words petered out. She looked helplessly at Adam and he sent her a look of reassurance.

'Did you see anyone, Rob?'

'No one. And you, Stepmama, should be in bed.' Robert eyed the table and the two half-drunk glasses. He quirked a brow at Adam. 'So... not content with failing to ensure my stepmother gets the rest she needs, you have encouraged her to partake of spirits.'

He strode back across the library, opened the door and stuck his head around it. Adam heard him request another glass and he took advantage of Robert's distraction to catch Kitty's eye.

'He did not see us.'

'I know. But I still find it hard to believe he

didn't notice anything amiss,' Kitty whispered. 'I could not help but panic... Edgar was his father and—'

Kitty fell silent as Robert returned.

'As I was saying,' he said, 'we saw no one, but we did find fresh hoofprints entering and leaving the wood from the road.'

He dragged a third chair to join the other two and then gestured for Kitty to sit. Once she was settled the two men both sat. Vincent brought in a third glass and Robert poured himself a generous measure of brandy and topped up Adam's glass. When Kitty wordlessly held out her own glass for a refill, he obliged with only a slight flick of one brow in Adam's direction. But Adam could settle for that. Better he blame Adam for leading Kitty astray with brandy than he should suspect what Adam really wanted to do with his stepmother.

'Did ye glean anything from those prints?'

'Nothing. I am afraid we are no closer to knowing who was responsible than we were before.'

Adam told Robert briefly what he and Kitty had been discussing.

'Tolly? Well... I should not like to think...but if that *was* an attempt to kill you, Adam, it makes sense it must be by someone who stands to benefit. And that can only lead to either your Uncle Grenville, or to Tolly.'

'Do ye doubt it was an attempt on my life, Rob?'

'No, but...' Robert frowned. 'Why wait until now? If it was your uncle or your cousin, they had ample opportunity while you were at Kelridge Place.'

'Could they think they're less likely to fall under suspicion if Adam is attacked away from Kelridge?'

'They could. But the timing makes no sense. Why now? Why not wait several months when it would be less obvious?'

'Or, for that matter—if it was Tolly, why didn't he try something in London?' Robert rubbed his jaw. 'That would make far more sense and it would surely have been easier to dismiss as a random attack by thieves, or an accident even. A spill off Westminster Bridge into the Thames has claimed many poor souls over the years. And I still cannot believe Tolly is capable of cold-blooded murder despite your theory he might be driven to drastic measures in the cause of love, Stepmama. I always said your imagination is too vivid for words.'

'Which leaves my uncle as the main suspect. Or a complete stranger, for reasons unknown. Or...it was, after all, an accident.'

Chapter Sixteen

Kitty arose early the following morning after a restless night. The sky held the promise of a summer's day, azure blue dotted with fluffy clouds, and her heart…her foolish heart…swelled with joy at the promise of time to spend with Adam. She steadied herself on the windowsill as she leaned towards the glass, gazing mindlessly at the garden below and the parkland beyond. What should she do? She knew Adam. At least, she knew the young man he had been. And the fire that now kindled openly in his blue eyes whenever he looked her way suggested he felt as passionately about her as he had back then. They'd not had a moment alone together yesterday after Robert returned from his search and, if she was honest, her main feeling had been one of relief. It had given her the whole of the night to think about what she wanted. About how she would react when Adam kissed her again, as he inevitably would.

Her skin prickled as a shiver chased over her. She wanted his kiss. Even more after yesterday. That kiss had been an entrée and had only whetted her appetite for more. More kisses. More caresses. More…*everything*.

But how much *everything* did she mean? That was the question that had her tossing and turning throughout the night. Her only certainty was that, whatever everything meant, it must be purely physical.

The door opened behind her and Effie entered, carrying a gently steaming pitcher.

'You're awake early, milady.' She crossed to the washstand and poured the water into the basin. 'Which gown shall I lay out for you?'

'Oh, any of them will—no. Actually, I shall wear my blue muslin.'

'Very well.'

'Effie, are the gentlemen up and about yet?'

'Yes'm.' The maid's voice was muffled as she rummaged in the clothes press. 'I saw Lord Kelridge going downstairs just now and His Lordship has been up for hours.' She straightened, the blue sprigged muslin draped across her arms. She shook the gown out and held it up, examining it with a critical eye. 'I don't *think* this needs pressing, milady, but maybe I should, just in case.' She turned for the door.

'Effie…no. The gown is barely creased and what there is will soon drop out.'

By the time she had washed and dressed and was alone again, Kitty was no nearer a decision on that all-important question. She would not… *could* not…risk opening her heart to the pain she had suffered before, yet she did not wish to deny the cravings of her own body. Cravings she had never before experienced…or, at least, not with such intensity. Before, in her marriage, there had been the odd fleeting hint of greater pleasure in the marital act. Nothing more than a glimpse of something more exotic, more intoxicating, that quickly evaporated, like the fast-fading memory of a dream upon waking. Now, her curiosity had been piqued.

Could she satisfy that curiosity without risking her heart? Men did it all the time—satisfied the lusts of their bodies without their emotions being involved.

But this is Adam. Your emotions are already involved, whether you like it or not.

She acknowledged the truth of it. So, the question became…was her curiosity, and that deep-down hum of need, strong enough for her to take the risk of heartache if she followed her desires?

At least, this time, she knew there would be no fairy-tale ending. Not when Adam would need an heir. This time, she would not expect a pot of anything at the end of the rainbow.

She went downstairs and into the parlour where breakfast was laid out on the sideboard.

'Good morning. How is your arm today?'

Adam paused in the act of raising his coffee cup. The table before him was bare of crockery or food, suggesting he had finished eating. As Kitty helped herself to a boiled egg and a slice of toast, he returned her greeting, adding, 'It is still sore to the touch but, otherwise, much better, thank you. I trust you slept well?'

'Very well, thank you. And you?'

'Well enough. Well—if I'm honest, I was rest-less.'

Kitty sat opposite him. 'I am not surprised. Being shot would have that effect.'

He captured her gaze, and that same fire in his eyes—banked low for now—quickened her pulse and fractured her breathing. Heavens! Did she have any choice but to explore this further? If he could heat her blood with one look, what more might he do with a kiss? A touch? The mem-ory of the day before—those feelings—shivered through her.

'Coffee, milady?'

She jumped at Vincent's quiet murmur close

behind her. The coffee pot appeared next to her. He filled her cup and his arm withdrew. The interruption had allowed her to bring her emotions back under control. She scraped butter on to her toast and bit into it. Behind her, she heard Vincent leave the room.

'It was not being shot that disturbed my sleep.' Adam's comment was no less forceful for being so quiet. 'It was you, Kitty. *You* were on my mind.' His eyes burned into her. 'I—' He broke off as Robert's voice rang out from outside the room. 'We need to talk, Kitty. Come to the library later, after Rob goes out. Please?'

Kitty nodded her head as Robert—full of cheer and early morning energy—breezed into the room.

It was almost eleven before Robert left the house, intending to visit his bank. Kitty—her nerves winding ever tighter at the thought of a tête-à-tête with Adam—suggested she might accompany Robert and pay a visit to her dressmaker, but Robert fobbed her off, saying he intended to be in and out of the bank in a flash and there was far too much demanding his attention back here at the Hall for him to have time to waste while Kitty shopped. Kitty recoiled at his brusqueness, so unlike Robert.

'My apologies, Stepmama. I had no right to

snap at you. This business with Adam is bothering me…he told me this morning he intends to ride out this afternoon. I cannot stop him, I know, but I cannot help but worry there may be another attempt on him. I need to be back in time to accompany him.'

'But…you will then put yourself at risk, Rob. You must not.'

And neither must Adam.

He gave her a brief hug. 'Don't you worry about me! Besides, why are you not hard at work writing? I thought you would relish the opportunity to spend more time on it while Charis is away.'

'I am not in the mood for it today.' She was far too distracted to even try to lose herself in her story. Her heroine must wait patiently until Kitty was in the right frame of mind to rescue her from that cliff face she clung to, praying that hero Jason would find her before the evil Lord Sidney—desperate to stop her revealing his plan to kill young Arthur—spotted her hiding place and hurled her into the foaming seas far below.

Robert smiled down at her. 'That is understandable. We are all of us unsettled. Give me a few days, until we have a clearer idea of what happened, and then I will gladly escort you to town to visit your modiste and to shop to your heart's content.'

Kitty thanked him, knowing she would not accept his offer. She had no wish to shop…she had, like a coward, impulsively seized upon the idea as an excuse to delay the forthcoming talk with Adam. She was still no more certain of what she would say or do.

She approached the library with dragging feet.

But when Adam looked up and saw her…when he jumped up and rounded the desk…when he strode towards her…all indecision fled. She stepped into his arms. They folded around her and she leaned into his strength, breathing in his spicy maleness, her head against his chest. The steady thump-thump-thump of his heart reassured her; the heat of his body relaxed her. It felt like coming home.

Kitty thrust her hands between them and pushed against his chest, only the fabric of his shirt separating her palms and his skin. As yesterday, he had discarded his jacket and was dressed in shirt sleeves and unbuttoned waistcoat. When his embrace loosened, she stepped away. She folded her arms.

'Robert tells me you intend to ride out this afternoon. Are you mad?'

She hadn't meant her first words to be so confrontational, but she couldn't bear to see him put himself into danger.

Adam quirked a brow. He crossed to the place

where he had been working, then turned to face her, hitching one hip up to perch on the desk, and folded his own arms.

'I will not skulk indoors shivering in my shoes.'

Of course he would not.

'He…they…might try again.'

'Then that will give me the opportunity to discover who he is. Or who they are.' His lips quirked in a smile. 'Kitty… I will not be alone. Robert and two grooms will be with me. And I will be on my guard. Yesterday, neither of us had any notion that someone might mean mischief. I don't know about you, but I was giving none of *my* attention to our surroundings.'

His smiled faded. His gaze heated. His voice deepened. 'I was far too interested in my companion.'

Awareness coiled deep in her belly and her pulse leapt.

'You wanted to talk?' The question emerged as a squeak.

'I did.' He stood. 'I do.'

He beckoned and Kitty moved towards him. All at once it no longer mattered that she still had no plan about what to say or what to do. This, she realised, was about instinct. It was about feelings. It was about spontaneity. It was about doing what was right for her in *this* moment. She had lived her life looking forward, not back. But this need not be about the future. That would happen come what may. This was about now.

She paused an arm's length from him. 'What did you want to say?'

Alive to every nuance in his expression, she saw his eyes narrow infinitesimally before creasing in a smile.

'I want to say…words are overrated.' He took her hands, his thumbs circling her palms as he held her gaze. Her breath grew short. 'Actions. Now they have more…value.'

He moved then, walking backwards, still holding her hands, thumbs still caressing. She followed. Not coerced. Not pulled in his wake. She followed willingly as he backed around the painted screen that shielded the reading corner from the rest of the room. He released her hands and she raised them to his shoulders as waves of longing heated her blood and sweet anticipation coursed through her.

Strong fingers flexed at her waist as his mouth swooped on hers, crushing her lips in a fiery kiss. She pressed close, her hands tangling in his hair, her fingers curving around the solid shape of his skull. That distant thrum of need strengthened, growing ever more insistent as her insides melted and her body moulded to his.

He tore his lips from hers. 'Kitty.'

His groan lingered in the air as he trailed hot kisses across her jaw and down her throat. Her head fell back, her eyes drifting shut as everything faded away. Everything but Adam and the feelings conjured up by the magic of his lips on her skin and the caress of his hands as they swept her body, stroking, fondling. She savoured the sheer joy of all that latent power, harnessed and controlled, as Adam skimmed her skin with the finest and tenderest of touches. His fingers released the buttons fastening the bodice of her gown and he opened it, spreading it wide to allow him to release both of her breasts from her corset. He kneaded them, his thumbs rubbing her nipples before he dipped his head and tasted her, sucking one hardened bud deep into his mouth, flicking it with his tongue as his fingers played with the other.

Need climbed within her and she thrust her fingers through his hair as pressure built inside…a craving for more. And more. How had she never felt this before?

She pressed her hips closer to him and the hard ridge of his arousal pressed against her belly aroused an urgency she'd never experienced, and she slipped a hand between them to stroke his length. His groan vibrated against the bare skin of her shoulder, where he'd pulled aside her gown to press hot kisses, as her other hand reached for his breeches' buttons. She released him, wrapping her fingers around him—all silken skin sheathed over hard, hot iron—following her instinct as she squeezed and stroked, and caressed the rounded tip with the pad of her thumb. Never had she held her husband in such a way.

'Kiss me,' she whispered and hungry lips seized hers. Tongues tangling, they moved as one to the wing-backed chair, set with its back to the window. Adam sat, his hands on Kitty's waist. He looked up at her.

'Tell me you want this, Kitty. Tell me you want me.'

'Oh, yes,' she breathed.

She could not tear her gaze from his erection as it jutted proud through the open placket of his breeches. Adam grasped her skirts and gathered them high, then pulled her between his splayed legs to press his mouth to the soft curls at the juncture of her thighs. She jerked as his tongue probed her secret, feminine lips, clutching his hair as her womb clenched and something hot and fierce leapt within her. He slid forward, nudging her back until he sat on the front edge of the seat, his hands on her hips, still holding her raised skirts clear. Then he pushed his legs between hers, forcing hers apart, and leaned back until his body stretched out before her. Beneath her.

Her intimate folds were swollen and wet and

ready and aching with need. Her heart hammered. Her chest rose and fell ever faster. She was wanton; desirable; *glorious*. The tip of his shaft touched her entrance. Adam's eyes were on her, watching, the flames leaping. His tongue snaked out to moisten his lips.

'Just lower yourself,' his voice rasped.

She did, her eyes locked on to his.

She sank down until he filled her. Stretching her. *Fulfilling* her.

She closed her eyes. And she closed her mind against the warnings clamouring to make themselves heard. At this moment, she did not care. For this moment, *any* risk was a risk worth taking. For now, her heart filled with joy as she began to move and as the sensations began to build within her. She propped her hands on his shoulders, feeling the edge of the bandage beneath her fingertips, reminding her not to grab at his arm. Her movements quickened and excitement bloomed and spread within her as she strained to reach the wonderful reward that she knew instinctively lay before her.

For now...*this* was everything.

Adam moved beneath her, thrusting up again and again in time with her own movements. His lips closed around her nipple and he sucked hard, then nipped. Her gasp feathered through the quiet of the library and her fingers clenched, grabbing folds of his shirt. Higher and higher she climbed, but that pinnacle stayed just out of reach until he reached between her legs and stroked that secret nub of flesh she hadn't even known existed.

She reached the edge and took flight, sucking in a huge lungful of air. Then his mouth covered hers, swallowing her cry as ecstasy pulsed through her, turning her entire body into a quivering, fluid mass. She collapsed against him, tearing her mouth from his as she panted, her energy spent as those ripples slowed, the spaces between them lengthened, and her brain scrambled to make sense of the conflicting emotions tumbling through her.

It was wonderful…she wanted to experience that all over again. And again.

And that scared her. No. It petrified her. Had she truly believed she could satisfy her curiosity and her lust so easily? As she steadied and those tumbling emotions quieted, the realisation growing that this was not enough, would never be enough…that she would always crave him, as long as he was near… *that* was what petrified her.

Could she cope with occasional liaisons until he decided to marry? Would that ever be enough for her? Could she still protect her heart?

She could no longer deny her love for Adam, but even if he had marriage in mind for their future—and even if she could find the courage to marry again—she could never accept him because she could not give him the heir he would need.

And though she loathed self-pity, the burn of tears at the back of her eyes told her she was in danger of wallowing in it. It seemed so unfair. She had always longed for a child of her own and now her barrenness would rob her of any chance of a future with Adam, doubling the torment of her failure as a woman as she added the loss of the man she loved to her childlessness.

But she must find the courage from somewhere to protect them both—her from the future agony that was now inevitable and him from the self-sacrifice of marrying a barren woman and living to regret it.

She lay still, snuggled into Adam's strong chest, safe for now in his embrace, reluctant to move and to face reality.

Chapter Seventeen

Adam hugged Kitty close, tucking her head into his shoulder as his chest heaved.

God! Dear God! Never...

He tightened his arms. He never wanted to let her go. She fit him so perfectly. He could stay like this for ever.

Gradually, though, the fear that someone might enter the library and catch them urged him to move. Even though they were hidden from the door by the screen it would be obvious what had taken place and Kitty did not deserve the gossip that would surely follow. Adam pressed his lips to her hair, breathing in the scent of her.

'We must move, my sweet.'

She snuggled closer for a minute, with a soft moan of protest, then pushed herself upright.

'Yes.'

Her obvious reluctance to move pleased him.

She slid from his knee and rose to her feet, smoothing her skirts before adjusting her clothing and making herself decent. Adam, too, stood. He buttoned the placket of his breeches as Kitty began to tidy her hair, gathering the scattered pins.

When she was decent, he took her hand and led her back to the table where the plans he had already drawn were spread out.

'I am sorry I did not withdraw, my darling,' he said. 'But, after all, it will not matter if there should be consequences... I can think of nothing more delightful than you, holding our baby in your arms.'

Kitty's face paled. 'I... Adam... I—'

She broke off as the door opened. Adam gave her a reassuring smile as he realised he had said nothing about marriage. He would soon remedy that, however, with a proper proposal such as she deserved. Although...he recalled her claim that she would never remarry and a voice of caution whispered that she might take some convincing that marriage was the right solution for them both.

'My apologies for the interruption, my lord.' Vincent entered, carrying a silver salver on which lay two letters. 'These have just been delivered from Kelridge Place.'

Adam frowned as he took the letters from Vincent and perused the direction on each of them.

'Who brought them? Is he still here?'

'He is, my lord. He gave his name as Carter. Your steward. He brought them himself in case you have any instructions for him. He is in the entrance hall.'

'Thank you. I shall read these and then speak to him.'

Vincent bowed and withdrew. Adam examined the letters again.

'This one is from my mother, but the other is an unfamiliar hand.'

He broke the seal on Ma's letter and read it quickly, then reread it, giving himself more time to digest her words.

> *My dearest Adam,*
> *Thank you for your letter. You can-*
> *not know what it means to me to have this*
> *chance to properly heal the rift between us.*
> *Since you left I have tortured myself, won-*
> *dering if I did the right thing in not fully*
> *explaining my actions over all these years.*
> *But, as I said before you left Edinburgh,*
> *I could not know if Kelridge had changed*
> *and I did not want to compound the harm*
> *I had already done by further damaging*
> *your opinion of your father. I am happy Bar-*
> *tholomew told you something of your fa-*
> *ther's character and, from what you wrote,*

it seems that even Grenville now accepts that Gerald was a violent man!

You ask why I settled for the life of a housekeeper when I was a lady. Well, at first I was terrified Kelridge would find us—because, of course, he had the legal right to take you from me and he would have done so, make no mistake. I could not allow that to happen. Not when his violence towards me had already spilled over into violence towards you. So, rather than keep house as Angus's widowed cousin, as he originally offered, I masqueraded as his housekeeper.

But, whatever my title, what I do is no more than I would do if I was Angus's unwed sister—I run his household and oversee the servants.

My experience of marriage killed any appetite for knowing any other man and Angus was and has always been a godsend to me—the brother I never had. I have been most content, I assure you. I have never been comfortable socialising—it was my father's ambition to see me marry into the aristocracy, not mine—and I am happy with my own company, as you know.

Thank you for your invitation to visit you at Kelridge Place. Not without some qualms, I accept. I thought to come next month and

I am looking forward to seeing how you are settled into your new role, although I am also a little apprehensive at meeting again with those people I knew from before.

I must also say, yes, of course you may pass on my address to Araminta—or Lady Datchworth I should say, I suppose. I remember her with some fondness, despite her outspokenness! It was useful to have a friend so full of confidence when I felt so awkward and diffident in my first and only Season. I shall look forward to meeting her again.

Adam—Angus would like to accompany me, if you are agreeable? I know you blame him as well for not telling you the truth, but you need to know that it was my decision to keep silent and that Angus had no choice but to respect my wishes.

I still feared your father, you see, even when you were a grown man. I feared his power to corrupt you. And, from the tales Angus heard about your father when you both worked on that job at Fenton Hall fifteen years ago, I was right to hold that secret.

I look forward to seeing you next month, Son.

Your proud and loving,
Mother

After Adam's second reading he looked up to find Kitty watching him, concern writ large on her face. She had regained her colour and he made a mental note to find out soon what she had been about to say when Vincent interrupted them.

'All is well,' he said and she smiled. 'My mother has accepted my invitation to come to Kelridge Place. Both she and Sir Angus will come next month and she writes that she hopes I have had enough time to settle into my new role.'

He huffed a laugh, shaking his head. 'I've made a poor job of that so far. I ought to have stayed and stamped my authority on the place and my staff.'

Instead of which, at the first opportunity I ran away.

He knew he ought to go back and begin work on setting things straight, but he couldn't leave Kitty. Not yet. It was too soon. He was certain in his own mind now that he wanted to marry her and, until that was settled, he would stay. He laid aside Ma's letter and broke the seal on the other. He quickly scanned the writing.

'Oh. It is from Tolly. He writes that he and my uncle are leaving Kelridge Place.' He read the date. 'It was written yesterday. Their intention was to leave before noon and to stay in London for a few days before travelling on to Brighton.'

Kitty frowned. 'Did he give a reason? Surely he does not mean they are leaving for good?'

'No, it is not permanent. He writes that he has persuaded my uncle that a breath of sea air would do them both good. And that it will give me the opportunity to take the reins at Kelridge Place.' He thrust his fingers through his hair, the news raising conflicting emotions. 'If they left on time, then neither of them could have shot at me.' Which was both a relief and a worry, for if it was not Grenville or Tolly, who could it have been? 'Of course, we cannae know that they *did* leave on schedule. And we also cannae know they did not divert their route to stop by here.'

'No. You are right. But, if they did so, then it must mean they were in it together.'

Adam prayed that would not prove to be the case. The news that his uncle and cousin were no longer at Kelridge Place presented him with a further dilemma, however, as he realised that now he *really* should go back. But he didn't want to. He wanted to stay with Kitty.

'I must complete these plans before I leave.'

Kitty half-turned from him, her shoulders tense. 'I am sure Robert will not object to a delay. Or you could take them with you and work on them at Kelridge Place.'

'I dinna want to leave ye,' he said. 'Not yet.'

Not ever!

Kitty faced him again. 'Do not fear I shall accuse you of seduction and abandonment, Adam.'

Her amused, slightly mocking tone brought a frown to his face. The Kitty, full of passion, who had writhed on his lap not fifteen minutes ago was now concealed behind a cool, distant mask and she was once again the Kitty he had met in London, but he had no idea why she had retreated behind her barrier. He'd thought it well and truly demolished, but here they were again with, seemingly, not a brick out of place.

'I did not imagine ye would,' he said, matching her light tone. 'If you will excuse me, I shall go now and speak to Carter.'

His skin heated under the cool appraisal of her grey gaze and his doubts and uncertainties about her...about what she truly thought and felt...intensified.

'Do not forget to ask what time your uncle and cousin left yesterday,' she said.

Adam strode from the room, his thoughts in turmoil.

Joseph Carter waited in entrance hall, his hat in his hands, under the watchful eye of Vincent.

'Might we use Lord Fenton's study, please?'

He could have bitten his tongue as he registered the hint of contempt in Vincent's tone as he replied, 'Of course, my lord.'

How many times had Lady Datchworth warned

him it was not done to speak to servants as though one was asking a favour, or to thank them for merely carrying out their duties? But being un-mannerly to *anyone* simply wasn't in his nature.

'Carter. This way.'

The steward followed him to the study.

'I was surprised to learn my uncle and cousin have left Kelridge Place. Was it a sudden deci-sion?'

'I believe so, milord.'

'What time did they leave?'

Carter's lips pursed as he pondered the ques-tion. Adam waited.

'About noon, I should say. I didn't take note of the exact time.'

'And I presume they travelled in the carriage?' At Carter's nod, Adam continued, 'My cousin made no mention of when they might return. Did they say anything to you, or to Green?'

'Not to me. Have you any instructions for me to convey back to the Place, milord?'

'Aye. I do. Please advise Mrs Ford that my mother and her cousin, Sir Angus McAvoy, will visit next month, so the work to refurbish the guest bedchambers needs to be completed as soon as possible.'

'Very good, milord.'

Adam frowned. 'Why is it you chose to deliver

the letters yourself, Carter? Surely a groom could have ridden over with them?'

'With the mast—that is, with Mr Trewin away, I thought I ought to report to you direct, milord. We lost some sheep yesterday. To poachers.'

'*Poachers?* How many sheep? When?'

'We can't be certain exactly when, milord, but Eddings found the remains of three beasts at the far edge of South Kell Wood. Soon after Mr Trewin and Mr Tolly left, it was. That was why the letters weren't delivered yesterday—we were looking for tracks and tryin' to work out what happened. It looks like they'd been shot, then butchered where they fell. The meat and fleeces were taken away. We found hoofprints.'

'No one heard the shots?'

He shook his head. 'If anyone heard them, they were far enough away for them to take no notice. They'd have been muffled by the woods, too.'

Adam frowned, his mind whirling. 'Was that before the thunderstorm yesterday?'

'It was, milord. Though me and Eddings got wet through riding back afterwards.'

'Very well. You were right to report this in person, Carter. Thank ye. You may get back now and please tell the men to keep a sharp lookout for any strangers hanging around.' Adam strode to the study door and out into the hall, leaving

Carter to follow. 'I shall return to Kelridge Place in a day or so.'

Carter bowed. As he exited the front door, Robert entered.

'Who was that?'

'My steward.'

Adam filled Robert in on both Tolly's news and the report of poachers as they walked to the library. Kitty was no longer there and Adam found himself unsurprised. Putting aside the fact that she desired him physically, she clearly still had reservations about him. He didn't fully understand why, though. He'd explained his reasoning in not agreeing to elope with her all those years ago and she had agreed he had done the right thing. If she had told him of her father's plan for her…well…yes, he probably would have found a way to rescue her. But she had not confided in him and he'd made his decision based on what he knew.

He'd find her. Try to talk to her. He needed to understand what was going on in her head.

'Poachers…' Robert frowned. 'That might put a different interpretation on what happened here yesterday, but let us concentrate on your uncle and Tolly first. They left Kelridge at noon, driving south, and their route to London would bring them close to Fenton Hall. But you were not attacked until much later.'

'They could have waited. In fact, whoever it was who shot me—if it was his *intention* to shoot me—must have hung around for some time.'

'But…the Kelridge carriage standing at the side of the road for that length of time…would they take such a risk? No. I cannot believe it.'

Adam sighed. 'Nor I. Plus, the culprit was on horseback. *If* those hoofprints you found belonged to him. Although—and I'm reluctant to even think this—if Grenville and Tolly *were* in it together, it is possible that one of them made the journey in the carriage while the other switched to horseback and rode on to Fenton land with the sole purpose of trying to kill me.'

His words repeated in his head, souring his stomach. 'I cannot credit that but, if there is any chance my uncle and cousin were to blame, that is the only scenario that fits the facts. Surely it must make more sense for it to be poachers after all. The argument that wildlife would take shelter with a thunderstorm approaching does not apply to sheep. *They* cannot take refuge in the undergrowth or in burrows and there *were* sheep in the meadow next to the woods, all huddled together with their backs to the rain.'

Robert paced the room. 'I'll be happier if we can fully eliminate Grenville and Tolly before we hang the blame entirely on poachers. I confess, I have never experienced poaching on that scale—

it sounds more like an organised gang than the work of a local poacher wanting a bit of meat for the pot.'

'Could ye send a man to make enquiries?' Adam said. 'I assume Grenville and Tolly are well known in the area—someone must have seen them pass and will be able to confirm at what time.'

'I'll do better than that,' Robert said. 'I shall go myself. I'll ride south and enquire at the toll houses. The carriage has the Kelridge crest on its doors, as I recall, so I'm sure they will be remembered. Hopefully the gatekeepers will remember the time they saw the carriage as well as confirm both men were inside.'

'I shall come with you.'

'No. Please do not. It will not take two of us and, although I know you must now feel obliged to return to the Place as soon as possible, I really do hope you can finish those plans first, Adam. It is important to me.'

Adam puzzled over that. Kitty had mentioned Robert had ideas of matrimony but, in consideration of the time it would take to build that new wing, what difference would a few extra days—or even weeks—make?

'Very well,' he said.

As it happened, Robert's words suited Adam, for his conscience demanded his immediate return to Kelridge Place and here was the perfect excuse to stay at Fenton Hall, the perfect excuse to stay near to Kitty and to use the time to persuade her to change her mind about remarrying. And if spending more time with Kitty meant those plans would take even longer to finish, then, so be it.

'I shall leave immediately,' Robert said. 'In fact, rather than ride, I shall drive my curricle. There is no time to lose…the sooner I leave, the more likely it is that the gatekeepers will recall Tolly and your uncle passing through. May I leave you to inform my stepmother? And do not worry should I fail to return tonight. I intend to make damned sure they did not leave a false trail and double back.'

'It sounds as though you are enjoying this, Rob.'

Robert grinned. 'Oh, I am. I love a mystery to solve. And if, as I hope, we find that Grenville and Tolly could *not* have shot you, then I am sure we will all breathe a sigh of relief.'

He strode from the library, calling to his valet to pack an overnight bag. Adam—furnished with the perfect excuse—asked Vincent where he might find Lady Fenton.

'She is in her sitting room, my lord. But she asked most particularly not to be disturbed.'

Adam wanted to see her now. Right away. But

a sly inner voice reminded him that if he told her too soon, before Robert left, she might very well persuade her stepson he must return that evening. The prospect of dinner with just Kitty for company, not to mention the entire evening together, was simply too enticing. He could wait to see Kitty until Robert had safely left the Hall—there was no need to disturb her rest.

'Very well, Vincent. I shall be in the library. Please let me know when Lady Fenton is available.'

He lasted half an hour after Robert left the house. The Hall was quiet, the silence weighing down on him as he quit the library. He knew where Kitty's sitting room was…and there was no sign of Vincent to disapprove of or prevent Adam disturbing his mistress. He climbed the stairs, then hesitated outside the sitting-room door. It was quiet within. He wondered if she was sleeping, but he convinced himself Kitty would want to know of Robert's plan. He put his ear to the door and heard a faint scratching noise. He pressed the door handle down and eased the door open until the gap was wide enough for his head. Just one peep.

Kitty sat at a table in front of the window, her back to the door. Not asleep, then, but writing. Letters, he presumed. He tapped on the door. She started. Glanced over her shoulder, her eyes somehow vague, shadowed by low, bunched brows. Then her expression cleared. She coloured, pushed her chair back and leapt to her feet. She stood with her back to the table, which he could now see was littered with dozens of sheets of paper covered in writing.

Adam frowned. 'What are ye doing?'

Her nostrils flared. 'Waiting for you to tell me why you are here. I left strict instructions I was not to be disturbed.'

'I am aware of it. I assumed you were resting and, had that been the case, I would have quietly withdrawn.'

'What can I do for you, Lord Kelridge?'

Adam's brows shot up. 'Kitty? What is it? Why am I suddenly Lord Kelridge once again? Do ye... are ye...?' He stopped. Sucked in a deep breath as he recalled her earlier coolness. 'Kitty. Do ye regret what we did?'

She stared at him silently for several moments. Then she gave him a rueful smile. 'I have no regrets.'

Adam waited for her to elaborate, wondering what was going through her head. What it would mean for him.

'I am sorry for my reaction,' she went on. 'You startled me. My mind was...elsewhere.' She walked towards him. He grabbed the opportunity to look at her table again, but he was no clearer about what she was up to. If she was writing letters, there were a great many of them. Unless…

'Kitty. Are ye writing a novel?'

'And if I am?'

Adam shook his head. 'Well…nothing, really. You are entitled to do as ye please. Does Robert know?'

'He does.'

'And he approves?'

'He does not disapprove.' Her tone suggested that she would not care even if he did.

'Will ye tell me about it?'

She glanced back at the table, then looked at him. 'No. I would rather not.'

She sounded defensive and he recalled their conversation about novels. What had he said? He could not remember, but he hoped he had not given the impression he disapproved of such books. Even though, if he were honest, he thought them a waste of valuable time.

'Now, if you will excuse me, Adam… I have reached a critical point of the story and I do not wish to lose the thread of my narrative. Did you come here for a particular reason?'

'Ah. Yes.' He hesitated. 'But it will wait until you have finished writing. I'm sorry to have disturbed ye.'

Her eyes softened. 'And—again—I am sorry

for my reaction. I tend to get over-involved in my story and my characters are currently in the middle of an argument. The mood can spill over into real life at times, until I have adjusted from my fictional world to the actual world.'

She tucked her bottom lip between her teeth, looking contrite and far younger than her thirty-two years. Tenderness, spiced with lust, welled up inside Adam. He reached for her hand and raised it to his lips.

'I shall leave you in peace.'

'No. Wait. You wanted to talk to me…have there been any developments?'

Adam smiled at her. 'It will wait. We will talk later.'

Chapter Eighteen

The door clicked shut behind Adam, leaving Kitty staring abstractedly at the space where he had been. Her mind whirled, but she found no solution to her conundrum. Their relationship had changed and, whether she willed it or no, she had opened her heart to more pain. It was inevitable. Adam had spoken no words of love. Neither had he mentioned marriage, but the implication had been there, cutting her to the quick.

She loved him. She could no longer lie to herself. And that terrified her because nothing could ever come of it. There was Charis to consider. And Robert. And…

She growled low in her throat as she acknowledged the real reason there could *never* be a happy ever after for her and Adam. Children. Babies. *An heir.* She was barren and Adam was now Earl of Kelridge, and all noblemen needed an heir to follow them, to care for their estates and provide security and a living for their tenants and for the many local craftsmen who depended upon a thriving 'big house' in their neighbourhood.

I can think of nothing more delightful than you holding our baby in your arms.

Those words had flayed her, bringing harsh reality to the fore after she had successfully banished all thought of the future from her mind. And if he were to ask her to marry him, what reason could she give for a refusal? How could she tell him the truth—speak out loud those brutal, final words *I am barren*—without falling apart in front of him? How could she bear his sympathy or, worse, his pity? And what if he *still* felt obliged to urge her to marry him, even when he knew the truth? A man such as he might see it as a matter of honour. He might break down her resistance. And he would be stuck in a childless marriage and would come to resent her...blame her.

And that she could not bear.

Feeling sick, she turned back to the table. She would lose herself in her work once again and worry about Adam later. But, mere minutes later, she slammed down the quill in frustration, causing ink to fly and speckle the nearby sheets of paper. The magic was lost. Her head was full of Adam. And her heart was full of that pain she had so carefully protected herself from all these years. She pushed back her chair and went in search of Adam.

'He has gone to the stables, milady.'

She recalled his plan to ride out that afternoon. 'Is Lord Fenton with him?'

'No, milady. His Lordship is driving to…well, he is driving *towards* London.'

'*London?*'

Vincent lowered his voice. 'His Lordship did confide in me before he left, milady. After the occurrence yesterday, and the letter Lord Kelridge received, His Lordship is determined to track the movement of the Messrs Trewin yesterday. Gresham has gone with him and they hope to ascertain at what times the Kelridge carriage passed through the toll gates. His Lordship did say he may not return tonight and Lord Kelridge would have informed you immediately but—as you instructed me no one was to disturb you—I asked him to wait.'

'I see.' But Adam had come anyway, knowing she would want to know Robert's plans. And she'd given him no chance to tell her. 'Thank you. And Lord Kelridge has gone to the stables, you say? With the intention of riding out, even after what happened yesterday?'

'I did try to reason with him, milady. But he was in no mood to listen.'

And that is my fault.

Her first reaction had been dazed, as it always was when she was interrupted in the middle of a scene in which she was fully immersed. But afterwards…she ought to have insisted on knowing why he had interrupted her.

'Very well. Send word to the stables to saddle Herald, will you please? And if His Lordship has not already left, ask him to wait for me to join him. I shall change into my riding clothes right away.'

'Milady… I do not think—'

Kitty, already on the fourth stair, paused. 'Vincent. You are not paid to think. Now do as I ask without further ado. Please.'

The butler executed his stiffest bow before stalking towards the back of the house. Kitty ran upstairs and to her bedchamber to change into her riding gown, her heart pounding with fear.

Within ten minutes, she was clattering down the stairs again. She grabbed her leather riding gloves and crop from a stony-faced Vincent and hurried out of the already open front door. Davey, one of the grooms, waited outside, holding the reins of both Herald, Kitty's chestnut gelding, and a brown gelding that went by the uninspiring name of Brownie.

'His Lordship left word that one of us must

accompany you if you go out, milady.' Davey touched his cap. 'On fear of dismissal if we don't follow his order *to the letter.*'

'Very well, Davey. I understand.'

Normally she insisted on riding alone—it gave her imagination the perfect opportunity to wander. But normally there was absolutely no danger. She remained on Fenton land and Robert trusted her to do so. She couldn't fault such an order after yesterday and it would be unfair to blame Davey for following his master's instructions.

The groom cupped his hands to help her mount. As she gathered the reins and settled into the saddle, she said, 'Had Lord Kelridge already ridden out when my message reached the stables?'

'Yes, milady. About quarter of an hour since.'

'And did anyone accompany him?'

'Yes, milady.'

Kitty breathed a little easier.

'He told us he would head up to Fenton Edge.'

'Then let us go.'

They rode at a fast trot, breaking into a canter where they could, and before long they saw two riders ahead of them, heading up a track over the heathland that led to the Edge, an escarpment with views over the relatively flatter land to the north—a view that included Kelridge Place and its parkland. Before long, Adam halted and looked back, presumably alerted by the thud of horses coming up at speed behind him. His hand had already withdrawn a pistol from his pocket and more relief flooded Kitty that he had at least come prepared.

When they drew to a halt, Adam's expression was as menacing as yesterday's thunderclouds. His horse—a piebald gelding called Jester—danced sideways, made skittish by his rider's clear annoyance.

'Why are ye here?'

Kitty, somewhat breathless from their fast pace, ignored him to speak to Dexter—Adam's companion and second in rank to Gresham in the hierarchy of the stable yard.

'Kindly drop back with Davey, will you, Dexter? And stay alert for anyone else in the area.'

Dexter, a man of few words, nodded and touched his cap. The two grooms held their horses still as Kitty nudged Herald into a walk. Adam, audibly grumbling—although she couldn't make out his words—followed, ranging his mount alongside hers.

'Why are ye here?' His demand was quiet, but no less forceful. 'He could be out there anywhere.'

'Precisely! And *I* am not his target. Or so we agreed yesterday. Why are you putting yourself at such risk? What do you hope to achieve by this… this act of stu—bravado?'

'Ye shouldna have come.' His tone milder now. 'I can look after myself, but you…'

She glanced up at him. His stern profile as he stared straight ahead. The tightness of his lips and the frown that creased his forehead.

'But I…?'

His lips quirked then, in a brief smile, and he flicked a sideways look at her before turning his attention once again to their surroundings.

'Ye're a terrible distraction and ye ken it. How am I meant to concentrate when your scent is weaving through ma senses, firing ma blood?'

Her heart thumped at his words. As if she wasn't already hot enough after that ride. 'Why, Lord Kelridge…' she strove to keep her tone light '… I never imagined that gruff exterior concealed such a poetic soul. You kept that well hidden.'

He smiled at her. Such a sweet smile. 'I canna help it, lass. You have that effect on me…ye're a woman to turn any man inside out.'

The track they were following up the gentle southern slope of the Edge petered out as they reached the open land at the top. Kitty reined in and twisted to look all around. There was no sign of life other than a few sheep grazing the sparse, coarse grassland on the top. Adam pointed.

'There. That is Kelridge Place. My new home—' he pointed at a speck in the distance, a light-coloured cube that perched on a rise in the land '—and that is the boundary—that woodland. South Kell Wood.'

Kitty had never been to Kelridge Place even though there was only six miles between it and Fenton Hall.

'Ye canna see it very well at this distance, I ken, but after what Carter told me I felt the need tae come and see it for myself.'

'What did Carter tell you?'

She'd never even thought to ask him earlier about the steward's visit and now she listened as Adam told her about the sheep that had been shot and butchered.

'But…is that not good news? Oh, not for the poor sheep, or that they have been stolen from you. But does it not support the theory that poachers shot you by mistake? And is that not better than believing the worst of your uncle and cousin?'

'Well, aye. Of course it is.'

'But I do not understand why Robert has gone haring off after Mr Trewin and Tolly.'

'We need to be certain, Kitty. It is no use our lowering our guard on a supposition. Rob will, I hope, find the evidence to confirm it was impossible for either my uncle or my cousin to have fired that gun. And, in the meantime, he has ordered the men to keep watch and even to patrol the outer reaches of the estate to look out for strangers or for further attempts to steal sheep.'

'That makes sense, I suppose.'

Kitty stared across to the distant Kelridge Place, the knot of fear in her stomach easing for the first time since the shooting. But she was still burdened—not by fear, but by anxiety. There was still the conundrum of what the future held for her and Adam. She had made matters worse by succumbing to her desires and was unsure how to handle what their relationship was now and what it might become.

'Are you pleased with the turn your life has taken, Adam? Is it what you want?'

'I wasna happy. At first. I admit it.' He shifted restlessly in the saddle, then dismounted. 'Will you walk with me?'

He lifted his arms to Kitty. She put her hands on his shoulders as he grasped her waist and lifted her from the saddle.

'Dexter. You and Davey hold these two, will you?' she called. 'His Lordship and I wish to stretch our legs.'

The grooms rode over and dismounted, taking control of Herald and Jester.

'Lord Fenton said—'

'Have no fear, Dexter,' Kitty interrupted the groom's concern. 'We will not go out of your sight. I promise. And we will remain alert.'

She laid her hand on Adam's arm and they strolled across to the edge of the escarpment.

'I adore this view,' Kitty said. 'I love that you can see for miles. It is worth the climb just to enjoy it.'

Adam tipped his head to one side and eyed her as he laughed.

'Why is that so funny?'

'It is clear you havena travelled over-much, Kitty, my love.'

Her heart clenched at the endearment. She could never be his love—not fully, not legitimately—even if he meant it.

'I have been to London. I know that must seem nothing to you, but I love my home and my family. I have never looked to travel away from them.'

'I didna mean that. I laughed at your calling this a climb. This, dearest Kitty, is but a pimple compared with the hills and mountains of the north.' He paused. 'And of bonnie Scotland,' he added in a wistful tone.

'So you do have regrets about the change in your life?'

'Some.' His arm flexed, squeezing her hand into his side. 'But they become less important by the day.'

He halted, capturing her gaze with his, raising a quiver of awareness as she recognised the fire smouldering in his blue eyes. She tugged his arm to keep him moving. 'Do not forget we are being watched.'

They strolled on, their pace slow, their eyes on the view, their attention on one another.

'I should like you to see Scotland, Kitty. The rugged mountains and glens of the Highlands. Edinburgh, with its castle towering over the city. The rolling hills and lochs of the Lowlands and the border country.'

'I have seen paintings and illustrations. It does look magnificent.'

'Aye, it is. But ye canna fully comprehend just how magnificent without seeing it with your own eyes, breathing the scent of the heather and feeling the caress of the air over your skin.'

That wistfulness was even more evident. Robert had speculated that Adam might not be content to make Kelridge Place his permanent home... that he had spoken of returning to Edinburgh and leaving his steward in charge of his estates. But Kitty had no wish to remind him of that, so she resolved to lead his thoughts away from Scotland and any homesickness. There might be no chance of marriage between them but, if he made his home at Kelridge Place, she would at least still meet him on occasion.

They might even have an *affaire*. They would have to be discreet. No one could know. She could not risk any hint of scandal tainting either Charis or Rob, but she was a widow, after all, and widows were allowed a certain amount of licence. A thrill ran through her, raising gooseflesh.

'Vincent said Robert might not return home tonight.'

'That is true. It depends, I would think, on how quickly he can establish whether or not my kinsmen could have been at Fenton Hall yesterday afternoon at the time I was shot.'

Is it so wrong that I hope Rob will *be forced to spend the night away from home?*

She ought to feel ashamed…*shocked*…by such a hope. But she did not.

'I suppose,' Adam said, slowly, 'we shall have to amuse ourselves if he does not come home.'

Their gazes fused again. Kitty swallowed. 'I suppose we will.'

Robert was not home by the time dinner was served. Kitty had never felt so on edge. She ate her meal, but she took no notice of the food as she chewed and swallowed. She did not look at her plate to see what she was eating and paid no attention to taste.

She could not tear her attention from Adam, seated opposite her.

Every mouthful, every look, every word spoken fuelled the fire that smouldered deep in her belly. Every sip of wine, as their eyes locked over the rim of their glasses, sent sparks sizzling through her veins. Finally it was over, and they rose from their chairs.

'Would you care to bring your brandy to the salon, my lord? There is no need to sit here alone.' Her voice, somehow, sounded utterly normal.

'Thank you, my lady. I will do that.'

'I shall not stay up late,' she continued as they left the dining room, for the benefit of Vincent and the other servants within earshot. They headed towards the salon, side by side. 'I find I am tired after a restless sleep last night. And you, I make no doubt, must also be weary.'

'I am.'

'Vincent, have the tea tray brought in as soon as it can be arranged, please.'

'Yes, milady.'

Somehow, as they walked towards the salon, side by side, Adam's hand found Kitty's. Strong fingers stroked her inner wrist, her palm and the length of her fingers. She stifled her gasp, but closed her fingers around his for the briefest caress before he moved his hand away.

'I doubt Robert will return at this late hour,' Adam continued. 'I will keep ye company while ye drink your tea, then I shall retire.'

Less than an hour later, Kitty was ready for bed. She dismissed Effie and then, after a moment's thought, she stripped off her plain cotton nightgown. In her chest of drawers, she found what she sought—a white silk nightgown, trimmed with lace, its neckline threaded with green ribbon. She pulled it on and regarded her reflection in the cheval mirror. She had bought it shortly after she'd married Edgar. It had never been worn. She had quickly realised that although there was affection and regard within their marriage, there was no romance. And little lust. The marital act had been perfunctory and had, invariably, taken place in the dark. And she had failed in her duty as a wife. Failed to get with child. But thank God—as Edgar had reminded her on a monthly basis—he already had his heir and spare in Robert and Edward.

Resolutely, Kitty cast Edgar from her thoughts and considered the lit candle by her bedside. Although it was still twilight outside, the curtains were drawn and the room was dark. Would he come to her? She thought he would and, when he did, she wanted to be prepared. She took her bed candle and used it to light the pair of candles standing on the narrow mantelshelf over the unlit fireplace, and another on her dressing table, its flame reflected by the mirror hung on the wall behind. Then she replaced her bed candle and climbed into bed to wait, ruthlessly quashing all thought of the future, all doubt, any whisper of heartache. For now, she would simply enjoy Adam and allow nothing to spoil this time together.

Before long there was a tap at the door and it opened a crack. Adam just looked at her, raising his brows. Kitty smiled and nodded. He came in, closing the door behind him, then turned the key in the lock.

They needed no words.

Touch, smell and taste dominated as they learned one another without haste and as they discovered how to give—and how to receive—pleasure.

As dawn broke, Adam embraced Kitty, stroking her hair back from her face as he peppered kisses over her forehead, eyebrows, eyelids, nose and cheeks, finally taking her lips in a long, slow dreamy kiss.

'Sleep now,' he whispered. 'I shall see you later.'

Chapter Nineteen

'Good morning, Adam. I hope you slept well?'

Kitty entered the parlour as Adam broke his fast the following morning, a smile stretching her lips. Adam's pulse quickened at the memory of those lips and their exploration of his body, and blood rushed to his groin. He cleared his throat.

'I had a wonderful night, thank ye, Ki—Catherine. And a very good morning to ye, too.'

Kitty sat opposite Adam and the footman in attendance filled her coffee cup.

'May I serve you with some food, my lady?'

'Not now, Terence. But I shall want more coffee—is there enough in the pot?'

'I shall go and fetch more, milady.'

The footman left the parlour, closing the door behind him. Adam caught Kitty's gaze.

'Are ye not hungry?'

She sipped from her cup and then set it down on the saucer before replying.

'I was,' she said. 'But I satisfied my appetite in bed.' Those fascinating dimples appeared, squeezing his heart. 'Effie brought me chocolate and rolls this morning before I arose.'

'Tease!' Adam had emptied his plate and pushed it aside.

Kitty raised a brow. 'Do I take it you are now replete?'

'Oh, indeed. Fully satisfied, in fact.'

The door opened and Terrence returned, carrying the coffeepot.

'Until the next meal,' Adam continued, allowing his gaze to lower to Kitty's breasts before returning to her mischief-filled eyes. 'I find my... um...appetite somewhat stimulated recently.' He patted his stomach. 'I shall have to ensure I do not gain too much weight.'

'Oh, you ought not to be overconcerned.' Kitty's lips pressed together, suppressing her smile. 'My advice, if you are concerned about your weight, is to take plenty of exercise. You may then indulge your appetite to your heart's content.'

Adam drained his coffee cup and gestured to Terence for a refill.

'Thank ye,' he said. He didn't bother to notice if Terence responded adversely to his thanks. He'd made his mind up he would no longer strive to be something he was not and he would start now. And when he returned to Kelridge Place, if his staff disapproved, then he would employ men and women who were more amenable to his ways.

'Thank ye for your advice, Catherine. And, to demonstrate my attention to your sage advice, I intend to take a walk around the gardens after breakfast, before I continue working on the drawings for the new wing. Would ye care to accompany me?'

'Why, thank you, Adam. I accept.'

The presence of gardeners prevented anything other than the most innocuous of conversations as they strolled, but it felt good to have Kitty on his arm.

'How soon will you complete the plans for the Hall?'

'Is that a subtle way of enquiring how soon I will leave?'

She lightly pinched his arm. 'You *know* that is not what I meant. I wondered how much longer we shall have the pleasure of your company, that is all.'

'I should think they will be finished in a couple of days.'

It was a fib. He *could* finish them today if he pushed himself. But reluctance to leave Kitty made him inclined to drag the job out. Except…

'I do know I *ought* to return to the Place as soon as possible, especially after those sheep were poached. But, also, I have a lot to learn and now would be the ideal time, with Grenville absent. The servants will have no choice but to refer matters to me first, rather than through ma uncle.'

'Would you rather complete the drawings at Kelridge Place? That way you can return sooner, if you think you should.'

But...he wanted to stay with Kitty. His hopes were high...he was *almost* sure she felt the same for him as he did for her. And yet...there was still a caution there...a reserve. Odd, after yesterday and after the night they had just spent together. Her body expressed love, but her mind...she still seemed reluctant to allow that breakthrough. She was holding back, reining in her emotions. And he didn't understand why. They were both adults. Both single. Did she think Robert might object? Or her other stepchildren?

No, he would not rush to complete his work. He needed to stay here and try to finally breach that barrier surrounding her heart.

It was early afternoon by the time Robert returned.

'Well, you may clear your uncle and cousin of any wrongdoing,' he said without preamble as he strode into the library.

Adam put down his pencil as Robert pulled a chair up to the table where he was working on the plans.

'What did ye find out?'

Robert shook his head. 'Wait a moment. I have asked Stepmama to join us—it will save me repeating myself.' He grinned at Adam and raised his brows. 'I trust you contrived to entertain yourselves last night without my scintillating repartee to make the evening fly?'

'You were sorely missed, my friend.'

Robert laughed. 'Very droll.'

Puzzled, Adam ran the conversation through his head again. Was Robert hinting that he was aware of the attraction that had simmered between Adam and Kitty ever since they met again in London, or was that merely an innocent quip? It was hardly something he could ask him—do you mean did your stepmother and I take advantage of your absence to indulge in bed sport? He was relieved when Kitty came in, saving him from trying to bluster his way through an awkward moment.

'Rob!' Kitty hurried across the room and embraced her stepson. 'What happened?'

'It was not them. It could not possibly have been them. We tracked them all the way to Highgate and the gatekeeper confirmed they passed and kept going towards London. Both Grenville and Tolly were present at each tollgate and there were no unexplained delays in their journey. They are innocent.'

Adam had been unaware of the tension that gripped him until it dissolved.

'I am verra relieved,' he said. 'And it surely now points to poachers such as those who struck at Kelridge Place. I wonder if there have been any other incidences in the area.'

'I did enquire at a few inns we passed—and we passed Datchworth on the road as we drove home, and I asked him, too—but no one has heard stories of an increase in poachers in the district. Nor is there any whisper of organised gangs. I think that is the most likely explanation, however. What is your opinion?'

'I think the same. And I am mightily relieved. I have nae wish to spend my life looking over my shoulder.'

'The men have reported no suspicious sightings around the estate,' Robert went on, 'but I have ordered them to stay on the alert.'

'But…what about when you return to the Place, Adam?' Kitty said. 'It might not be poachers. Just because your uncle cannot have pulled the trigger himself does not mean he did not give the order.'

'Nae. It is one thing for a man to attempt to kill another for his own sake. I canna credit that any man would do so at the bidding of another.'

'You would be surprised what many men will do for money, Adam,' said Robert. 'But… I know Grenville Trewin. He was a cavalryman—he has killed before, albeit during battle. But if he wanted something done, he would do it himself. He is no sneaksby.'

'I am inclined to agree with ye, Rob. If it were my uncle, he would more likely do it to my face.'

'Well, we have done all we can for now. Tell me, how are those plans coming along?' Robert slid one around until it faced him and bent over it. 'This looks complete.'

Adam cursed silently. He had told Kitty a couple of days and now he could feel her eyes on him. He looked at her, noting the crease between her brows. With Robert's return he would not have the luxury of time to court her and to persuade her to rethink her objection to remarrying. Her reasons for not marrying again—the ones she had listed during their dance at Almacks—well…if Robert intended to wed, and if Charis found a husband, she had already told him she would re-move to the Dower House. Her other interests—she must have referred to her writing. Well, he would not interfere with that. And her final ob-jections—neither need nor desire to remarry… surely last night must have given her reason to think again?

'If you will excuse me, gentlemen, I shall leave you to it,' Kitty said and left the library.

Adam sighed in resignation as he suppressed his urge to follow her. He switched his attention to the plans.

'We do need to discuss some of the finishing touches still.'

'Ah. That sounds as though you will need me here. In which case, might we leave it until to-morrow? My bed was so lumpy last night I barely slept a wink and my brain is far too foggy to pay proper attention to detail.'

'Of course it can wait until tomorrow.'

Robert grinned and slapped Adam on the back. 'Good man! I'll see you at dinner. I'm off out to attend to estate matters.'

He strode to the door leaving Adam wondering what had prompted Robert to lie, for he appeared nothing like a man who had missed a night's sleep and, until that very moment, had been perfectly alert.

Still…grateful for the reprieve, he went in search of Kitty. She was nowhere in the house or the gardens. At the stable yard, however, he learned from Dexter that she had ridden out. Alone.

'She refused to allow anyone to accompany her, my lord,' the groom said when Adam ques-tioned him. 'And being as it was you that was shot at and she has always ridden alone on Fenton land... Well.' He shrugged. 'What could we do?'

'Did she say where she was heading?'

'No, milord, but she went in that direction.' He pointed. It was the same direction Adam had taken yesterday. Towards Fenton Edge.

'Saddle Jester, will ye please, Dexter?'

'Very well, milord.'

It was the reverse of the day before. Adam set off at a fast trot, heading for the heath and Fenton Edge. This time, it was he chasing Kitty and his doubts about her feelings for him eased as he recalled her anger when she had caught him up yesterday—anger that had been fuelled by her worry for his safety. Anger that proved she cared for him. Hell, her every touch, every caress proved she cared. She was not the sort of female who would give her body without having *some* feelings for her lover.

They reached the beginning of the heath and he urged Jester into a canter. The horse's stride lengthened willingly and he soon flattened into a gallop. Of course, Adam couldn't be certain Kitty would head for the Edge, but instinct told him she would. If she felt anything like he did, she would yearn for the chance to gallop up that long, gentle slope that led to the top.

Jester slowed as they reached the top and the ground levelled. There was Herald, tied to a bush.

And there was Kitty, her back to Adam as she gazed north. She hadn't noticed their approach and his worry gave way to anger of his own. He leapt from the saddle, tied Jester to the same bush and strode across the open ground to where Kitty stood.

'Kitty.'

He spoke before he reached her, not wanting to startle her, but she jumped anyway and spun around, her cheeks pale.

'Oh! You frightened me!'

Adam's chest swelled as he held in his temper. 'I did not mean to, but it proves how vulnerable ye are up here alone. I could have been anyone.'

She shook her head. 'Yes. You could have been. But you are not. I have been riding up here alone for fifteen years, Adam. There is no danger.' She tipped her head to one side. 'Why have you followed me?'

'We need to talk.'

Her grey eyes searched his and then a smile of resignation curved her lips. As though she knew what he would say and was solidly certain of her own reply. That smile gave Adam pause…what if he waited? If he didn't give voice to his hopes… his heart's desire…then she could not refuse him. His feelings had grown steadily since they met again and he now knew with absolute certainty that what he felt for Kitty was love…he had loved her fifteen years ago and he loved her now and he wanted her in his future. To keep silent about his feelings was the coward's way and so, even though his confidence balanced on a knife's edge, he hauled in a deep breath and took a leap of faith.

'Kitty…ye must ken how I feel about you. I love you.'

Her eyes closed, as though she were in pain, and she shook her head slowly from side to side. Adam gathered her hands in his, squeezing, as though to impress his words upon her.

'I know you have feelings for me. Ye canna disguise them, ye know, even though you try. I *love* you, Kitty, my darling. I want to spend the rest of my life with you.

'Kitty…will ye marry me?'

She shook her head again. 'No, Adam.' She opened her eyes. 'I do not have feelings for you. Not in the way you mean. I cannot marry you.'

Cannot…not will not.

He gazed into her eyes, chasing after hope, clinging to belief. 'You are as stubborn as ever. And as…adorable.'

Her eyes sheened.

'What have I said? I thought… Kitty… I dinna understand ye. Tell me why not—ye canna deny you were as eager as me last night.'

Kitty sighed. 'No. I cannot deny that.'

His heart leapt.

She gave a helpless shrug before gently disentangling her hands from his. 'When I cannot deny I was eager, Adam, I am speaking of lust. Pure and simple. A physical need that we both felt... a natural urge for adults such as we are now. It does not mean I have any wish to rekindle a...a... an *emotional* relationship. That is not on offer.'

He stilled. 'Not on offer?' He thrust his hand through his hair. 'Then let us understand one another. You were willing to give your body to me, but ye willna give me your hand in marriage? No!' The word burst from his lips. Disbelief battled with pain. 'I canna believe...ye will truly refuse me, after last night? And dinna tell me ye have no emotional feelings for me, for I shall not believe you!'

'It is for the best.'

Regret shone in her eyes, contradicting her words, leaving him even more confused. How could she expect him to believe she did not love him? Her body could not lie so convincingly. Could it?

'Adam. I *told* you I have sworn never to marry again. I have never pretended that is what I wanted from you.'

He stared at her in disbelief as her words ripped his heart. Tears burned behind his eyes and he blinked to keep them at bay.

'Adam... I cannot admit to a desire for you

other than physical, but… I am a widow. If we are discreet, surely we may indulge our passions from time to time?' Her hands clutched his and then, just as quickly, released them. 'Think about it. Please. Before you, I have been intimate with no man other than my late husband and your touch has awoken a strange force in me…an urge that I long to explore.' Her hands gripped one another before her, her knuckles white. Her chin rose as she sucked in a deep breath. 'If my offer is unacceptable to you, however, then we shall forget this conversation ever took place and we may each get on with our own lives.'

Adam's throat ached with the effort of holding tears back, his heart leaden even though her offer—her body with no strings attached—would surely be most men's idea of heaven. But it was not enough for him. He wanted all of her, mind and body and soul. He wanted the essence of her. To live with her and to see her every day of his life.

'I canna accept such an offer, Kitty. I shall never be content with the occasional loan of your body…how can I bear to live so close to ye and yet not see ye every day? How can I bear not to have the right to hold ye in my arms every night?'

Her grey eyes were stricken. 'You will not return to Scotland, though?' Her voice was little more than a whisper.

'I dinna ken.' Again, he thrust his hand through his hair, holding his emotions in check by a mere thread. 'In a straight choice between you and Scotland, ye win every time. But now… if I canna have ye…' His voice cracked and he cleared his throat to add, 'I still canna believe ye truly mean it, Kitty.'

He trusted himself to say no more. He pivoted on his heel and strode away from Kitty, his vision blurred by tears and his only thought to return to Kelridge Place as soon as he could.

Chapter Twenty

Kitty swallowed desperately as the pressure of tears built in her throat. She bit back the near-overwhelming urge to call Adam back, to reassure him of her love for him, to ease some of his pain. But she did not, for she must still refuse to marry him.

What choice do I have?

Even if she could find the courage to speak of her barrenness, Adam would no doubt claim it made no difference—and maybe it would not, at first. But it would. Eventually. She was convinced of it. Every peer of her acquaintance was obsessed with one thing and that was to sire a son to continue his line and to succeed him to his title. And Adam had already spoken of the joy of their own baby.

Her way was surely better. Once Adam calmed down, he would see they could enjoy one another's company discreetly and no one need ever know. It would be safer for her to continue with her contented life with Robert and Charis, and her writing. If she allowed Adam to persuade her to wed him, she could not bear to see his regard for her slowly turn to resentment as her failure to conceive eroded his love for her and he grew to realise exactly what that meant to him and to the earldom.

Adam had not hesitated in his stride. Kitty watched with heaviness in her heart and tears in her eyes as he reached the horses, untied Jester, leapt into the saddle and raced off down the slope.

When she had arrived home, Vincent had informed her that Lord Kelridge was at work in the library and, that evening, Kitty and Robert were both seated at the dining table before Adam put in an appearance.

'My apologies for my tardiness,' he said. 'I became engrossed in my work and lost track of the time. Rob... I have finished the plans. I would appreciate it if we might meet early tomorrow to go over them. After the news Carter brought, I have decided I must no longer neglect my duty and must return to the Place as soon as possible.'

'Of course,' said Rob.

He caught Kitty's eye and frowned at her. Unable to interpret what that frown signified, Kitty did not respond and instead she began to drink the white soup placed before her. Although she and Robert did their best, the conversation that evening was strained, and it was with some relief that Kitty rose to withdraw. When Robert joined her in the salon only ten minutes later, he said that Adam was feeling unwell and had gone to bed early.

'Do you know what has upset him?'

Kitty started at Robert's bald question and she wilfully misunderstood his meaning.

'I have not the slightest idea—it cannot be anything he ate, for neither you nor I are unwell. I am sure he will be recovered by morning.' She stood. 'However, I am also very tired and, if you will excuse me, I, too, will retire early.'

She willed herself not to blush at Robert's quizzical stare and, after Effie had left her, she wondered if Adam might come to her room, if only to talk. But he did not, and she had too much pride to go to him uninvited.

The next morning, Adam had gone by the time Kitty went downstairs and, although the news was no surprise, she none the less had to blink back the tears that he had not even said goodbye.

But what did I expect? He has his pride. And I had no choice—this has to be for the best.

She had repeated that refrain countless times through the night, reminding herself of Adam's words, just two days ago. *'I can think of nothing more delightful than you holding our baby in your arms.'*

That could never happen. But her heart was breaking. What if he went back to Scotland? She might never see him again…could she bear that? *Should* she have told him the truth?

'Stepmama?' Robert popped his head around the parlour door where Kitty lingered over her coffee. 'Would you come to my study when you are finished here, please?'

It had taken Kitty some time to get her emotions under control. When she felt more secure, she went to Robert's study, where he sat at his desk, and sat opposite him.

'May I tell you a story, Stepmama?'

'Of course.' She tried a joke. 'Does it begin with once upon a time?'

'As it happens, it does.' Robert stood then and stared out of the window, his back to Kitty, arms folded. 'There once was a boy who had lost his mother in the worst way imaginable.' His voice quivered a little, confirming he spoke of himself. Kitty knew the story, from both him and from Edgar. How they had battled to save Robert's mother from the fire. 'And he felt lost. Then a young man came to stay and he was kind to the boy, who looked up to him as his hero, because he took him fishing but, mainly, because he spent time talking to the lad—unlike the boy's father who had withdrawn into himself. But, sometimes, the young man would disappear and the boy felt hurt. Abandoned. So, one day, the boy followed the young man into the woods.'

Kitty gasped. Robert turned to face her.

'You saw us?'

Robert nodded.

'Why did you never say anything?'

'What would I say?' He shrugged. 'At the time, I felt guilty for spying on you both. I knew what I was doing was wrong. And I didn't want to risk losing Adam's friendship. I guess I didn't really think ahead to when he left. And one day, he was gone. And I saw you crying. So I...'

He paused. He sat again at the desk. Kitty narrowed her eyes at the sympathy and the guilt in his.

'So you told your father?'

He nodded again.

'I always wondered what made him walk through that part of the woods. He never said.'

'I didn't tell him about Adam. I just...it sounds naive now, but I saw my father, so sad and withdrawn, and I saw you with your heart breaking, and I hoped you might help each other.'

'And we did, so your plan worked.' Kitty swallowed past the painful lump that had thickened her throat. 'Why are you telling me this now?'

'Because I was hoping you and Adam might end up together after all.'

'A happy ever after?'

He smiled. 'Like in your novels.'

'Real life isn't as neat as fiction, Robert.'

To her horror, a sob began to build up in her chest. In a flash, Robert was round her side of the desk and handing her a handkerchief. He waited until she had herself under control.

'Tell me… I could never work out why Adam was so angry with you. When you and he first met again, in London.'

'He was hurt that I'd married your father so soon after he left.'

'But…he knew you had to escape your father's plans.'

'I never told him the truth. I was too ashamed that my own father would do such a thing and I didn't want Adam to take me out of pity. So I just begged him to take me—he'd said he loved me and I thought, naively, that would be enough. And when, on that last day, I tried to tell him why, he wouldn't listen. He didn't want to know. He said it would make no difference, our positions in society were too far apart and I would be ruined. As if I cared for that.'

'And why has he gone now? What happened?

I've seen the way you look at each other… I've felt the tension in the air whenever you are together…what went wrong?'

She had no pride left to lose. Robert, it seemed, already knew her heart was breaking, as it had fifteen years ago. What was a bit more humiliation? So she told him.

'He proposed to you and you refused? In the name of God, why?'

'I cannot leave you and Charis.'

'Nonsense! You have raised us all selflessly. It is time to put your own happiness first. Charis will be quite happy home here with me and it is not as though you would be far away at Kelridge Place, is it?'

A thought occurred to Kitty. '*Are* you looking for a wife, Rob?'

'Ah.' He had the grace to blush. 'No. That was a bit of subterfuge to bring you and Adam together.' He scowled at her. 'Without success as it turns out.'

'So I have no need to worry about you and Lady Phoebe Crawshaw?'

'Lady *Phoebe*?' Robert shouted with laughter. 'Is that what you feared? As if The Incomparable would look twice at a mere viscount!' He raised his brows at her. 'And do not think to divert me on to the subject of *my* matrimonial plans, Stepmama, for they are non-existent. We've established you cannot use Charis and me as an excuse, so what is now to stop you accepting Adam?'

She really did not want to discuss such personal matters with Robert, but she could see no way out of admitting the truth.

'Adam will want an heir.'

Robert shrugged. 'I should think he will, now he has something worth handing down. What of it?'

Kitty cringed inwardly. 'Have you never wondered why your father and I never had any children, Rob?'

She watched a tide of red rise up his neck to flood his cheeks. 'Er…no. I assumed… I thought, maybe, you did not…that is…'

She took pity on him. 'Your father sired four children in his first marriage. None in his second.'

'And what did Adam say?'

'I did not tell him. It is personal.'

'So he doesn't know the real reason you refused him.' Robert frowned. 'You do realise you are in danger of repeating history? You are concealing the truth from him, just as you did before, and denying him the chance to make his decision based on the facts.'

Kitty hunched her shoulders as if against a blow. He was right and part of her had known it ever since Adam had stormed away from her up on Fenton Edge.

'Do you love him?'

She nodded, wordlessly.

'And I am certain he loves you. So, is it not *Adam's* decision as to whether having an heir is more important to him than his love for you?'

Kitty slumped, dropping her face into her hands at Robert's accusation.

'He would feel obliged to claim it did not matter,' she mumbled. Then she looked up, 'But it would, Rob. In time. He will want an heir and he will resent being tied to a woman who cannot give him one.'

Robert shook his head, his expression grim. 'Well, I cannot force you to be honest with him and you need not fear I shall interfere any more than I have already but, if you will take my advice, you will tell him the truth. He is a grown man. He is perfectly able to understand the implications and deserves the chance to decide for himself whether or not he can accept never being a father.'

Kitty's thoughts whirled, seeing her dilemma more clearly after hearing Robert's opinion.

If I am honest with Adam...if he understands precisely why I refused him then, even if he decides siring an heir is more important to him, maybe he will accept my offer of an affaire?

At least he might not then disappear back to

Scotland because, if he did, how could she bear never seeing again?

'Very well,' she said. 'And thank you for the advice. I shall write to Adam and ask him to meet me. I shall tell him the truth and he can make his decision in possession of all the facts.'

Her heart felt immeasurably lighter as she penned her letter. She sent it to Kelridge Place, via a groom, with the instruction he must hand it direct to Lord Kelridge himself.

Adam found it strange to return to Kelridge Place when neither his uncle nor his cousin were in residence. He felt like an intruder, as though he could be challenged at any moment and thrown out, and it was an effort to portray a confidence he did not feel in front of the servants. As a distraction from Kitty's rejection, he immediately settled down to educate himself about the management of the estate. By one o'clock in the afternoon, however, his eyes were already sore from deciphering Carter's miniscule letters and numbers in the stock records and ledgers, and his notebook was full of questions to which he needed answers. He sent for Joseph Carter.

While he waited, Adam leaned back in his chair and rubbed his eyes, for the first time allowing himself to properly think about what Kitty had said and, more importantly, *why* she had refused his offer of marriage. No matter what words came out of her mouth, he knew—viscerally and wholeheartedly—that she loved him. Some women might fake their responses during intimacies such as they had enjoyed, but not Kitty. She was too honest.

Yesterday…his anger and pain had roiled inside him, threatening to erupt, and he'd acted on instinct with the desperate need to get away from Kitty amid all those churning emotions…the need to give himself time to calm down and to recover his pride. Such a volatile situation demanded silence, yet accusations had been clambering over one another in his head, battling to be spoken out loud. All he'd been capable of thinking was what a fool he had been to believe he and Kitty could ever truly put the past behind them. There was too much past hurt and he'd been convinced she would never forgive him for abandoning her, no matter how good his motives at the time.

Now, though…the question still remained unanswered. Why in God's name would a respectable widow like Kitty be prepared to be his lover, but not his wife? It made no sense.

He propped his elbows on the desk and dropped his face into his hands.

I will put this right. Somehow.

But he had no idea how.

He straightened up at a knock on the door. 'Come in.'

'You sent for me, my lord?' Carter waited just inside the door.

'Ah. Yes. Good afternoon, Carter. Do sit down.' Adam wrenched his thoughts back to estate matters and ledgers. 'I have several questions about the estate records and, from what Mr Trewin said, I understand you have been keeping the books for the past several years?'

The steward's brow puckered. 'Is there aught amiss, my lord?' His defensive tone caught Adam's interest and he studied the man opposite, who avoided making eye contact but sat back and folded his arms across his chest. 'I do my utmost to ensure accurate records are kept, I can assure you. Neither your father nor Mr Trewin ever found reason to complain about my work.'

'This is not a complaint, Carter.' Adam spoke calmly. There was no point in antagonising the steward if there was indeed anything wrong with the books. But his interest was piqued and he determined to examine them with even more thoroughness as soon as Carter left. 'I merely require clarification upon a few points as I am unfamiliar with the running of an estate.'

Carter visibly relaxed. 'Of course, it must be difficult for you to decipher such records, my lord, being as you are unused to country matters and to estate business. I shall be glad to answer any questions you might have.'

'Thank you. Now…first…crop yields. Wheat, barley and oats are, I think, all grown here?'

'They are.'

'As I know nothing about yields, I looked back over the records for the past five years.' Carter's expression stayed open. Unconcerned.

Perhaps I am wrong?

Adam ploughed on. 'Even non-country folk like myself were aware of the disastrous harvest in 1816 and that it was hardly better in 1817.' The entire country had suffered through a summer when the sun simply did not shine—all the result of a volcano that erupted the year before on the other side of the world, so it was said. There had been widespread failure of crops up and down the country, and much starvation as the price of corn rocketed. 'And yet…' Adam indicated the note-book where the crop yields were recorded, then swivelled it around to face Carter '…the last three years' yields at Kelridge Place are barely better than they were in 1817. I found that strange.'

'Our yields in '16 and '17 did not drop as much as they did elsewhere so they would not show as much recovery, would they?'

'Where are the records for the years prior to 1816?'

'They are in my room, my lord.'

'Will you please fetch them?'

'It may take some time to lay my hands on them. Were there any other queries first? In case I need to look out more old records for you.'

'Very well. Yes. I have a question about stock numbers. There is an anomaly in the record of sheep numbers at the start of the year, the number of lambs born and the current flock size. What is the explanation for that?'

'Sheep die all the time, my lord. They are notorious for it.'

'Deaths are recorded. There is still a difference in numbers.'

'Poachers and thieves, my lord. We lost three just the other day, as I told you when I spoke to you at Fenton Hall.'

'Indeed ye did. Well, I suppose that explains it. What steps have ye taken to protect the flock?'

'I have ordered the men to—'

He broke off at a knock on the door. It opened and Green entered.

'I am sorry to interrupt you, my lord. A groom from Fenton Hall has arrived with a letter and he refuses to leave. He says he is under strict instruction to deliver it direct to you.'

Adam's heart leapt with hope. Kitty. Surely it must be from Kitty. Could she have had a change of heart?

'Please send him in.'

Green's lip curled. 'He is a *groom*, my lord.'

'I do not care if he is the night soil man. Send him in.'

Green bowed and walked ramrod straight from the room. He soon returned, and stood aside for Davey to enter, cap in hand.

'Beg pardon, milord, but milady said most particular that I was to hand it to no one but you.' He slid a defiant glance at Green. 'No one.'

'Thank you, Davey. You may bring it to me.'

With hands that, of a sudden, shook, Adam took the letter and opened it, his gaze quickly picking out Kitty's signature at the end of the brief message.

Dear Adam,

I am aware I did not properly explain the reason behind my decision yesterday and would appreciate an opportunity to do so, if you will allow.

I shall be on Fenton Edge at three this afternoon. I hope you will meet me there.

Your friend,

Kitty Fenton

It did not say she'd changed her mind, but Adam would grab this chance with both hands. Whatever her reason, he would persuade her she was wrong. He must.

He took out his pocket watch. He must make

haste. The Edge was a good four miles from Kelridge Place and he must find the best route to the top from this side. He looked at the three men waiting patiently. He grabbed a clean sheet of paper, scribbled a note to Kitty—simply, *I will be there*—and blotted it before folding and sealing. He addressed it to Lady Fenton and held it out to Davey.

'Make sure ye give this to Her Ladyship the minute ye arrive home, Davey. Thank you.' The boy bowed, then hurried out.

'Green?' The butler bowed. 'Please send word to the stables to saddle a horse for me. I am going out.'

He still didn't know the horses in the stables well enough to have a favourite. That was another matter requiring his attention—it would give him great satisfaction to buy his own horse, and a pair for his curricle, rather than keep using his uncle's pick of animals.

Adam pushed away from his desk and stood. 'I am sorry, Carter. We will have to finish our discussion another time. In the meantime, though, perhaps you can locate that old crop-yield notebook and leave it on my desk?'

Carter had already risen to his feet. He inclined his head. 'Of course, my lord. If I might… I will just check the exact number of that book to ensure I find the correct one.'

'By all means.' Adam gestured at his desk and Carter reached across, moving Kitty's letter aside to find the crop book. 'I will be gone a few hours so I will speak to you again tomorrow.'

They left the study together—Carter back to his work and Adam to the most important meeting of his life, his head full of hope and fear and doubt and dreams.

Chapter Twenty-One

Kitty's stomach fluttered with nerves as she set Herald's head up the long sweeping slope to Fenton Edge. There was no hurry, so she held the horse to a steady trot. She had come early deliberately. Adam had said he would come in the note Davey had brought back from Kelridge Place, so she would get there early and watch his approach—at least until he disappeared into the trees at the base of the Edge. He would have to ride around to the south side before he found a way up and that would give her time to prepare herself and to plan what she wanted to say. Not that she hadn't already planned it, and practised it, *ad infinitum*. But she needed to make sure she missed nothing out. She had all her logical answers ready and must make sure she didn't allow emotion to cloud her judgement. And she would pray that her honesty would tempt him to stay at

Kelridge Place where they could at least see one another from time to time.

She would stand firm. She would refuse to be swayed, even though she loved him to distraction and believed that he loved her. And it was because she loved him she must let him go. She would not…could not…trap him in a childless marriage. He would say it did not matter to him, but it did. It should. He had many others relying on him now… his workers, his tenants. It was Adam's duty to sire an heir to take on that responsibility.

She reached the top and dismounted, tethering Herald to the same bush she had used before. She stripped off her riding gloves, removed her hat and unbuttoned her jacket—she had dressed with such care in her best riding dress, with her midnight-blue spencer and matching hat, but now, with the sun still high in the sky and not a breath of wind, she was close to being uncomfortably hot. She hurried across to the edge of the escarpment, eager to catch her first glimpse of Adam.

There he was—and her heart leapt to see him—astride a grey horse, cantering along a track that crossed a field far below. Kitty squinted, trying to make out his expression even though he was clearly still too far away. She estimated he had ridden three of the four miles that separated Kelridge Place from Fenton Edge, which meant she had plenty of time before he joined her, so she sat on the grass and watched his steady progress as she rehearsed her arguments in her head. He disappeared from view as he reached a tree-lined lane that edged the field. Kitty watched, waiting for him to reappear. And waited. She frowned.

Where is he?

He should have turned to his left once out in the lane. After about a quarter of a mile, there was a junction, where he would turn right on to the road that curved around the base of Fenton Edge, bringing him round to the gentler slopes to the west and south. Kitty jumped to her feet, her heart suddenly thundering.

What has happened?

She moved closer to the steep drop, peering down, trying without success to penetrate the canopy of the trees. Then, she spied a movement. Her heart leapt but, within seconds, her stomach lurched, filling her mouth and throat with the sourness of bile. The grey horse was there, yes. But he was tied to the back of a carriage drawn by two brown horses. A man—she could only see the top of his cap, but he was all dressed in black—drove and…she squinted again…she could just make out another figure through the carriage window. Although she couldn't quite make him out, she would swear he was not Adam.

She whirled around and ran for Herald, tore his reins free and mounted, using a nearby rock.

She urged him into a canter and sent him careening down the slope, angling him to the left as they descended. He seemed confused, wanting to head for home, but Kitty insisted. As the terrain levelled out, she urged him even faster, bending low over his neck, his mane whipping her face. There was no time for thought. Or to plan. If she was wrong, if for some reason Adam had met friends and accepted a ride in their carriage, then she would laugh at her own stupidity later. Once she knew he was safe. But the image in her head, as she headed for that road that would lead her around to the other side of the Edge, was of Adam, his arm bleeding after he had been shot.

Stupid. Stupid. Stupid. Why did we all so easily dismiss the threat?

Too late to regret it. She thrust aside the pointless recriminations that threatened to engulf her. They would slow her down too much. All she could do now was concentrate on catching that carriage. After that...no point in even thinking about it. She would catch it and then she would do whatever she could.

They reached the road at last and she reined Herald to the north. They did not slow until they reached the junction with the lane the carriage had been on. No sign of anything or anyone. She listened, but heard nothing other than her own heaving breaths. But there was only one direction they could have taken. She set Herald to a ground-eating trot, sitting erect in the saddle, craning her neck to try to see…anything.

Ten minutes later, she slowed. A roadside gate afforded her a view across a paddock and, on the far side, she spied a small, enclosed carriage with a pair of brown horses hitched to it—their steaming coats glistening with sweat—next to a ramshackle wooden-sided barn. The barn stood in a yard behind an abandoned cottage, its thatched roof long caved in and its window glass shattered, which was set back from the road and fronted by a large garden enclosed by stone walls. Kitty could see no sign of the grey horse, or of Adam or the men she had seen earlier.

Kitty slid from Herald's back and tied him to the gate before running along the road until she reached the track that led up to the side of and behind the cottage, only to find the barn and the carriage were now hidden from her sight. A flash of white further along the road caught her attention, however, and she looked in time to see a riderless grey horse disappear from view. Her insides curdled with fear and she looked around her helplessly. She had no weapon. What could she do? She eyed a nearby hedgerow. A stick? Hopeless. What use a stick against two men? A rock? The broken-down stone wall that edged the cottage's garden would provide plenty, but what would she do with one? Or even a hundred? Never had she felt her own sex and its lack of strength so keenly.

She hesitated at the end of that short track, ideas darting into her head, only to be dismissed almost immediately. Then her nose twitched and she fought a sudden urge to sneeze, squeezing her nose between two fingers, as the creak and rumble of carriage wheels reached her. She jerked her head up in time to see the horses' heads emerge from behind the cottage and, beyond them…her heart bounded into her throat as she took in the lazy spiral of smoke above the cottage roof, rising and spreading in the still, summer air.

Oh, dear God! Adam! Then… *Don't panic! Don't freeze.*

She could do nothing to help if she was seen. A glance up the track confirmed she still had time to hide before the driver spotted her, so she scrambled over the wall and crouched low, her heart beating so loudly she was afraid they would hear it. As the carriage drew level with her, she risked a quick look through a chink between the stones and caught one fleeting glimpse of two men on the box of the carriage. Her blood chilled and her insides turned liquid as she saw they were masked, with mufflers drawn up to cover their lower features. Sick with fear, she realised they would see Herald if they turned back towards

Fenton Edge, but luck was on her side. The carriage turned north, away from the Edge and towards the village of Kelworth, beyond which lay Kelridge Place. She risked lifting her head high enough to peer into the carriage window as it passed her by, but there was nothing, and nobody, to be seen.

She didn't bother clambering out into the road again, but sprinted through the abandoned garden, brambles catching and tearing the skirt of her gown. She reached the cottage and raced around to the back, terrified at what might await her. She skidded to a halt, taking in the three fires spaced out along the base of the front of the barn, including one at the bottom of the big double doors that had been firmly wedged shut by two large poles, one end against each of the doors and the other ends jammed into the dry earth in front of them.

'Adam!' Her scream reverberated and she both longed to hear him answer and dreaded hearing him, still clinging to the hope she had misunderstood everything and that he was even now waiting impatiently for her on top of Fenton Edge.

She started at a loud crack from the far side of the building and peered up to see thicker smoke rising, pluming black above the ridge of the barn roof. The sight jolted her into action and she fell to her knees, scrabbling at the bare dry earth in front of the doors and throwing it on the fire set there. It took time…too much time…to smother it. The other two fires had taken hold of the tinder-dry grass and brambles that grew right up to the side of the barn. There was no dry earth close by either fire and a quick scan of the yard revealed no shovel to help her douse them in time to stop the flames that even now licked up the side of the barn.

She leapt to her feet and lunged at the nearest pole, tugging at it for all she was worth, but it was wedged too tightly and wouldn't budge. Sobbing with frustration, she tried the other pole but, like the first, it was wedged solidly into the earth. Then, with a flash of inspiration, she moved to stand underneath it, allowing her to push it upright instead of trying to pull it. She shoved at it with all her might until the top end lifted away from the barn door. She didn't have the strength to topple it right over, but she had loosened it sufficiently for it to slip sideways down the barn door until the entire pole lay on the ground. Grunting with the effort, Kitty rolled it, bit by bit, until she could open the door wide enough to slip inside the barn.

Smoke had fingered its way inside, roiling and curling up to the roof and escaping through the many gaps in the tiles. It immediately caught in Kitty's lungs and she coughed, her eyes smarting. Remembering Edgar's nightmares about his frantic, futile efforts to save his first wife from the blazing wing at the Hall, and the things he blamed himself for not knowing—that he should have covered his nose and mouth, he should have kept close to the floor where the air would stay clearer of smoke—Kitty dropped to her knees and screamed Adam's name again.

She ripped off her spencer and held it to her nose and mouth, her eyes darting all around the dim interior of the barn. She could see further, down here at floor level, and she could see a man, lying on his side. Unmoving.

'Adam?'

A pathetic, choking sob, muffled by her jacket. She crawled to the huddled figure, grabbed its shoulder and heaved with all her might until it toppled over on to its back. He groaned and his arm flailed.

Oh, thank God!

Sobs of relief swelled her chest and choked her throat, but there was no time for emotion. If they were to get out of the barn, she must rouse Adam. Somehow. A glance overhead confirmed the flames had not yet reached the roof beams, but it was surely only a matter of time.

She shook Adam. He groaned again, his eyes screwed shut. She put her lips to his ear.

'Adam.' She fought to keep her voice steady and low, but the tremor was there nevertheless.

'It's Kitty. You have to help me. I can't move you by myself.' She slipped her hand behind his head, feeling the sticky warmth of blood. 'Adam.' It was an effort not to scream at him...shriek at him to *wake up*...but she needed him to come back to her, not to retreat back into oblivion, driven away by shrill pleas that would serve no purpose. 'Come. You can do this. Adam... I love you. I cannot *bear* to lose you again.'

A sob broke free. She grabbed his shoulders and shook him. *'Please...'*

She was sure he was coming around. His breathing was erratic, his forehead puckered and his eyes were still screwed shut. If he were unconscious, surely all his muscles would be limp? She didn't really know, but she took them as good signs. She twisted to look at the door. So near. When she again glanced up at the roof a thrill of fear leapt through her as she spied flames licking along the heavy beams.

She scrambled to her feet. She grabbed Adam's hands, stretching his arms over his head, straight out behind him. She leaned back and pulled with all her might. He didn't budge. Worse, he snatched his hands from hers and she was powerless to stop him. But that must mean he had some idea of what was happening to him.

'Adam Monroe!' she bellowed at him before bending double as she was seized by a paroxysm of coughing. She dropped again to her knees by his head. 'Fire! Fire! Fire!'

He stirred, mumbling.

'Move, Adam. Fire! You have to move because, as God is my witness, I will *not* leave you. If you choose to stay here and burn, then I will burn right alongside you.' She cradled his face and lowered her mouth to his, kissing him. 'I *love* you, Adam. Help me. We can only do this together.'

One eye slitted open and his hand went to his head. 'Hurts,' he whispered.

She shook him again. 'It will be better soon. We have to get you—'

Again, she was overtaken by a spasm of coughs, but she saw Adam's other eye open and a look of horror suffuse his features as his gaze swept their surroundings. She put her lips to his ear.

'Adam. If you do not help me, we will both die.'

She didn't waste her breath with more words. She shuffled around on her knees and thrust her arm behind his neck, straining to lift him into a sitting position. His groan was almost smothered by the crackle of flames. She glanced behind them again. The doors were still untouched by the fire, but for how much longer?

'Adam! Stay awake! When I pull you *must* help me.'

She scrambled to her feet and stood behind

him, then stooped to push her hands under his armpits.

'Bend your knees. When I pull you must dig your heels into the floor and push with your legs.'

His head was still upright, so he was awake. She prayed he was aware enough to understand what she wanted him to do.

'Now!' She pulled back and could have sobbed when she saw him bend his knees up, just a little, and then straighten his legs, using his feet to shuffle himself backwards.

'Again!'

Little by little, they neared the door.

'Hie! Is there anyone in there?'

Her blood turned to ice, despite the heat that had slowly built inside the barn. The sweat trickling down her back raised gooseflesh and she shivered. Those men. Had they come back? She didn't even have a clue what they looked like. Then an ominous, low roar grabbed her attention and, with horror, she saw the main roof beam engulfed in fire—the flames almost alive as they danced across the inner surface of the roof, greedy and gleeful as they hunted more fuel.

She had no choice. 'Help!' It was barely a croak. She took the two steps to the door and thrust her arm out, waving frantically. She could have gone outside, but she would not leave Adam. The air was fresher there, however, and she filled her lungs, which just made her cough even more. She crouched down, waiting for the fit to pass. Then tried again. 'Help!' This time, it emerged as a shriek. She waved again, then returned to Adam, who was again flat on his back.

'Push with your feet or, heaven help me, I will *never* speak to you ever again,' she growled into his ear.

He moaned, but he did as she demanded, and they continued to inch towards the door.

Then everything happened with a whoosh. Literally. As the doors were flung open, the fire leapt with life, the walls all around the barn alive with flames. Strong hands grabbed Adam, and Kitty found herself swung up into the arms of someone who ran out of the barn, cradling her. Dazed, she stared over his shoulder at the burning barn and she winced as, with a loud crack, the roof caved in. Tears leaked from her eyes. She raised them to her rescuer's face.

Grenville Trewin.

She gasped and the energy she had lacked a moment ago now surged through her. She struggled.

'You! Let go of me! Put me down!'

Chapter Twenty-Two

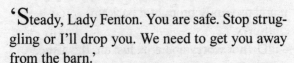

'Steady, Lady Fenton. You are safe. Stop struggling or I'll drop you. We need to get you away from the barn.'

Pain racked Kitty's chest, her lungs burning and throat burning as she was seized by another bout of coughing. That surge of energy had drained away, leaving her limp and close to tears. Mr Trewin carried her from the yard and then lowered her to a grass verge, a rough stone wall at her back. In front of her was the track that led to that abandoned cottage and on that track stood a carriage. Fear flooded her. They'd come back to make sure Adam was dead.

'Where's Adam?'

'Safe. Tolly has him.'

'But you…'

She put her hand to her chest, pressing, incapable of more words. Her breathing was shallow

and fast, but she willed herself not to pass out.
Not until she knew for certain Adam was safe.
Mr Trewin went to the carriage and rummaged
about inside, emerging with a water canteen such
as soldiers carry.

'Here. Drink this.' Mr Trewin held the flask
to her lips. 'Lucky I always carry water,' he said.
'A result of all my years on campaign...water can
mean the difference between life and death.'

Water had never tasted so sweet. Kitty gulped
it and promptly brought it back up.

'Sorry.'

'Do not worry about it. Just sip this time.'

She did.

'Better?'

She nodded.

'Shout if you need anything. I'll not be long.'

Mr Trewin stood up and walked away. Kitty
grabbed the opportunity to look around. She
could see Adam, lying on the ground, through the
legs of men clustered around him. She frowned.
Where had they come from? What was Grenville
Trewin doing here? He was supposed to be in
London, as was Tolly, who she could see barking
orders at men who had formed a line between the
barn and a well. She ought to object...she ought
to warn somebody that Mr Trewin had tried to
kill Adam...she ought to...

Her roving gaze stilled at the carriage that

Grenville Trewin had, without doubt, arrived in, as it had the Kelridge crest upon the door. It looked…big. Her eyes travelled slowly to the horses. Four, not two. Black, not brown.

Tears welled again, this time of relief.

This time, when Adam woke up, his brain felt…clearer. More normal. He was able to string thoughts together to make some sense. He was only vaguely aware of other times he had surfaced…people tending to him. Urging him to drink. His eyelids so heavy…

But, this time…his thoughts froze. Kitty. His nightmare…she had been there right alongside him. Burning…

Gritting his teeth, he levered himself up on his elbows.

'Adam.'

She was there, cool hand on his forehead. Smiling. He flopped back to his pillow, and pain shafted through him. He raised his hand to his head and fingered the bandages. His eyes sought hers. Grey. Brimming with love. That hope he'd felt when he rode to meet her…

'Masked,' he muttered.

'Don't worry about that now. It is all under control. Your uncle—'

'Not uncle. Voices…'

'No, it was not your uncle,' she soothed. 'But

he has everything under control. We'll talk about it when you feel a bit better. Sleep for now.'

She brushed his forehead with warm, soft lips and Adam closed his eyes, calmed by her presence. Her words echoed in his memory: *I love you. I cannot bear to lose you again.* He forced one eye open and sought her beloved face.

'D'ye really love me?'

Cool fingers caressed his cheek. 'I do.'

Now he could sleep.

Kitty was still there when he woke again. She helped him to sit up and to drink some water.

'There is someone to see you,' she said and Adam's gaze moved past her to the end of the bed.

'Tolly.' His voice still rasped in his throat and he sipped more water. 'You here?'

Tolly moved around the bed, to the opposite side from Kitty.

'I am,' he said. 'And happy you are on the way to recovery.'

Adam frowned as hazy images jostled each other in his head, his recollection of the day before still muddled. He only had a vague memory of what happened after a masked man had tackled him from his horse and he'd been knocked out by a blow to the head. But he did remember Kitty's sweet voice in his ear telling him she loved him and threatening to stay there and burn with him if he did not help her get him out of the barn. And his own pathetic efforts to help—pushing with legs as weak as a baby's.

Horror filled him at what she had risked. For him. He reached out, groping for her hand, and gripped it when she put it in his.

'Ye put yourself in danger, Kitty. Ye saved me. How can I ever thank ye?'

Kitty shook her head as she perched on the edge of the mattress. 'It was Tolly who saved you, not I. He saved us both.'

'You are far too modest, my lady,' said Tolly. 'Adam…believe me when I say that without Lady Fenton, you would not be here now. Had you been further from the door when we arrived, we would not have had time to get *either* of you out. She'd managed to coax you to move until you were both right by the door, even though you were barely conscious. My father grabbed Her Ladyship and I managed to drag you clear just before the roof collapsed.'

Adam raised Kitty's hand to his lips and pressed a kiss to her soft, sweet-smelling skin. 'Thank ye.' Her warm smile enveloped him. He tore his gaze from hers to focus on Tolly. 'How did you and my uncle come to be at the barn? I thought you were gone to Brighton.'

'We hadn't left London when we heard the news you'd been shot.' Tolly looked grim. 'Father worried one of us might be thought respon-sible, so we came straight home.'

'Who told you about the shooting?'

'It was Lord Datchworth,' Kitty said. 'You haven't met him, of course, but he is Lady Datch-worth's son.'

'And how did Datchworth know?'

Kitty huffed a laugh. 'Robert did, if you re-member. He met Lord Datchworth on the London road after making his enquiries at the tollgates.'

'Ah. Yes. That.' Adam felt his face burn. 'Sorry, Tolly...but we had to be sure it couldn't be either my uncle or you.'

Tolly shrugged. 'I'd have done the same. We were the most likely suspects, I can see that.'

'Anyway,' Kitty continued, 'Robert asked His Lordship if he'd noticed any increase in poach-ing and told him about you being shot so, when he met Tolly in town, he told him.'

'And we headed for home right away,' Tolly said. 'And, as we passed the cottage, we saw the smoke. We might not have thought much of it, but I'd noticed a horse tethered to a gate we'd just passed and so we decided to investigate. And, of course, as the smoke rose higher, it was visible from the village, so other helpers soon arrived.'

'And ye got us both out in time.' This time, Adam reached for Tolly's hand and gripped it.

Hard. 'I canna thank you enough. You *and* my uncle.'

'Nor I,' said Kitty.

'So…did ye find out who attacked me? And why?'

'Oh, yes. We found out almost immediately,' said Tolly. 'It was Carter and Eddings.'

Adam sat bolt upright. '*Carter?* The steward?'

'Yep. And we caught them red-handed, thanks to Lady Fenton here,' said Tolly. 'If she hadn't re-membered the details of the carriage, and the pair that drew it, I'm not sure we'd have found the evidence we needed to implicate them.'

'I was petrified when your uncle carried me out of the barn,' Kitty said, 'and I was convinced that he and Tolly were the masked men I'd seen for, otherwise, why were they there when they were meant to be in London? And they had a carriage…but when I calmed down a little, I realised the carriage was bigger than the one I'd seen earlier, and it was drawn by a team, not a pair. So, I soon realised your uncle and Tolly hadn't been involved and so I told them all I knew. Your uncle suspected right away that the brown pair of horses I'd seen were Kelridge horses.'

'We went to the stables immediately,' Tolly continued, 'and sure enough, there were the horses, which had clearly been worked. One of the grooms confirmed that Carter and Eddings had taken the small carriage out and had only recently returned.'

Adam shook his head, aghast to discover Carter's villainy. 'Where does Eddings fit in?'

'He is the brother of Carter's wife,' said Tolly. 'It transpires that Carter has been stealing from the estate for years by falsifying the accounts. The abduction was a last desperate attempt to stop you uncovering the truth. All three of them have been benefitting from the extra money Carter swindled and Eddings helped by reporting livestock deaths and thefts that never actually happened. Father is mortified he never noticed what was going on and that he allowed Carter such freedom in keeping the estate books. He thought he could trust him.'

'I had found some irregularities in the record books,' said Adam, 'but I had not even begun to imagine that anyone was deliberately falsifying the entries. Poor Uncle Grenville. But I can hardly blame him…he really *does* have no head for figures. At first, I thought he was deliberately trying to confuse me when he answered my questions so inconsistently, but I believe he genuinely does mix numbers up. No wonder he left the bookkeeping to Carter.'

'That is true,' Tolly said. 'He has always been the same…absolutely no head for numbers. But he does have his uses…he was so furious about all this that he…er…*persuaded* Carter to admit to everything before the constable came to arrest him.'

'Yes,' said Kitty. 'He admitted it was he who shot at you that day at Fenton Hall. He had ridden over to deliver Tolly's letter—choosing to do so himself in case he saw an opportunity to kill you...' her voice hitched and she swallowed before continuing '...and then, when his shot failed, he returned to Kelridge Place, taking the letter with him, knowing you might be suspicious if he turned up that same afternoon.'

'So...' Adam frowned. 'Was that story about the poachers and the three sheep even true?'

'No. He concocted it to divert us all from believing someone was targeting you. And he succeeded.' Kitty stroked Adam's hand.

'He got the idea of killing you after your horse threw you when you first arrived at Kelridge Place,' said Tolly.

'So that incident was not down to him?'

'No.'

Adam shook his head again. 'Well, at least they are safely locked up now and can do no more harm. I guess I shall have to start looking for a new steward.'

'Not right away, though, Coz,' said Tolly. 'You look done in. I'll leave you in peace.'

He squeezed Adam's shoulder and left the room. Adam leaned his head back and closed his eyes. What a sorry tale… He forced his eyes open and looked at Kitty, clad in a soft green gown, drinking in her lush curves and her beautiful face with her clear grey eyes and pink, full lips. How he loved her…

'Here,' she whispered, 'allow me to help you lie down.'

With her help he wriggled down into the bed. She adjusted his pillows and pulled the covers up as exhaustion rolled over him and his eyelids drooped.

'Kitty…we need to talk…' It took great effort to get his words out.

'Hush.' Kitty soothed his forehead. 'Sleep now. I will still be here when you wake and we will talk then.'

The next time Adam roused it was morning and she was still there, in the chair by his bed, her eyes closed, her long dark lashes a crescent on her cheeks. Her chest rose and fell gently as she breathed peacefully. He watched her silently, all the while taking stock of how he felt after his ordeal. He was pleased to find his headache had all but gone, his throat no longer felt scratchy when he swallowed and his mind felt as sharp as before.

Adam's heart swelled with contentment. All was right with his world.

Well. Nearly all.

'Kitty.'

Her eyes snapped open, as though she had not been sleeping, merely resting. She reached out to feel his forehead and smiled. A smile so full of love his pulse raced and his spirits dance with joy.

'How do you feel?'

'I feel fine.' He pushed himself into a sitting position and began to swing his legs from the bed.

'No.' Kitty grabbed his shoulders, preventing him from rising. 'You must not...the doctor said you must rest.'

But Adam was in no mood for more sleep.

'I wish tae get up. I have been confined to this bed for days,' he grumbled.

Kitty shook her head. 'You have not. You are exaggerating. The fire was just two days ago, and it is only ten o'clock in the morning now.'

Adam scowled. 'We need to talk, Kitty, and it is not a talk I wish to have while lying in bed. I want tae get up and I want tae get dressed. I have waited two days to hear why you refused me and I willna wait any longer.'

He recalled all too clearly his stomach roiling with a mix of conflicting emotions as he rode to meet her: doubts and hopes; fear and joy. She'd told him in the barn, time after time, that she loved him, but did that mean their problems were resolved and that she would agree to marry him?

'I need to understand, Kitty. I need to know. I

cannae rest with these vexatious questions nipping at me.'

She bit into her bottom lip, and desire surged through him. That decided him—if he was well enough to want to drag her into the bed and kiss her senseless, he was damned well fit enough to get dressed and sit in a chair to talk. He threw back the bedcovers.

'Ye have two choices, Kitty, my love. Ye can wait there and watch me while I wash and dress myself, or ye can ring the bell for Corbett to come and help me and then ye can wait downstairs.'

Wordlessly, Kitty went to pull the bell. 'I shall await you in the drawing room.' She stuck her nose in the air—making Adam grin—and then she left the room.

Corbett—Uncle Grenville's valet, who had been attending to Adam's needs while he was confined to bed—had soon appeared and helped Adam with his ablutions before assisting him to dress. By the time Adam was fully clothed he felt more human, and more than ready to discuss their future with Kitty. Apart from a slight tenderness from the bump on his head, he appeared to be suffering no residual effects from the attack.

He went downstairs and to the drawing room where Kitty was sitting, waiting. She watched him through narrowed eyes as he entered the room and crossed to sit in the matching chair to hers.

'I am not an invalid,' he said. 'Ye need not watch my every move.'

'If you say so,' Kitty said, with a sweet smile. 'I ordered a tea tray. Shall I pour you a cup?'

I'd rather something stronger.

He needed fortification, but tea would have to suffice. He could bear no further delays. His gaze grazed over Kitty, finding comfort in her presence as he drank in her creamy skin and her clear grey eyes. Those full, pink lips. The craving to taste them again filled him, but he put it aside for the time.

Kitty had promised him the reason behind her refusal of him and the need to know...the need to understand...overshadowed any number of cravings for a kiss. She had stayed at Kelridge Place since the fire and, as far as Adam was concerned, she could stay for ever. He could not bear for her not to be here, with him, near him. This was where she belonged, but he was aware that if Kitty had refused his offer of marriage despite loving him as she claimed, her reason must be a powerful one. And this would be his best, and possibly only, chance to persuade her to change her mind.

His nerves wound tight and he hauled in a breath.

'Why did you say no, Kitty?'

Chapter Twenty-Three

Kitty's hand jerked at the suddenness of Adam's question, slopping tea into the saucer of the cup she was pouring. Her gaze snapped to his and she saw a tumult of emotions in his blue eyes: pain; fear; hope. Her heart cracked.

She was the cause of all those feelings. Her main reason for refusing his proposal might have been a selfless one, but at what cost?

There had been several reasons—or maybe they had been excuses—why she had shied away from getting too close to Adam after meeting him again. Some of those reasons had dropped away as time passed and no longer could she fear opening her heart to love again, for it was too late. The barriers she had erected had tumbled. She already loved Adam; her heart was open and vulnerable and already hurting.

But the main reason remained. Insurmountable.

If only she could make him understand how her inability to have a baby would risk blighting their love in the future. She feared he would be reluctant to listen to her reasoning, but she hoped his pain would be less, knowing she refused him out of love.

The silence stretched as tight as Kitty's nerves and, as she handed the teacup and saucer to Adam, her hand was shaking. Adam took the cup and frowned.

'Ye asked to meet me yesterday to tell me the truth as to why ye said no even though ye say ye love me. Please…tell me now. And tell me what I can do to change your mind.'

She rubbed her hands over her cheeks, searching for the words to help him understand.

'Kitty…' Adam put his cup down and slid to the floor, kneeling before her. 'I *love* you.' He cradled her face between his hands. His blue eyes pierced her, searching. 'I have loved you for fifteen long years… I fell in love with ye then and I have loved you ever since. Ye know now that I only denied my love for you to stop ye throwing yourself away on an architect's apprentice, fearing that, in time, ye'd grow to resent being tied to a man of my lowly status.'

Kitty laid her hand over his as it cupped her cheek. His words had struck a chord with her. It was the same message she had been telling herself…the same reason she had refused his offer of marriage without explanation…the fear that, in time, he would come to resent being tied to a woman who could not give him a child.

But there would be no magical reprieve for her: Adam had found himself to be the son of an earl; Kitty would still be unable to conceive a child and give him the heir he would need.

'Adam…' She turned her face into his palm and pressed her lips to his warm skin, swallowing past the painful lump that constricted her throat. She had almost lost him yesterday and now she must risk losing him for good. 'I know you were shocked when I refused to marry you, but was willing to have an *affaire* with you, but I had… have…a very good reason for that offer.'

She paused, willing her emotions under control. This reason…this reality of her life…had caused her so much pain in the past and now it was to cost her the man she loved if she could not persuade him to accept her offer.

'Adam, I am barren. I was married to Edgar for ten years without getting with child.'

Adam's dark eyebrows bunched as his eyes searched hers.

'Kitty, ye cannot think that matters to me.' His hands slid from her face to clasp her shoulders. 'I want you as my wife and that is far more important to me than whether we have children. I love you. I want to have ye in my life for ever. Till death us do part.'

She saw by his puzzled expression that he had not appreciated the full implications of her bald confession. She quelled the misery and the pain that the subject cost her, knowing she must make him understand.

'Adam, this is not just about whether or not you become a father. You are now a peer of the realm. You have a duty to secure the lineage of your family and of the earldom, quite apart from your responsibilities to your workers and your tenants. You must at least give yourself a chance to sire an heir.'

Adam's frown deepened. His hands slipped from her shoulders to the arms of her chair, which he used to push himself to his feet. He sat back down on the companion chair, his blue eyes never once straying from her face, while she fought to keep her expression from revealing the full depth of her misery.

'Kitty…my darling…do you really…?' He stopped, and swiped one hand through his hair, pushing it back from his face. His chest expanded and he shook his head. 'You speak of duty and of responsibility. I think only of love. Of need. Of making my life, and yours, as happy as I can humanly make them. Kitty…my love…a few months ago I had no notion of titles or estates.

I did not ask for them. I will go so far as to say I did not *want* them. If not for you...' His voice trembled and he cleared his throat. 'If not for you, Kitty, I should have returned to Scotland within a fortnight and left the lot in my uncle's hands.'

She searched his expression, hope rising despite her best efforts to deny it. Could it be that easy, after all her anguish and heart-searching? Did he really not care who might succeed him? The notion was utterly foreign to her...never had she ever known a nobleman who did not care whether or not he had a son capable of continuing his bloodline.

Adam leaned towards her, reaching out, and she placed her hands in his. With one powerful tug he pulled her across to his lap and wrapped his arms around her waist. He nuzzled her neck, kissing her.

'I never expected any of this, Kitty, and I do not care who might inherit it when I am gone.'

'You cannot mean that, Adam. You—'

He pressed his fingers to her lips. 'I do mean it. Every word of it. I am sorry for your sake you cannot have a child, but you must believe me when I tell you that what is important to me is *you*.'

She shook her head, still trying to deny that swell of hope. 'You do not mean it. You have not thought properly about it.'

He gripped her chin and turned her face to his, capturing her gaze.

'Who is my heir now, Kitty?'

'Your Uncle Grenville.'

'And after him?'

'Tolly.'

'And Tolly…he is a good man, is he not?'

Kitty nodded, that sense of hope burgeoning as she gave up the fight to suppress it.

'Then tell me again why I must sire an heir when there are two good men ready to take on the mantle of the earldom. Although I confess I would rather live long enough to deprive my uncle of that honour.'

'But—'

'But nothing, my sweet. I have no need to think about it. Tolly will make a fine earl—let *him* worry about siring an heir and perpetuating our line. *Our* marriage will be no different to countless other couples who get married every day. They wed, and they face the possibility they may not be blessed with children. It is a gamble. Some married couples produce one child. Some produce a dozen, or even more. But nobody knows, when they make their vows to one another, what their destiny will be.'

Kitty gasped. 'I never thought of it like that.'

Adam kissed her, tiny kisses peppered all over her face.

'I promise you, my dearest love, that is *exactly* how I will view our union—if you will have me. The fate of the title and the estates simply do not feature in my plans for the future.'

Emotion welled up, blurring her vision. So much wasted time. So much pain. Adam gently passed his thumb beneath her eyes, one after the other.

'Don't cry, sweeting,' he whispered. 'Don't cry, or you will have me in tears, too.'

Her throat ached as she summoned up a smile. 'A big brave man like you, in tears?' she teased.

'I am brave enough to admit I have cried,' he whispered, his voice raw. 'I cried when I left ye fifteen years ago and I cried when ye turned me down.'

His fingers curled around her scalp, urging her face to his. She opened her mouth as his lips covered hers, pouring every ounce of her love for him into her kiss.

Too soon, he pulled back and captured her gaze again.

'Kitty...' His eyes glowed with love, tinged with uncertainty. 'Will ye *please* put me out of my misery? Please say ye will have me. Say ye will marry me.'

Her heart bloomed with love for him.

'Oh, yes, my darling Adam. Yes, I will marry you.'

The doubts that had plagued Adam ever since

they met again vanished and he finally...*finally*... could allow himself to believe in a happy ever after for him and for Kitty. He seized her lips in a searing kiss that lasted a long time. A *very* long time.

When he eventually drew back, he tipped his head to one side. 'Will I have to ask Robert his permission?'

Kitty gave him a puzzled smile, then laughed. 'He is my step*son*, not my step*father*,' she said, giving his shoulder a light slap. 'Of course we do not need his permission, as you well know. Besides...he already knows, more or less.'

She told him how Robert had followed Adam into the woods and seen their trysts. Adam laughed.

'I suppose we must be grateful we did nothing more scandalous than kiss in those days. I should hate to have corrupted such a young lad.'

He took her lips in another long, dreamy kiss. This time it was Kitty who ended it, leaning back against his encircling arms to search his face with suddenly serious grey eyes.

'You will still permit me to write my novels, Adam? My new one is almost complete now and I have had the most splendid idea for an exciting finish.'

He shook his head, then concealed his smile at her suddenly crestfallen expression.

'Kitty…you goose! I will not permit you because you do not—and will never—need my permission for anything you wish to do. Unless, of course, ye decide to run inside a burning building again. For that, my dearest love, ye will *never* have my permission. No more heroics. Are we quite clear about that?'

'Crystal clear, my darling.'

She kissed him, her smooth lips caressing his as the tip of her tongue teased his mouth to open. He needed little encouragement, tightening his arms around her waist again as he tasted her sweetness. Then she straightened.

'But,' she said, 'the fire *was* a valuable experience. Just think how real it will be when I write it—it will be truly authentic.'

'Authen—? *Kitty!* Is *that* the exciting ending you have planned?'

'Well…' She hung her head, then peeped at him from the corner of her eye. Adam bit back a laugh, keeping a frown on his face.

'But, Adam, my darling…it will be truly marvellous. The heroine rescues the hero, who then realises how very much he loves her and—'

'But I already knew how much I loved you. It was *you* who was hiding her true feelings.'

Kitty waved a hand dismissively. 'Details,' she said. 'I am sure my readers will prefer the hero to be the one who refuses to submit to his true feelings.'

He couldn't help it. He laughed.

Trust his Kitty. And, at last, *this* was the Kitty he remembered.

* * * * *

MILLS & BOON

Coming next month

THE HIGHLANDER AND THE WALLFLOWER
Michelle Willingham

Regina sank into a chair, burying her face in her hands. She didn't know whether to weep or groan with frustration. 'Why did you come, Lord Camford?'

'Because you didn't read Lachlan's note, nor any of mine. You refused my calls, and I had no other way to tell you that the laird married someone else.'

'His governess,' she predicted, feeling as if the bottom had dropped out beneath her. She had burned his letter without reading it. And he had been trying to call off the wedding. Dear God.

'Aye,' Camford answered. 'I am sorry to be the bearer of such news.'

Her emotions gathered into a tight ball of humiliation, but she managed to say dully, 'The wedding is off. We'll send the guests away and be done with it.' She already felt miserable, and the last thing she wanted was to face everyone else or see the sympathy in their eyes.

But then, this was what she deserved. She had been using the laird as a means of escaping her problems. She hadn't wanted to marry him, and it was now quite evident that he hadn't wanted to wed her either. If only she had opened his letter or allowed Camford to pay a call, she would have known the truth.

The viscount came close and knelt at her feet. 'I know

that you wanted to marry him to escape London. Because you're afraid of your father's blackmailer.'

She didn't look at him, so afraid she would break into tears. He took her hands, and she felt her heart begin to pound. 'But there is no reason why *I* cannot give you what you're wanting.'

What did he mean by that? Regina stared into his green eyes, uncertain. Then Lord Camford said, 'Marry me, instead. I will take you to Scotland, and you can escape London as you wanted to. I will also ensure that no one ever blackmails you or your father again.'

Continue reading
THE HIGHLANDER AND THE WALLFLOWER
Michelle Willingham

Available next month
www.millsandboon.co.uk

COMING SOON!

We really hope you enjoyed reading this book.
If you're looking for more romance, be sure to
head to the shops when new books are
available on

Thursday 23rd July

To see which titles are coming soon, please visit
millsandboon.co.uk/nextmonth

MILLS & BOON

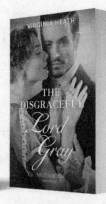